GOODBYE

HIDEOUT

A Chance and Choices Adventure

Book Eight

Lisa Gay

This book is a work of fiction. The names, characters, places, and incidents either are the product of the author's imagination or used factitiously. Any resemblance to an actual person, living or dead, business establishment, or event is entirely coincidental.

ISBN-13: 978-1-945858-17-8

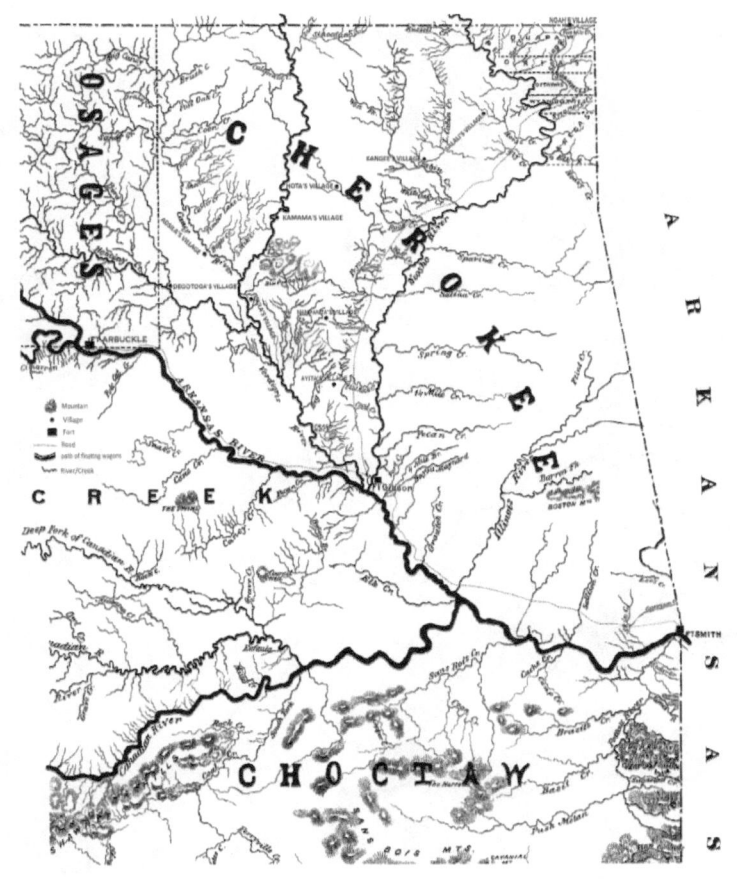

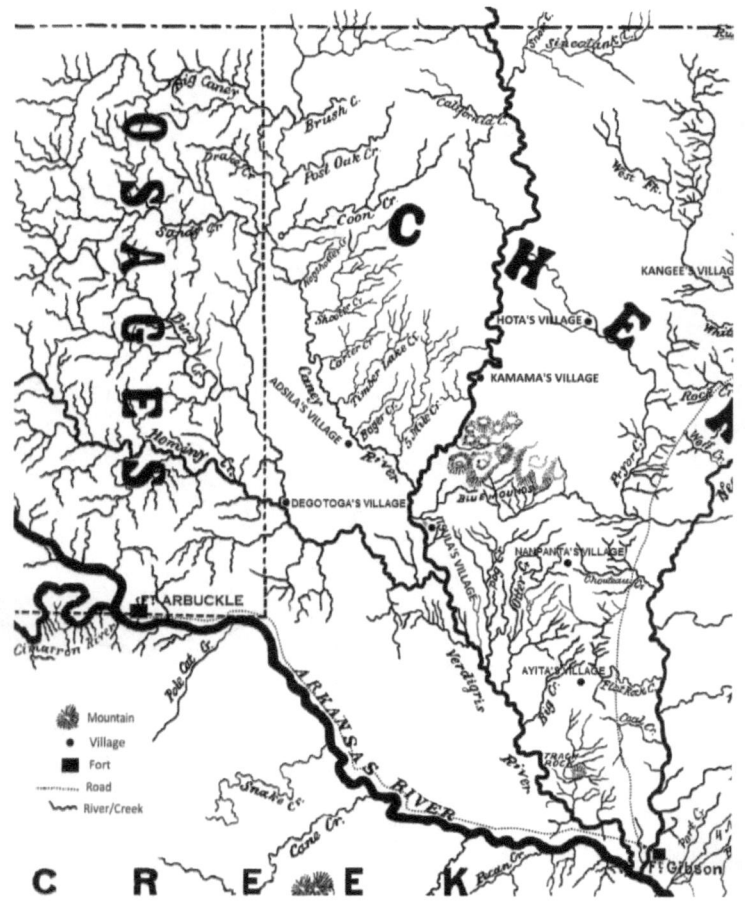

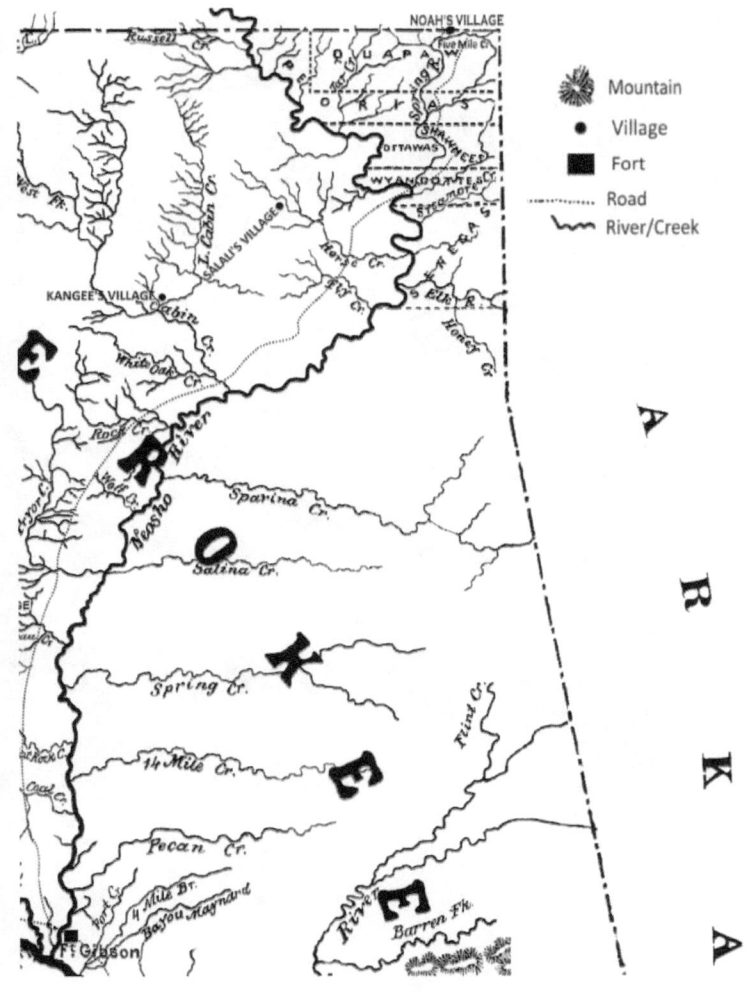

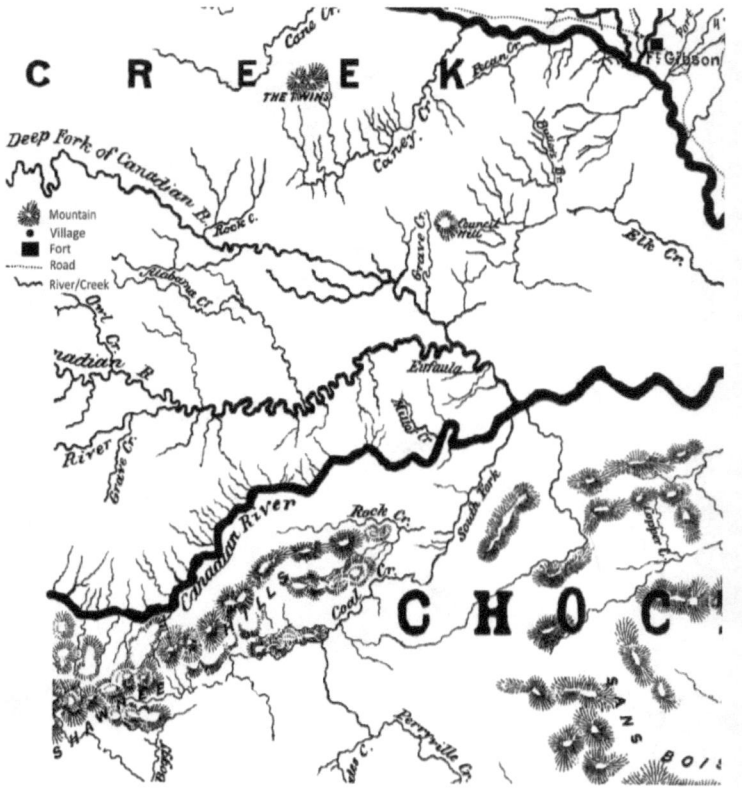

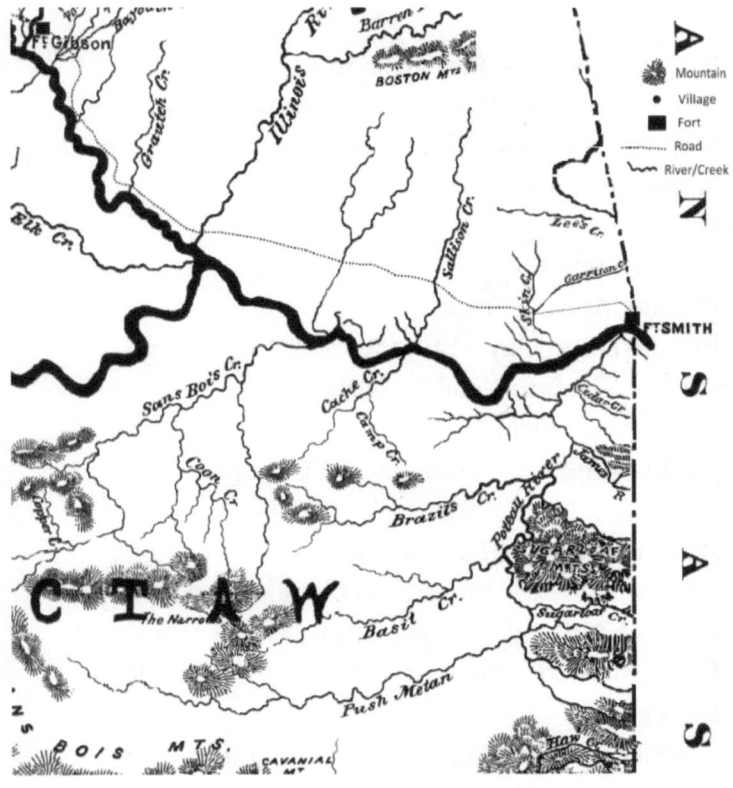

Those Involved in these incidents:

Place of Origin – Fort Arbuckle
Joy - baby girl
Mac – Joy's father
Amanda – Joy's mother

Place of Origin – Fort Gibson
Colonel Stephen Howland – Commander
Sergeant Matthew McCormick - Master of Supplies
Sergeant Timothy Anders (Tim)
Private Ezra Knuckles
Private Ham Blanders
Private Morgan Finch
Private Donnelley – Store worker
Private Kenneth – stable worker
Lieutenant Olson
Orville King – ferryman at Fort Gibson

Place of Origin – Fort Smith
Roy Butterfield – Butterfield Gang member
Richard Atwood – Judge of State of Arkansas
Edith Atwood – Richard's wife and sister of Roy
Butterfield
Colonel Josiah Habersham - Commander
Artrell Seibel– Army doctor
Gad Mead - private with a broken jaw
Henry – soldier on guard duty at the infirmary
Bruce – private working the dock
Promise – army horse purchased by Noah
Biscuit – army horse purchased by Noah
Beatrice – army mule

Place of Origin – Harmony
Ann Williams – oldest sister and Noah's wife
Stephanie Yates – middle sister and Eli's wife
Sally Williams – the youngest sister
Eli Yates – Stephanie's husband
Tom Yates - Eli's father/owner of Yates Mercantile
Hattie Yates – Eli's dead mother
Eyanosa – Noah's horse

Place of Origin – Indian Territory
Quapaw Land:
Noah Swift Hawk – Ann's husband (Tahatankohana)
Christopher – Noah and Ann's baby (Chris)
Chetan – Noah's father
Bethany – Noah's mother
Luyu – Chetan's mother
Hanataywee – Noah's oldest sister
Ehawee – Noah's next oldest sister
Ke – Noah's brother
Chumani – Noah's youngest sister
James Williams – Ann, Stephanie, and Sally's uncle
Wakanda – village mystery man
Mina – Woman who had previously been in love with Noah

Cherokee Nation:
Waya - warrior of the Cherokee
Dustu – grandson of Waya and twin of Adahy/ Hanataywee's husband
Adahy - grandson of Waya and twin of Dustu/ Ehawee's husband
Petang – married a girl in Noah's village

Salali - chief of her village

Ahyoka – a woman whose husband died

Kangee - chief of her village

Magaskawee – the second rank woman in Kangee's village

Cheasequah – the man who lost his wife

Tsiyi – man gored by a buffalo

Inola – the woman whose leg healed incorrectly

Hota- leader of Waya's village

Kamama – Waya's grandniece

Wyanet - a woman of Waya's village

Hangka – Dustu and Adahy's cousin

Atohi – a guide for Noah and the family

Doya – Atohi's wife

Diwali – Atohi's brother

Yona - Atohi's mother

Coowescoowe – Atohi's father

Tsula - chief of Yona's village

Adsila - chief of her village

Kanuna – the man forced to allow Noah's family to spend a night in his lodge

Nanpanta – a guide for Tom and Adahay

Degotoga – the man who took Ann, Noah, and Chris to Fort Arbuckle

Ahuli – Degotoga's son

Osage Nation:
The'-ha – Kangee's Spoils of War slave (Awan)

Place of Origin – Pine Bluff
Roscoe Bacon – the previous owner of Bacon's Trading Post

Roscoe's donkeys:
Little Jenny – miniature donkey
Little Jack – miniature donkey
Big Jenny
Shaggy
Spot
Blanco
Chocolate
Smiley
Honey
QuickSilver

Roscoe's mules:
King
Rose
Hector
Molly
Jumper
Blue
Chief
Diamond
Eli and Stephanie's mules:
Redeemed
Ace

Place of Origin – Little Rock
Daniel Hall – Judge of State of Arkansas
Robert Teal - man who betrayed Noah and Ann
Beauty – severely injured mule given to Sally
Dollie – mule with injured eye purchased by Sally
Mules 7 & 8 – injured mules purchased by Sally
Honor – injured mule purchased by Noah
Justice – injured mule purchased by Noah

Place of Origin – Fletcher Creek
Morris – sent to warn Ann and Noah
George - Morris's son, sent to warn Ann and Noah
Matt – sent to warn Ann and Noah
Justin - Matt's son – sent to warn Ann and Noah

Place of Origin – Maumelle
Edwin Snow – sent to warn Ann and Noah
Zi- Noah's mare

Place of Origin – Perryville
Raymond Pence – a local farmer
Joe Smith - an assassin working for Judge Hall
Sebastian De La Cruz – a local resident
Lola De La Cruz – a local resident

Place of Origin – New York
Helen Yates
Amanda – mother of Joy
Mac – father of Joy

Place of Origin – Dover
Ben – Butterfield Gang member
Charlie – Butterfield Gang member
Pete – Butterfield Gang member
Al – Butterfield Gang member
Gus - Butterfield Gang member
Starlight – a mule, bought by Eli and then traded to Roscoe
Brandy – a mule bought by Eli and then traded to Roscoe
Gumdrop - mule bought by Noah
Glory - mule bought by Noah

Goodbye Hideout

ONE

Ann Williams' green eyes blazed. She and her husband were betrayed. Now, she had only one viable choice, and it was only barely so. On a frigid day, she held her newborn son inside a stack of buffalo hides and attempted to escape in a covered wagon. *So cold!* As if Christopher understood her words, she spoke to her tiny baby. "Don't freeze."

Wearing long blanket coats and heavy furs, her family remained on high alert. Christopher cuddled to his mother. His eyes peeked out at Noah Swift Hawk, who brought Ann news of yet another threat. "Waya says Kangee will kill everybody in a wagon train without even a chance to explain. He went to her village alone."

Ann replied to her husband, "Your grandmother married a fearless man."

A village sentry studied the lone man approaching. An elk skin hat covered the man's typical Cherokee skullcap centered at the back of his

1

head. The furry buffalo hide wrapped around the man's sleek, muscular body concealed his Cherokee clothing. The mukluks on his feet did not look Cherokee either, but the approaching man signaled that he was one of their people. The watchman allowed the stranger to get close enough to see his face. Blessedly, the lookout had been present at Waya's marriage to Luyu. "Waya, why are you here?"

"I need help."

"Come." The sentry did not take him to the lodge of Kangee, the village leader and female warrior, well known for slaughtering entire villages. He escorted Waya to his lodge and whispered to his wife.

The woman ordered, "Waya, come."

A young man opened the door of Kangee's lodge. "Praise the Great Spirit! Is Tahatankohana with you?" exclaimed The'ha.

"Yes."

"Bring him now! Kangee needs him!"

Waya informed the man, "My entire family needs to stay in your lodges tonight."

Even though he was Kangee's Spoils of War Osage slave, The'-ha was able to command the woman who had brought Waya because she knew it was for Kangee. "Magaskawee, find them places. I need to get Tahatankohana."

Waya followed the woman back into the bitter cold. "We will trade."

Goodbye Hideout

The'-ha ran to the wagons. "Tahatankohana! Something is wrong! Kangee has terrible pain!"

Noah responded to his Quapaw name. "Where?"

The'-ha pointed to his lower right abdomen. "Here, and she is throwing up."

Noah got his book about surgery, the medical cane Ann's sister Stephanie had given him, and the surgical kit he had bought in Perryville. He spoke to Ann's youngest sister. "Sally, get everything we need to make the sedative, then come to Kangee's lodge."

Bethany, Noah's blue-eyed, blonde-haired mother, hurried behind The'-ha, her son, and her daughter-in-law, who carried Chris inside her coat.

Luyu, however, knew Cherokee women led their villages and that Magaskawee would prefer to negotiate with her. She turned toward the woman. "We will trade to spend this night inside your lodges and for warm water for our animals."

"I soon come back." Magaskawee hurried Sally to Kangee.

In Kangee's lodge, The'-ha went behind a curtain. "Kangee, the Great Spirit has answered my prayer. He has sent Tahatankohana."

"Bring h—" Kangee vomited.

Bethany looked around, found a pot, and filled it with water. Ann sat beside the fire and let her son nurse. The baby pulled at the dark hair that curled above his mother's shoulder.

Believing, even in her current condition, that the fierce muscular woman who had slain many enemies could easily kill him, Tahatankohana notified Kangee, "I am going to touch you." She nodded. He felt her side. "Have you eaten anything different?"

"No," The'ha answered. "She has not, but she has been feeling worse and worse for the last few days. Please help her."

Tahatankohana continued to direct his words to the woman. "Something inside you has gone bad. This white man's book says I have to cut it out. I can put you to sleep. You will not feel it."

The'-ha refused. "You cannot cut out pieces of her. I will not let you."

Kangee touched The'-ha's arm with obvious affection. "I trust him, and you will watch over and protect me. If you do not let him do this, I will surely die." She looked into the blue eyes of Tahatankohana. "Do what you have to do."

Sally came into the lodge with several bags. "I have what we need."

"Come here." Bethany checked the water.

Tahatankohana looked at The'-ha. "I need many clean cloths, much water, and many pots."

The slave dashed away. A minute later, he returned. Shortly after, women brought the requested items. In the first pot of boiling water, they made the sedative. In the second, Tahatankohana put the surgical tools he needed to operate. His mother started food, and they boiled water in others for whatever need arose.

Outside, the temperature plummeted as the sun went down. Tahatankohana's family crowded their four goats and four sheep together in the center of the animal organizer hanging inside the special tent they had made. They put mules and donkeys around them, hoping they would stay warm enough. The other twenty-eight mules and horses they crammed into their two unfinished animal tents. With all the animals fed, watered, and hopefully protected from the bitter cold, they went to their assigned lodges.

Inside Kangee's home, Sally carried a cup of sedative tea to the patient. "May I ask my God to watch over this operation and direct Tahatankohana's hands?"

Kangee drank the concoction. Her body immediately ejected it. Sally brought more. Kangee tried a sip. *It stayed inside.* She took a swallow. "I don't need the help of your God." She drained the cup. Her stomach contracted violently. Tea and stomach fluids erupted from her body. "Pray for me!"

"Dear God, Kangee is very ill. She needs you to heal her. You made Tahatankohana, You filled him with knowledge about medicine, and You put him here. You planned to save this woman from the beginning of time, and You planned to do it this way.

We thank You for your guidance and direction of Tahatankohana's eyes, mind, and hands, so he can find the problem and fix it. I pray to You in the name of your son, Jesus."

"I hope you are right." Kangee attempted to keep down the sedative. After six cupfuls and much spewing, she had finally absorbed enough sedative to put her to sleep. Kangee and almost everything else reeked of bile.

Sally retrieved a pot of hot water. Tahatankohana again read the relevant pages of his book while Sally cleaned. The'ha watched the fifteen-year-old girl with hazel eyes, bouncy, shoulder-length chestnut-colored hair, long thick lashes, and heart-shaped lips. However, his only interest in the gorgeous girl was that she was helping the woman he loved. They laid out a fresh blanket, then placed Kangee on it.

Tahatankohana placed a clean cloth beside Kangee, got the tools out of the boiling water, and lay them on it. He took a deep breath, made a small incision, and then turned to The-ha. "I cannot see through this little hole. I have to make it bigger."

The'-ha nodded his go-ahead.

"Hold this skin back." Tahatankohana handed an implement to The'-ha. "Sally, come here." He held out another of the same tool. "Hold the flesh back."

While Sally and The'-ha held Kangee's body open, Tahatankohana sucked out the pooling blood with a syringe. "See how swollen and red it is?" As a surgeon who might be executed, Tahatankohana wanted The'-ha to see that he was doing the right thing. "That book shows a picture and says if an appendix looks like this, you have to cut it out."

Once again, The'-ha nodded his approval. Tahatankohana picked up the scissors and snipped off the offending organ. He put it in a bowl then sewed shut the hole he had made in Kangee's colon with many stitches. Even though the book did not direct him to do so, he poured warm, strained yarrow tea into the wound then sucked it out, along with blood. He searched for severed vessels, which he seared with snuffed out lucifer matches. Finally, blood no longer puddled. "I think I got them all."

Tahatankohana proceeded to sew the muscles together and then the skin. Next, he poured yarrow over the incision, placed a folded bandage over the stitches, and then applied gentle pressure. The dressing quickly soaked. He poured more yarrow over the cut, lay another clean cloth over it, and pressed again. After a few rounds, the external bleeding stopped. Tahatankohana dabbed antiseptic wash on the incision, covered it, and wrapped a bandage around his patient.

Late in the night, Kangee woke. The'-ha gave her a cup of sedative mixed with yarrow. After a brief period of pain, she again slept.

TWO

The morning sun rose above the flat land. "Stay a few more days," The'-ha requested.

"A killer is trying to find Ann and me. He has orders to take us to the white man's prison or to kill us. From what we know, I am sure he would not take us alive! We have to go."

The'-ha offered a trade. "Stay and make sure Kangee will heal. I will kill this man if he comes here."

From the corner, Ann said, "We should stay for a few days for Kangee but also because it is much too cold. Christopher won't survive outside."

Bethany said, "I'll go speak with the rest of the family." She left before her son could object.

Several minutes later, Luyu arrived. "Nobody wants the baby outside, but since we're trading to stay inside, Waya wants to go to Hota's village with his grandsons, your sisters, and me. They want to show us off." Luyu put one hand to her cheek and the other beside her hip to accentuate herself as a bride on display.

Goodbye Hideout

The'-ha replied, "Kangee will pay for all the days you stay here and over there too. I will speak to my people." This time, The'-ha left.

Sally said, "I would not have thought he would think of this village as his people."

The'ha returned with Waya and Tahatankohana's father, Chetan. The'-ha said, "It is good. You do not need to trade anything more."

"We are going to my village," Waya informed the others.

Chetan looked at his wife. "You, Chumani, Ke, and I are going too. We will only take our horses and bedrolls." He turned to his son. "Someone will bring you and everything else when you are ready."

"The others will come here. I will cook for you," The'-ha concluded.

"All right. I see it is all arranged." Tahatankohana no sooner had agreed than their adopted family member, Roscoe Bacon, and the four members of the Yates family arrived.

"I'm glad we're together." Stephanie Yates put her things in her designated place, then hugged her older sister. Stephanie's husband Eli, Eli's father Tom, Tom's mother Helen, and Roscoe settled in.

THREE

Days later, those in Kangee's lodge felt sure she would survive. The'-ha knew how to make the different teas, and when to use each kind. Tahatankohana stocked him with plenty of the plants and explained where he probably could find more.

Kangee asked the man she knew as Tahatankohana, "What can I do to thank you for saving my life?"

"You do not need to do anything."

The'-ha said, "I see you have fed almost all of your hay to your animals. We have plenty of tall grass. I could ask our people to cut it and put it in your wagons and the nets under them."

Kangee directed her slave, "The'-ha, get Magaskawee."

Magaskawee came into the lodge wearing her new red flannel shirt. Kangee ordered, "Get all the people to cut grass. Fill the wagons and nets as directed by Tahatankohana."

Goodbye Hideout

"Yes, Kangee." Magaskawee left to get the work started. She was delighted that the wind that could freeze a person to the bones was not howling across the prairie.

Kangee knew the red shirts would be a source of problems if only a few people in the village had one. "I want to buy shirts for everybody in this village?"

"We do not have that many reds. We can sell you blue shirts but for adults only. How many do you need? Do you have money or want to trade?"

"I need twenty-three more. I have no gold. The'-ha tells me you do not have covers for all your animals. You need eight for horses, and he told me your women have been making something to feed your animals inside your white man tents. I will ask our women to help while others cut the grass."

Tahatankohana contemplated. *We do need the tents finished and enough blankets to protect all our animals, and we need hoods with side blinders too.* "We have other things we need too. My women will show what we want and decide who can sew well enough. We will pay a blue shirt, including to older children."

"The'-ha, will you tell our people?"

The'-ha smiled. *Kangee did not order me.* He went to do as asked.

Willing women came to Kangee's lodge. Ann, Sally, and Stephanie explained in universal Indian sign language. "One shirt for two hoods. Our men will show you which animals to fit. Bring back all the unused material and tools with the completed hoods." To each woman, they doled out enough of a wool blanket to make two hoods, along with a small spool of cream-colored wool thread, a large needle, scissors, and an awl.

A married woman asked, "May I have enough to make two sets and also get a shirt for my husband?"

"I am delighted that you are willing to make four." Sally handed the woman more material.

Later in the day, the women returned with the completed hoods. Ann told each woman, "Very nicely done. Thank you. You may keep the needle if you want it." Every one of them tucked the needle safely into her medicine bag.

By the time the hay wagon and nets were crammed full of freshly cut grass, they also had forty-six of the fifty-six hoods they needed and a completed animal divider for the second tent. Ann told Magaskawee, "Any person who will make one more of the last ten hoods we need, may have the remains of the spool of thread and a package of fish hooks or a package of needles. We also need one more tent divider and poles."

Since Magaskawee had already gone into the white man's tent to look, she understood what Ann wanted. "We will get our girls to make the hoods. What will you trade for helping to make the inside part of the tent?"

Goodbye Hideout

The family had already decided what to offer. Ann negotiated. "Attach one divider and one feed bag, or one pole sleeve on the tent wall, or two short pole sleeves of the divider. You may pick any one of these." She laid out a pair of scissors, an awl, a steel butcher knife, a whetstone, a package of fishhooks on top of two fishing lines, and needles with a spool of cotton thread. "You may pick the color of thread. We have ten of each item to divide between you. We can use all of you to make the tent divider, but you cannot all work at the same time. Divide into two groups. If you are going to help, decide now, so we can determine by lot the order of choosing your item."

The eight youngest of the girls able to sew adequately, who had not already made a hood, took their supplies and selected in trade what instructed to get by their parents. One of the girls stood between parents quarreling over fishhooks or needles. She waved her hand. "Would you give a package with," she held up one hand of fingers, "fish hooks and" she displayed her other hand of fingers, "needles?"

Tahatankohana spoke up loudly, "We can rearrange the packages. You may have half fishhooks and half needles if you would rather have that."

The girl's parents immediately agreed, which resulted in all the other families changing to that option as well. Ann retrieved what she had previously doled out. Sally got a few sheets of paper and a pair of scissors to divide and rewrap needles and hooks.

Meanwhile, Stephanie carried a jar holding folded papers marked one to forty-six. When everybody to help with the tent had one, they opened them.

The selections went smoothly until the last five people. Four packages of hooks, needles, fishing line, and thread, and an awl remained. The woman whose turn had finally arrived was not happy. "I want scissors, but I cannot have any, so I am not helping."

"All right." Tahatankohana skipped the woman. The following person said, "I would rather have a whetstone, but I will take a needle, thread, hook, and fishing line package." The next took the same because that was what she wanted. The following was the husband of the woman who had refused to help without getting scissors. "I will do a section without pay if my wife can have scissors."

"Hold the thought," Tahatankohana told him.

The last person said, "I already have a package of hooks and needles from the first night, so I will take the awl, but I also would have liked scissors."

Tahatankohana waved Sally over and softly spoke to her. She left the lodge. "Other than you four, is everybody happy with what you selected?" They all agreed they were. "Thank you. We will start after supper. Do you want to decide for yourselves which shift or decide by lot again?"

Magaskawee said, "We all have children to look after. We will decide."

Sally returned with two pairs of scissors, two

knives, and two whetstones. She gave scissors to the woman who had refused to help without scissors, took the awl from the other woman and gave her scissors, and then retrieved the hooks and needles from the man who wanted a whetstone and gave him the stone. Sally stepped up to the last man. She had the awl, a whetstone, a knife, and three packages of hooks, fishing line, needles, and thread. "Pick."

"You are very wise. I need to keep the scissors sharp." He took the whetstone.

Sally held out the butcher knife. "Because you were willing to work for nothing, so your wife could have what she wanted." She took the rest of the items to the wagon and packed them away.

Kangee had remained in her bed and listened while the negotiations had taken place. Many villagers had told her they were happy that she was recovering as they had gawked at the dried-up organ in the bowl.

The'-ha saw the commotion wearing on Kangee. He went to Tahatankohana. "You need to make the tent in a different lodge." He turned to the people. "Go home. We will give you more instructions soon."

Kangee heard The'-ha's desire to protect her and smiled.

FOUR

In Kangee's emptied lodge, Tahatankohana spoke with The'-ha. "Find out who will let us use their home. We can divide into three groups. One with ten for the outer tent, another with eight for the divider ring, and a small group of four for the inner divider. Find families who have not already received much if you can. Tell them I will come later to negotiate what we will trade for the use of their lodge."

While they ate supper, Tahatankohana informed their host, "Kangee, we will leave in the morning."

The patient turned to The'-ha, "My love, please get my pipe."

Kangee never calls me her love! The'-ha wanted to hold her and tell her he loved her too; instead, he did as asked.

"All the Cherokee people will recognize this pipe." Kangee held out her Calumet toward Tahatankohana. "They will not harm you, and they will protect you anywhere on Cherokee land if you have my Peace Pipe."

Goodbye Hideout

Tahatankohana accepted the gift. "May the Great Spirit continue to heal and bless you."

Kangee drank the tea she knew would put her to sleep. "Let me hold your child. The-'ha, help me sit up." Ann put Christopher into Kangee's arms. "Soon, I will be holding one every day."

"What?!" The'-ha exclaimed.

"Well, my love. You are going to be a father. I believe you will be a very good one. Because you have loved me so very well, I know you will love our child the same."

The'-ha knew this could happen, but had believed that somehow it never would. "I want to talk with you alone if we can."

Kangee passed Christopher back to Ann. "Thank you for letting me hold him."

"You're welcome." Ann and Tahatankohana went to the other side of the lodge but still heard The'-ha's conversation.

"You called me your love twice, and you said I have loved you very well. Do you want me to love you? Do you love me?"

"Yes, my The'-ha, I want you to love me, and I love you. You could have let me die and been free, but you wanted me to live. Even though I killed all your people, you have been very loving from the very beginning. I do not understand why you love me, but when I thought I was going to die, I realized what I have and that I want you forever. I cannot marry you because I claimed you as my war spoils, but I can love you and have your children."

"I will go out hunting and come home to your love and all our children. That is a life I will be happy to live." The'-ha kissed Kangee's lips and then lay beside her. After the tea put her to sleep, The'-ha left her side. "I go now."

He went to a woman with two children able to help as well as a daughter already assigned to make a hood. Her husband, Tsiyi, had been severely injured in a recent buffalo hunt. "It should not be too hard for you to have only two extra people in your lodge, and Tahatankohana will give you something good."

The couple agreed.

Next, The'-ha went to Inola, a woman who had broken her leg many moons before. It didn't look right, and it would barely support her. "I think Tahatankohana will help you if you let eight people work here."

Last, he went to the home of Cheasequah, whose wife had died only a month earlier. The man rarely left his lodge and had not helped at all. The'-ha hoped Cheasequah would realize how much better it was to have people around him. The man agreed reluctantly.

The'-ha reported the arrangements and explained what he thought the people needed. Tahatankohana went to look at Tsiyi, gored by a buffalo. "I need to open this, clean and fix, and sew you up again. I will put you to sleep first and leave you plenty of medicine plants."

Tahatankohana then looked at Inola's leg. Neither Inola nor her husband had volunteered to help with anything. "You will never walk unless this leg is broken again and then put back together the right way. I will make you sleep first. I will leave plants to stop pain, and The'-ha knows how to make it."

At the last lodge, he offered, "Cheasequah, if you find somebody to watch your children for seven sleeps and let us use your lodge this night, we will give food for your children while you go to Salali's village and speak with Ahyoka. Her husband recently died. Maybe she will help take care of your children, and you could hunt for them all."

He agreed.

Tahatankohana walked back to Kangee's lodge. "The'-ha, you know who should go where. Will you set it up and let everybody know where and when to go?"

"I will."

FIVE

By morning, packed into the appropriate wagon, were all fifty-six animal hoods, as well as the needed tent parts. Tahatankohana examined his patients and reviewed the instructions with their caregivers. When he was satisfied that they knew what to do, he asked Kangee for permission to give something special to The'-ha. "The'-ha has helped you, the people in this village, and us. I want to give him a bow and a quiver of arrows that I made. I know he is a captured slave, but there are already plenty of weapons around he could have used if he wanted to hurt anybody. Will you let me give them to him?"

"Thank you for asking me first. I agree that he does not want to hurt anybody here. You can give them to him. He told me what you did last night. I think we have gotten much more than you have."

"My son would not have survived without your warm lodge, and now we can protect all our animals. We are happy with our trades, but I would like one more thing. I want to give The'-ha a new name. He is not The'-ha, lower than the soles of our feet. I want him to have a spirit name. If you agree, we can have a ceremony with just you, my family, and The'-ha, or with the whole village if you are willing."

"I declared death to everyone in his birth village for burning down one of ours. He must remain my spoils of war, or I forfeit his life. Still, you can give him a new name, even with all my people, but first, ask him if he wants this."

Tahatankohana found the man. "The'-ha, to me, you are not lower than the soles of our feet. I have asked for permission to give you a new name before the whole village. Kangee agreed if you want this."

"No. That may be bad for Kangee."

"What if I give you a spirit name with only my family, you, and Kangee?"

"I would like that."

"Then come into the lodge and purify yourself."

Tahatankohana told Kangee, "The'-ha agreed but only privately. He does not want you compromised. He is a good man. Treat him well."

"I know he is. I will, and I want to give him the ceremonial outfit of my father." Kangee pointed. "Take it to him."

Tahatankohana held up a folded animal skin. "This?"

"Yes," Kangee replied.

Lisa Gay

After everybody was ready, they entered behind the drape Tahatankohana had hung from the roof. Wearing buckskin pants, a bone breastplate, a bone hairpiece, and a mink cape, he purified each person with sweetgrass smoke. Pretending not to be surprised by Tahatankohana's outfit, Kangee lay on a pallet. The others sat in a circle. The'-ha entered, wearing his just-received, embroidered elk skin clothes.

"Sit in the middle." With his eagle feather fan, Tahatankohana billowed sweetgrass smoke over The'-ha. "There was a man who was born an Osage. He became the Spoils of War. The'-ha: a man lower than the soles of our feet. He found the people in his new life to be like everybody else; people who needed aid from time to time. Instead of looking for revenge, he chose to help and to love a woman. He became purified just as this smoke purifies him now."

Tahatankohana put down the bowl of sweetgrass and the fan. He poured a ring of tobacco around the group. "Those inside this circle know this man is more than others might believe." Tahatankohana sprinkled The'-ha with water. "He has a clean heart."

"The spirits have asked me to give a name." He poured a drink made from dried chokecherries into cups on a tray. "If you acknowledge that this man is worthy of a spirit name, take this drink." Tahatankohana went to each person and held out the tray. Everybody took a cup. He walked to The'-ha. "If you are willing to receive your name, take a cup of this juice."

The'-ha retrieved a vessel of burgundy liquid. Tahatankohana took the last serving. "I had to protect my family. I was desperate. I asked, 'Who can help me?' The spirits told me somebody in Kangee's village. In the village, a woman said, 'I am dying. Who can help me?' Somebody prayed for her, and the spirits heard. I went to Kangee's village and found somebody. Somebody took me to the dying woman. He helped her, my family, and me.

"I said, 'I need to keep my family and animals safe after I leave. Who can help me?' Somebody said, 'I can ask the people to cut grass for you.'

"People in this village had a desperate need. Somebody said, 'I see you. I will bring help.'

"I did not know how to pick the people to fix our tents. Somebody said, 'I will do it.' Somebody put the needs of the people together with my needs and made all things get fixed.

"When the spirits were asked, every time anybody needed somebody, they brought The'-ha. That is why this man's real name is Awan, somebody." Tahatankohana held up his cup. "Drink this cherry juice and affirm this man as Awan." Everybody drank the chokecherry tea and put down an empty cup.

Tahatankohana pulled back the blanket on the floor behind him. He brought out the bow and quiver of arrows. "Within this circle of people and with the Spirits, you are Awan. Awan, you must go forward to provide for the woman and children given to you and to whom you have been given. You will need to hunt for them. You need weapons. This gift is for somebody." He laid the beautiful, well-made bow, quiver, and arrows in front of Awan. He swept a break in the tobacco circle with his eagle fan. "Awan, take your weapon and your name into the world."

Awan picked up the bow and quiver of arrows. He stood up and walked through the opening in the tobacco and then from behind the draped off area.

"Go back to the world as witnesses to the giving of this name."

Sally and Stephanie helped Kangee rise up, exit the circle, and get back to her bed. The others followed behind them and discovered that Awan was not in the lodge. Tahatankohana cleaned up the ceremonial items. Believing they would still be able to get to Waya's village before dark, they decided to share one more meal.

Only minutes later, Awan came into the lodge. "I am sorry I left, but I needed to be alone."

"I understand." Tahatankohana assured him, "It is perfectly fine, but it is too cold to stay out there very long. I am glad you are already back."

Goodbye Hideout

Awan went to speak with Kangee. "Was it too hard on you walking and lying on the floor?"

"I am fine, but I have been awake all morning, and I hurt. Bring me sleeping potion."

The'-ha brought the sedative and a big container of water. "Tahatankohana said you need water. Drink this too. I will get your food."

Ann and Helen had prepared the meal before the ceremony. Tahatankohana took her the food and examined the incision.

"I did not know you are a mystery man," Kangee remarked.

"Wakanda named me 'Mystery man to the world' the night before we left."

"He did the right thing. Thank you for saving me, helping my people, and giving The'-ha, I mean Awan, his new name and the bow and arrows. May the Great Spirit protect you and your family."

"And you and your family as well." He left so that Kangee could eat with Awan.

A short time later, Awan joined the others. "She is sleeping. We thank all of you for what you have done."

"You are welcome," Sally replied.

Tahatankohana said, "Tell me everything I told you about taking care of these people, how to make all the medicines, and finding more of the plants."

Awan recited everything correctly.

Lisa Gay

"Perfect. I'm going to check on Inola, Tsiyi, and Cheasequah one more time."

Awan informed Tahatankohana, "Cheasequah left early today. His children are with Magaskawee. You can check on the other two, but first, I have a suggestion. At each village, get a person who knows somebody in the next village to take you there. You cannot just hope to find a place. You will get stuck outside at night, your baby will die, and maybe others too. Also, make sure the person will be able to make the arrangements for you to stay because they trust the person who brought you. You should not just show up at a village."

"We will do that." Tahatankohana left to check on his other two patients still in the village. He returned and found everybody ready to go. As they left with the sentry who had brought Waya into the village, Tahatankohana told the man he considered a friend, "Goodbye, Awan. May the Great Spirit bless you and your family."

Washta found the statement odd. *That is not The'-ha's name, and I killed his entire family myself.*

Goodbye Hideout

SIX

Hota's village, the place Waya had lived for most of his life, was barely a day's ride west of the Indian Territory road running from Fort Smith north to Saint Louis. The temperature rose above freezing that afternoon, but it was almost the shortest day of the year, and they knew the night would be far below freezing. They prayed they would reach Waya's village before sundown.

As fast as the goats, sheep, and miniature donkeys could travel, the family hurried across the low, rolling hills covered in blown snow. Helen shivered. "I didn't know the prairie was so bleak."

Roscoe spoke of another way the prairie had looked. "You haven't seen the waves of gold when a gentle wind blows across the tall yellow grass."

Sally added, "You should have seen the prairie after the rain this summer. It was a garden of wildflowers as far as you could see. I spent a week in that garden butchering buffalo with Chaska. I was very happy." *I wish I would stop falling in love. I'm tired of leaving my heart behind.*

Since Noah hadn't spent as much time with Ann and Christopher as he wanted, he rode in the wagon with his wife and son. His oak bark colored hair was down to his shoulders after growing for ten months. It had been much longer before the doctor in Harmony had shaven him bald to sew up the gash put in his head by the outlaw Roy Butterfield. Ann's raven-colored hair was much wavier than it had been when Noah had first met her. At that time, her hair had also been very long. Noah liked the way Ann's locks curled around her face. He stroked her hair and looked into her green eyes. "You are so beautiful. I am very blessed."

"I am too. I love you and our son very much. Chris looks at me so intently sometimes. I wonder what he's thinking."

"He's thinking what a wonderful mother he has."

"Probably for sure when he's nursing. I didn't know you had Wakanda's breastplate and hairpiece."

"Wakanda had a short ceremony the night before we left. One mystery man naming another is only between them. I'm sorry you couldn't be there."

"I'm not upset. I'm proud of you."

"Thank you, my wife."

"You're welcome, my husband. Do you want to hold your son?"

"Yes." Noah looked into his son's eyes. "He does seem to be looking into my soul."

"I think he's very perceptive. Don't you?"

"Extremely." They laughed together. Noah whispered to his wife, "I love you, Ann."

"And I love you, Noah." They snuggled close with their son between them. After being awake for thirty-six hours, they inadvertently fell asleep. When they heard talking, it was dark.

Noah brushed his lips across Ann's. "Be right back." He got up and hugged the woman outside the wagon.

"Get Ann and Christopher. I'll take you to our lodge," Bethany told her son.

The village chief, Hota, arrived at the wagons. "Welcome, Tahatankohana,"

Noah thought it would be best to respond to the name by which Hota knew him and not offer his name, Noah Swift Hawk, for the assassin to track him. "Thank you for allowing us to stay in your village." Tahatankohana turned to his father.

Chetan waved him off. "Go on. We will put up the animals and wagons."

"Thank you." Tahatankohana hurried to the back of the wagon. "Come, my wife."

Ann had already wrapped their son in the yellow buffalo wool blanket Sally had made. "Here's Christopher." She got out of the wagon.

Lisa Gay

Tahatankohana gave her back the baby then wrapped a buffalo fur around them.

Ann stepped into the lodge. Chumani, Bethany's three-year-old daughter, ran over. "I hold Itofer."

"After he eats, then you can sit beside me and hold him in your lap."

"Itofer. Itofer," Chumani chanted as she did a happy dance around the room.

When his belly was full, Ann laid her baby in Chumani's lap. "Sit very still while you hold him." Ann squatted right in front of them.

Chumani carefully held her nephew. Christopher wrapped his tiny fingers around the one Chumani held out to him. "Itofer like me. Itofer hold me."

"I see that," Ann confirmed Chumani's take on the subject.

Chumani looked up. "You have Itofer."

Ann took her son. "Thank you for holding him."

"You welcome." Chumani was glad she had helped.

That night, even though they were still only a few days away from Noah's village, Noah and Ann agreed to stay until after Christmas. Noah thought his new brothers-in-law should spend more time visiting the people with whom they had grown up. Mostly, he wanted to keep his son out of the freezing weather. He prayed the assassin sent to kill him and Ann wouldn't find them.

SEVEN

Christmas morning in Hota's village, billows of tiny, dry snowflakes blew across the land while the family had a private time of thanksgiving for the birth of their savior. Bethany read the story of Christ's birth. "At that time, Emperor Augustus ordered a census to be taken throughout the Roman Empire. When this first took place, Quirinius was the governor of Syria. Everyone, then, went to register himself, each to his own town. Joseph went from the town of Nazareth in Galilee to Bethlehem in Judea, the birthplace of King David. He went to register with Mary, who was promised to him in marriage. She was pregnant, and while they were in Bethlehem, the time came for her to have her baby. She gave birth to her first son, wrapped him in strips of cloth, and laid him in a manger- there was no room for them to stay in the inn.

"Some shepherds in that part of the country were spending the night in the fields, taking care of their flocks. An angel of the Lord appeared to them, and the

31

glory of the Lord shone over them. They were afraid, but the angel said to them, 'Do not be afraid! I am here with good news for you, which will bring great joy to all the people. This very day in David's town, your Savior was born- Christ the Lord! And this is what will prove it to you: you will find the baby wrapped in strips of cloth and lying in a manger.'

"Suddenly, a vast army of heaven's angels appeared with the angel, singing praises to God. 'Glory to God in the highest heaven, and peace on earth to those with whom he is pleased!' When the angels went away from them back into heaven, the shepherds said to one another, 'Let us go to Bethlehem and see this thing that has happened, which the Lord has told us.'

"Therefore, they hurried off, found Mary and Joseph, and saw the baby lying in the manger. When the shepherds saw him, they told them what the angel had said about the child. All who heard it were amazed at what the shepherds said. Mary remembered all these things and thought deeply about them.

"The shepherds went back, singing praises to God for all they had heard and seen; it had been just as the angel had told them. Luke 2:1–20. And that is how it happened."

After Bethany read, Chetan prayed. "God in heaven, today, we celebrate your arrival as a human to be our example, comforter, and savior. We can never be good enough to repay You for the gift of Jesus, so we just say thank You.

"Make us forever grateful. We want to be your messengers to the world, so help us be the best we can be with love, compassion, and help for all. Thank You for every person here in this lodge, born or unborn."

The rest of the family added blessings as they served mussel chowder, freshly baked sweet bread, and sassafras tea.

After enjoying the meal, they took a package of fishhooks, fishing line, needles, and thread to each family. Hoping at least one person would want to know more, they explained why they were giving the gifts and what Christmas was about. Nobody cared to hear more. The family was still happy to have given the gifts and been able to tell the Christmas story to everybody in the village.

Waya's grandsons Dustu and Adahy, the twins who had married Noah's sisters, sat beside their cousin, Hangka. Dustu informed him, "We will move on in the morning."

Hangka's wife offered, "All of you come for breakfast. You will not have to cook or clean."

Just before his cousins left the village, Hangka handed both Dustu and Adahy a carved wooden horse. "I want you to remember where you came from."

Adahy examined his gift. "You have always made beautiful carvings. I will never forget this place, but I am excited to go to the western sea."

Dustu felt the same as his twin, mostly. "Me too. I will never forget my home."

EIGHT

After saying goodbye, Waya led his family southwest across the prairie for most of the day.

Christopher is too quiet. Ann moved the buffalo hide to look at her son. "Noah!" she screamed, "Christopher is red!" She unwrapped the wool blanket, removed his clothes, and slid her son inside her dress. Ann squeezed him against her skin and pressed his tiny fingers between her breasts.

Noah dashed to the wagon. "What can I do?!"

"Snuggle up behind him. He's freezing!" Ann willed her body heat into her baby.

Noah removed his outer clothes and did as Ann asked. "Heavenly Father, save my son." He pulled the coat and fur up behind him.

"Is he any warmer?" Sally stood at the rear of the wagon.

Stephanie asked, "Should we build a fire?"

Ann peeked at Chris's bright red fingers. "Yes."

Noah nixed the plan. "No! When the sun goes

down, we'll all freeze! We've got to keep going! See if he'll eat."

Ann brushed her nipple on Christopher's lips. Warm milk flowed into the child.

"Move your hand for a second." Noah looked at his son's fingers against Ann's breast. "Not much better. Keep him against your skin."

"Just like you did with Noah," added Stephanie.

Sally fumed. "If Christopher dies, I'm going to kill Judge Daniel Hall. If he'd stop worrying about you marrying Noah and hadn't sent Joe Smith to kill you, we'd still be back in our warm lodge. I hate that man!"

"I'll help you," spat out Ann.

Noah remained pressed against his son's back. "You will both be too late. I will have already done it."

Despite plodding through the snow, they made it to the village of Waya's birth before the sun dropped below the horizon. It was the first time since Waya had married Dustu and Adahy's grandmother that he had been to the village of his birth. He discovered that his pudgy niece, Kamama, whose name meant butterfly, was the leader of the group situated on the Verdigris River. "I am Waya. Do you remember me?"

"I do."

"We have a baby freezing to death! We need warmth fast. We are nineteen people, many animals, and six wagons. Help us!"

"Bring the baby."

Ann hurried inside. "We need warm water."

Goodbye Hideout

Ann tested the water that Kamama dipped from the large jug beside the fire. "Warm but not too hot." She signed, thank you, then lay Christopher in the warm wetness.

Waya handed his niece a red shirt and a sewing kit. "For allowing us into your home."

The baby screeched. Noah softly stroked his son's head. "God, please don't let him die!"

Luyu put her hand on Noah's shoulder. "The crying is good. Even though it hurts, it means warmth is returning."

Chetan's stomach churned. *I don't want to upset Kamama because Christopher needs to get warm, but Noah's life is in jeopardy too. We have to keep running. We have to get to the next village safely.* He forced himself to casually ask, "Is there anybody who could guide us to a shallow ford across the river and then to another village where somebody will take us in before sundown tomorrow?"

Kamama looked at the howling baby. *I can get more if I ask while they are worried.* "Are you going to trade for this?"

"Would this work?" Chetan held out the offering he had in case the shirt and sewing kit had not been enough to get inside a lodge.

Kamama examined the steel knife. She removed a small whetstone from its sheath. "I will take you. I see why you need a shallow ford. It will not be possible to

37

find one in every river. We can trade old hides to make shells for the two wagons not covered in pitch."

Hanataywee put down the bedrolls she had carried into the lodge. "Don't we already have unused hides?"

The two spare buffalo hides belong to me. Chetan offered, "If that's what it takes to save Christopher, I'll give mine."

Bethany answered, "Also, we had twenty-one antelope skins, but we used ten to wrap the pemmican and four to make dresses for Ann and Stephanie."

Ehawee spoke over the increasingly loud crying. "We need to make Helen a dress. She should stop wearing white woman's clothes in Indian Territory. That will take another two."

Eli held more bedding. "So, we have five we can use. That won't cover even one wagon."

Bethany looked at Kamama. "We need to take care of my grandson. Find what hides your people are willing to trade."

Kamama tried not to smile. "Wait here." She left.

Bethany joined the crowd around the screaming baby. She looked over the shoulders of her daughters. "Is he going to be all right?"

"He looks even more distressed." Noah stripped off his shirt. "I don't think this water is a good thing." He took his son from the washbasin. "Maybe it's too much of a change for a baby this cold. Give me his blanket."

Goodbye Hideout

Sally quickly held out the yellow, buffalo yarn blanket she had made for her nephew. Noah snuggled it to his son's back, wrapped his arms around his baby, and pressed him to his bare chest. The skin-deep warmth of Christopher soon dissipated. The baby felt like ice. "God, help him!" chanted Noah as he tried to warm his son.

Ann wrapped her coat around the three of them. While the baby howled in pain, the rest of the family pressed together around them.

Christopher slowly faded from bright red to pink before he finally felt warm in Noah's arms. His screaming changed to fussing. Ann watched her son's face. "He's not in anguish anymore. I think he's going to be all right."

No longer afraid that Christopher would die, the rest of the family left Noah and Ann to care for their son and prepared to trade.

NINE

The men got trading goods from the wagons. The women separated them. In group one, they placed Hudson Bay one-point wool blankets, sewing kits, steel hunting knives with the small whetstone, both of which were in a cow leather sheath, several fifteen-foot pieces of red cotton fabric, and more of blue.

The second pile had plugs of tobacco, butcher knives, scissors, awls, and blue flannel shirts.

The third collection of items included cotton handkerchiefs, crambo combs, fishhooks, fishing line, needles, and small spools of red, blue, green, yellow, white, and black cotton thread.

Before long, a middle-aged woman arrived with a child and a buffalo hide. In Indian universal sign language, she requested —show me sewing thing— then sat at the trading blanket across from Luyu.

Luyu opened the cloth wrapped around a sewing kit, which lay between them.

I trade— the woman held out the fur.

Luyu took the fur, looked at the burn in the

middle, and then stuck her hand through the hole. "One sewing kit, nothing else."

Two other women came in as the first walked away, chastising her daughter. "We were lucky we were able to get something for the hide you ruined."

"You need old hide. What you have?" one of the new arrivals asked.

"Let me see the hide." Luyu looked it over. *Its fur is wearing away, but it is bigger than the last one, and it doesn't have holes.* "Pick one item from each of these two groups and two from that group."

The woman picked scissors and an awl.

Luyu pointed. "If you want two from this group, you cannot have any from the first group, but you may pick four from the last group."

"I will trade if I can have the red cloth and these two things." She held the scissors and the awl.

Luyu wasn't giving in or the women would not respect her, nor would the next one. "If you also give me two buckets of buffalo fat and one of ashes, then you can have them and the cloth."

"I agree." The woman started to walk away with the items she had selected.

"You may take them when you bring the tallow and ashes. Waya will give you the buckets." Luyu set the items aside.

Except for Noah, who refused to leave Christopher, the men took the two hides and spread them beside the wagon. Waya went back into the lodge and whispered to his wife. "We will have to cut the one with the hole. Those two are not enough."

Luyu nodded. She held out her hand toward the third woman. The young woman offered a large, freshly removed hide with four large slits where the spears that had killed the beast had punctured the skin. Luyu looked it over. *This one is large enough to cover two people. It would be better to sew the holes and tan it.* She said to the young woman, "Your husband killed a huge buffalo, but he needs to learn better places to spear it."

"But it is enormous. He killed it close to his brother's village."

"Where is that?"

"South on other side of river."

"One from the first group." Luyu pointed. "Two from this one and four from the last pile."

"I heard you tell Wyanet she could bring buffalo fat and ashes. I want the sewing kit, the blue cloth, and all the colors of thread."

"How much tallow do you have?"

"All the rest you need."

"I do not want to take all you have."

"But I also want this for my husband." The woman picked up the knife and whetstone."

Luyu waved Chetan over. "Give five pails to this woman," then spoke to the woman again, "Fill four

Goodbye Hideout

with buffalo fat and one with ashes. I will let you have the sewing package, the cloth, and one spool of each color thread when you bring the fat and ashes. I will send a message to you about the knife. What is your name?"

"Doya."

"Doya, show my son which is your lodge." Both women came back with the fat and ashes and then carried away their treasures. No other person brought a fur. Luyu contemplated.

When Kamama returned, Luyu told her what she wanted. "I plan to ask Doya and her husband to take us across the Verdigris to the next village. Will you agree to this? If not, I understand. We did already agree to give you the knife to take us. However, we still need more hides, so I will give you the knife if you get at least two more people to trade."

Kamama thought. *I would rather not spend two days guiding Waya's family.* "I will try, but you may have to trade more because they do not have hides they think are bad."

Many minutes later, Luyu decided nobody else was going to trade. She packed up their trade items.

A woman with long, white hair and a face deeply wrinkled by many years in the sun stepped into Kamama's home. "I have tipi. I will never live in it again. It could be wagon cover. I want three-point blanket, also one of everything you have in your blanket, and five tobacco. I will not change my mind."

Luyu looked at her family vigorously nodding their heads. "Let my husband and I see it."

"Come." As they walked, the woman said, "So you married the wolf. I hope you will be safe."

A scowl passed over Waya's face, but he had learned to hold his tongue very early in his life.

Luyu replied, "Wolves are very devoted to their mates. I am blessed. Why do you trade your tipi?"

Waya smiled at Luyu's reply.

"When I was young, the tipi owner killed my husband and stole me. He made me his wife. I lived with him for two weeks. I hated him. One night, I stabbed him in his heart, buried him, took down his tipi, packed it up, and left."

In the snow, Waya and Luyu spread the seventeen sewn together hides painted with still visible designs. The owner informed Luyu, "When the tipi is standing, three people can sleep foot to head across it. I have not looked at it since I put it in that corner. You will need to soften it again with tallow and ashes."

Luyu and Waya looked at each other. "We will trade if we can also have the poles."

The ancient woman agreed. "Take them."

The men carried away the poles. Ann's and Noah's sisters rolled up the tipi. Luyu and Waya walked with Doya and her husband to their home.

Goodbye Hideout

TEN

In the morning light, Doya and Atohi joined the wagon train leaving the village. For taking them to where he was born and then across the river, Atohi selected the item his wife had wanted him to have, as well as a package of fishing hooks and two bundles of line. For helping to sew buffalo hides while they rode to the river crossing, Doya picked a red shirt for herself and another that fit Atohi.

Atohi led them south along the Verdigris River. The nine women and Christopher, held to Ann's warm body in a sling, rode together in the same wagon. Their backs leaned against one or the other side of the wagon. Their legs passed each other's to the opposite side.

Bethany got the smaller buffalo hide of the two Chetan had killed the previous summer. The women sewed the two whole buffalo skins to the halves of the skin with the burn hole. Bethany stowed the buffalo fur Atohi had killed to make it into a blanket for two.

Just after the sun passed its zenith, Atohi brought them to a sheltered glen full of green pennycress. At the Blue Mounds, the animals happily drank from a small stream and enjoyed the nutritious food.

Their large herd had consumed most of the cut grass. The nets under the wagon hung empty, and the wagon was almost bare. Not having to feed the animals while stopped was a blessing.

Helen and Roscoe prepared the meal. The other women continued sewing the hides into a shell to make the wagon into a boat. The men gathered all the downed branches they could find and squirreled them into the nets. After filling all their water barrels and canteens, they continued south.

Noah rode to Atohi. "Are we going all the way to Fort Gibson?"

"Only to the junction of the Verdigris and Hominy."

Eli's father, Tom, joined them. "If we go that far, we might as well go to Fort Gibson."

"By then, you should have your wagon covers ready. I was only going to take you to the village where I was born. Tomorrow, my brother will take you farther down."

"You agreed you would take us across the river," Noah reminded him.

"You are not ready, and from my family's village, you would cross three rivers to get to the Arkansas. If you go to the junction, you will be ready and have

Goodbye Hideout

only one river to cross. If you think I must, I will take you over in the morning, then you can find your way to another village, or you can hire somebody to take you. I will come back across to this side and go home."

I can't have my son outside at night. We need somebody to guide us to the next village, and Atohi did find the pennycress. Noah asked, "You are sure your brother will lead us?"

"Yes. He will like some of your trade items, but he doesn't have a wife to help you like I do."

ELEVEN

Atohi brought them to the home of Yona, his mother. "Wait here." He took his wife inside and explained the situation. "... If you take them all, you will get good things like this knife or blankets." He showed his knife to his brother. "Diwali, if you take them to the village of Adsila, you can get something. I got this knife and also fishhooks and line."

"Tell them to bring the trade items. I will decide what we want." Yona opened her door.

Atohi went outside. "All of you stay here. Bring your beds and your trade items."

As soon as their bedrolls were placed, Luyu picked up the blanket she had commandeered and filled with one of each trade item. She held it closed. Her family now had needs beyond a night's stay and two meals, but she started there. Luyu already held a nine-inch steel butcher knife and a sewing kit, which she had put together inside a scrape of antelope hide. "We offer these to stay inside your lodge, have a meal tonight, and another in the morning."

Goodbye Hideout

"That will be good." Yona held out her hand.

Luyu continued, "Do you have animal feed?"

"Wild barley we gathered for ourselves and our horses. I am sure you saw the stacks of grass, but it is not mine to give away." Yona directed her son. "Get Tsula."

Atohi returned with a tall, narrow-faced woman with sunken cheeks, who otherwise looked healthy. "Atohi says you need food for your animals, and you will trade."

Luyu replied, "This is true."

"Atohi says you have blankets. For ten blankets, I will show you the barley. You have to do the work." *I doubt there is any there. I'll get the blankets before we go.*

Luyu saw Noah point to himself and switch his fingers back and forth. He then waved his hand past everybody, leaned forward, put both hands together by the ground, then stood up with his hands still together. He held up two fingers then nodded his head up and down. She switched the direction of negotiations. "Do you decide about the grass?"

"I do."

"I see two stacks are very old. How many winters are they?"

"Only previous winter."

"Did you harvest as much this summer as last, and do you have more animals now than then?"

"We have enough to trade the old hay. Do you want both piles?"

Luyu believed the hay belonged to the whole village. She wanted everybody to benefit, not just one woman. "Both stacks. We will give each adult either one small blanket or a butcher knife, and either five fishhooks and one fishing line, or five needles and one spool of thread."

"Bring the items to me. I will give them out."

Luyu saw Atohi, his father Coowescoowe, Doya, Diwali, and Yona shake their heads back and forth. She knew they did not want Tsula to have control of all the items. "We will not carry it all to your lodge. Each person can come to our wagon and get their share."

"I will tell everybody what I have done for them. Do you want me to show you the barley for ten blankets?"

"Did you plant the barley?"

"We found it then took care of it."

"If we can find the barley ourselves, and we harvest it ourselves, we will give you two blankets if the fields are close to this village. If they are far away, we will not give you anything unless we cannot find the fields. Then we will trade six blankets for you to show us the location, and we will harvest the grain ourselves."

"You will not find it. Then you will come, ask for my help, and give me ten blankets." The woman left the lodge.

Goodbye Hideout

Noah believed Atohi knew where the fields were, but he decided he would not ask him. He suspected their guide had inadvertently already told him the answer. He had noticed the young man looking in a specific direction for a portion of the trip. Luyu informed Yona and Coowescoowe, "We will get our animals ready for the night."

Ann stayed inside with Christopher and Chumani while the others fed hay from the old stacks in the field. Noah, however, jumped on Eyanosa.

"May I come with you?" Ke, his seven-year-old-brother, asked.

Noah looked at his father, who nodded his head. "It's going to be dark soon, and I don't know the land, so let's go." Noah pulled his brother up in front of him. They rode toward the place where Noah believed they would find the barley.

After putting the outer layer of hay beside the animals for them to eat, the men loaded the fresher hay from the protected interior into the wagon. Stephanie, Sally, Hanataywee, Ehawee, Helen, and Bethany doled out the trade items as the people came to get their share. Inside the lodge, Ann made packets of fishhooks and line, and some of needles and thread.

Except for Noah and Ke, everybody sat inside and ate hot food. Noah and Ke rode back and forth across the cold land that Atohi had watched as they had traveled to his village. Three times, they moved closer to the river and then went all the way from one end of the area to the other. They didn't find a field of barley. The little bit of warmth of the day dissipated fast. When Noah could see the river, he headed back, disappointed. At the village, they fed Eyanosa, gave him water, rubbed him down, and put him with the others before they went to the lodge. Noah called out, "Tahatankohana and Ke are here."

Ann opened the door. "I'll get your food."

Everybody saw Noah signal that he had not been successful. Late that night, when he thought everybody was asleep, Noah woke his father. He motioned for Chetan to follow. Knowing the frigid air would enter and awaken the others, they dared not go outside. They moved as far away as they could. "We are using a lot of trade goods keeping our animals fed. We can't even carry enough food to last any amount of time. We've been lucky so far. That won't last. We may get stuck where we can't get more."

Chetan whispered, "We can probably use money around here, but farther away from the fort, it would be useless. We need to buy more trade goods."

Ann heard the conversation and slipped over. "We can't travel outside all winter. Christopher won't survive. Ezra told me about an abandoned military garrison named Fort Arbuckle. It's just below the Red Fork joining with the Arkansas River. We could have Diwali take most of us across the river and on to the village of Adsila. We go from there to Fort Arbuckle.

Goodbye Hideout

"A few of us take the two wagons without pitch and the other thirty-four animals to Fort Gibson. At the fort, buy pitch, and cover the wagons, then come to Fort Arbuckle with all the hay and oats they can carry.

"We would have only two and a half months until the prairie grass comes up next spring. By then, the pitch on the wagons will be set. Also, Stephanie will have her baby in a safe, warm building. In the spring, we can cross the Arkansas and move on."

Chetan thought for a minute, "I don't think we would be able to get enough hay."

Noah said, "We can make another trip to the fort and buy more. We could ask them to get more from Fort Smith if they don't already have enough."

After breakfast, Atohi and Doya headed home. Noah, Waya, Roscoe, and Tom went looking for the barley field. Chetan explained their plan to Yona's family. Coowescoowe offered, "I can take those who cross the river. I have a good friend over there. Diwali can take those who stay on this side."

Chetan agreed, "We will get started." They rearranged and stacked their supplies high.

Yona's family joined. She said, "We do not want to trade. We just help."

Luyu accepted. The family emptied the wagon assigned to stay on the current side of the river down to the crates of dynamite, the heavy blacksmith tools, and their carpenter tools. They also stretched the sewn-together buffalo hides around a frame they made with the branches from the glen and then pulled strips of buffalo hide through holes close to the edge of the fur.

"Pull tight," Coowescoowe instructed.

"If I pull any tighter, it will break," Diwali replied.

Chetan said, "I think it is tight enough. Tie off."

They stepped back and looked at the large, oddly shaped, furry on the inside, but sturdy boat.

"Put a rope around the frame on that side. I will tie one here." Eli drew a rope between the fur and the wood frame. "Flip it," he requested as Stephanie and Sally approached with buckets of melted beeswax from Fletcher Creek.

Yona helped work the substance into the seams. "I never saw beeswax before."

"What about honey?" Stephanie asked.

"Never."

"I will ask Ann if we can have some with dinner." Helen left the other women.

TWELVE

When the barley seekers returned to the village, the women still surrounded the buffalo-fur-covered bowl by the river. Except for Noah, the men went to look.

Noah assumed his wife and son would be in the lodge. He found Ann preparing dinner for both families with Yona and Coowescoowe's food. Christopher looked out from the cradleboard on his mother's back as she worked in the warm lodge.

Ann saw the smile on her husband's face. "Are you happy to see me, or did you find it?" she asked as they walked toward each other.

"Both." He took her into his arms as best as he could with their son on her back. He kissed his wife lovingly and enjoyed the returned love until the door opened. They stepped apart.

Helen entered. "Don't mind me. Go back to what you were doing. I just came to ask if we can have honey with the meal. They've never eaten any."

"I'll get some." Noah started toward the door.

"You'll never find it, my husband. You take Christopher. Helen and I will do it."

Noah took the cradleboard off Ann's back. She walked out the door as Noah untied the cover to get his son. Whatever Ann was cooking smelled good. Noah carried his little son in one arm and checked the food with his other. He tasted it. *Very good!* He sat down to admire and play with his son.

Chetan came into the lodge. "I hear you found it."

"It was Tom."

"But you took them to the general area. How did you know?"

Noah continued to bounce Christopher and make bubbles with his lips just as Christopher was doing. "As we were coming here, I noticed Atohi looking toward a specific area then paid attention to when he stopped looking. I thought there must have been something over there that had meaning for him. When Tsula said there was a wild barley field, I figured that was probably where it was.

"The ground looked flat, and we could each see the next person, so we assumed we were seeing everything between us. We almost rode past, but when Tom went away from his horse to relieve himself, he walked into a dip and found the barley.

"The plants still have many seeds on them. After we eat, we should harvest it. Even though it is rather far away, it is obvious they have been cultivating it. We should give them some blankets, but I do not think they should all go to Tsula."

"I agree." Chetan held out his arms. "Let me hold my grandson."

Noah handed Christopher over. "Is this how you felt about me when I was born?"

"I do not know exactly how you feel, but you were and are very much loved. We were very happy to have you."

"I just cannot even imagine life without him. Is it wrong of me? I almost love him more than Ann, and you know I love her so very much."

"You can love them both extremely. That is the way it should be. I love everybody in my family that way."

Together they enjoyed having Christopher to themselves.

"Did he just smile at us?" Noah posed the possibility that his son was happy that his father and grandfather were paying so much attention to him.

Chetan said, "Let us agree that it was a smile of pleasure no matter what he was feeling."

Helen and Ann returned. Helen carried a mostly full quart jar. "We were able to get to one of them."

Chetan stated what was on his mind since both Noah and Ann were there. "Tom and I should go to Fort Gibson. Everybody else goes to Fort Arbuckle."

Noah protectively brought his son to his chest. "Christopher needs to be warm."

"We can't stay here. According to Coowescoowe, it will be only five days to Fort Arbuckle. Ann and Christopher can wrap up in a blanket coat, and you can put furs around them. Neither of you can go to Fort Gibson. Sally and Roscoe shouldn't either. The four of you made a big impression when you were there last summer. Eli, Waya, Dustu, and Adahy will want to be with their wives. It's not that I don't love Bethany, but we've been together a long time. They just got married."

Noah answered, "I don't want to take any chances, and there are possible bad consequences with any option. Let's decide later."

"You shouldn't harvest the barley today. I know it will be more work, but we should leave the village without a guide, then circle back, and get the barley. That woman is not going to be happy that you found it." Helen set the honey beside the cooking food.

Chetan stated his opinion. "I don't want to be deceptive. Let's talk about it during dinner."

Ann changed the topic. "I want to see the boat."

Noah wrapped Christopher in his yellow, buffalo fur yarn blanket, put him in the sling across his chest, and then slipped his wool coat over both of them. Christopher looked up at his father from the opening at the top of Noah's coat. The four crossed the village and joined the crowd at the river.

Goodbye Hideout

"We'll be done in a few minutes," Stephanie informed them.

"We can eat as soon as you finish. I want to enjoy moving freely while Noah carries the baby. May I work on the boat? I rarely get to do anything to help."

Ke handed her a bucket of beeswax.

Ann pushed it into the remainder of the seam then double-checked the whole joining.

The men flipped it right side up and then put it in the river, flowing slowly across the flat land.

Roscoe held one rope, and Tom had the other. Chetan stepped inside to force it deeper into the water. He asked his youngest son, "Will you help me test this?" Ke got in. "We are sitting on the riverbed. We need to go out farther. Push us."

Once floating, they felt around the seams. Ke informed everybody of the verdict. "No water!"

As they pulled the buffalo hide shell back to the shore, a cheer went up from the village folks gathered at the river. Chetan passed Ke out before he stepped out of the makeshift boat. They pulled the boat out of the water and tied it to the wagon. Since the show was over and it was frosty outside, the crowd broke up and went to their homes.

When everybody was content with full bellies, Luyu looked at Yona. "You know what is what around here, so I want to ask your opinion. How upset will anybody be if we found the barley and harvest what is still on the plants?"

"You found it?" Yona asked with surprise.

Coowescoowe told them what everybody in the whole village knew. "Tsula will not like it. It will make life much harder around here if she does not get what she wants, but you found it, and the field does not belong to her any more than the rest of us."

Yona remarked, "I thought we got all the seeds."

"More must have ripened. We would be taking what you would not have used anyway."

Yona looked at her husband and son then said, "Why should you give us something for what we did not know exists? It would be better if Tsula thinks you never found it. She would not know that you got any if you harvest it after you leave."

Luyu knew her family wanted to be fair. "You know that grain exists. We will give you two more blankets and another shirt. Then you will each have one."

"Peace is worth more than blankets." Yona looked at her husband for confirmation.

Luyu thought of a different solution. "Then we will give you ten feet of red cotton cloth and the other four colors of thread if you feed us tonight, let us stay one more night, and feed us in the morning."

Yona, Coowescoowe, and Diwali smiled. Yona spoke for them. "We agree to this."

Eli tapped his chin as he stared into the corner. "Several of us can say we are going to look again, take tarps and empty sacks, and go harvest. We leave the sacks of barley wrapped in tarps somewhere safe. Tomorrow, all you have to do is put them in the wagon."

Roscoe said, "Since we are now desperate to find the field and everything else is ready, more people could go without drawing suspicion."

Yona advised, "Do not sneak out the bags. Make sure you are seen taking them. Just do not let it be known how many. Everybody thinks you have to get the barley today. When you come back with empty sacks, nobody will realize you found it."

Coowescoowe said, "You should all go? It is a big field?"

Noah said, "Ann needs to stay here with Christopher, and I am not leaving them alone." *Or everything we own.* "We will get the wagons and hay across this afternoon. We will get however much we can with those who stay here tomorrow."

"I agree." Chetan slipped on his blanket coat.

Roscoe got up right behind him. "I'll get King, Ace, Dollie, Beauty, Blanco, and Shaggy."

Dustu told Adahy, "Let us get the hay into tarps."

"We'll help you," said their wives.

"Me too." Ke got his coat.

THIRTEEN

They harnessed mules to a wagon and filled tarps with the stacked grass. Tsula watched them crunch around on the frost-covered ground. In their warm lodges, the other villagers avoided the cold.

"Forward ho," Roscoe called out. The feet of King and Ace went into the water. They were up to their knees when Dollie and Beauty stepped in. The wagon still sat on the dry land. Water touched the underside of King and Ace when Hector and Diamond joined the other four animals in the icy water. A third of the way across, the lead mules still walked on the riverbed.

Chetan reported. "Looks like a channel of deep water ahead."

Roscoe knew if they stopped, they would not be able to start again. He tapped King lightly and warned his lead mule that there would be a sudden drop. "Forward deep." Roscoe felt King change his gait to test each step. Just before he thought they would reach the channel, Roscoe again called out and tapped

Goodbye Hideout

King's rear. King prepared to swim. Ace knew 'forward' but not 'deep.' However, he did understand that something different was coming. He learned deep when his hooves lost the riverbed.

The mules behind saw those ahead of them drop and prepared for the transition. The current of the river wasn't strong, and the heavy wagon still rolled on the riverbed. The wagon slowed.

"We can't stop. We have to get the wagon into the channel." Roscoe cracked the whip. "Forward run!" He hoped his mules would interpret the command as swim hard. They did and swam with all their might. Even so, the wagon slowed more. They were close, but they would not be going anywhere in only seconds. "We won't make it."

"I'll cut them loose." Chetan took off his coat, mukluks, hat, scarf, and gloves and then lowered himself into the frigid water. "COLD!" He pulled his knife. The front wheels touched the edge of the channel. The wagon's weight pulled it down the slope. The top of the wagon's bed floated only inches above the water.

"Get back in here," Roscoe ordered.

Chetan was more than willing to leave the mules to pull the wagon with its fur-boat-tag-along of hay. He stripped off his wet pants and shirt and jumped into the dry items he had brought. Even wrapped in an animal blanket, he shivered.

The current slowly carried the contraption downriver. Eli tied the end of the rope that needed to stay on his side of the river to the pommel of his saddle and then rode along the bank.

Only minutes after they had started in, mule hooves again touched the riverbed. The wagon left the water on the western side. They hurried upriver until they arrived opposite the village.

Roscoe and Chetan got the mules out of the harness, dried them as best as they could, and then covered them with the animal blankets. The second they had unloaded the hay, Chetan got into the boat. He started across the river as Roscoe stacked firewood to warm the mules.

On the eastern side of the Verdigris, Eli secured his end of the rope and made a giant loop across the river fastened between two wagons. "We can't take more than twenty-four animals to Fort Arbuckle, and we'll have to take every bit of this hay. Most of the animals need to go directly to Fort Gibson, and whoever takes them will have to buy hay."

Helen stood in her long, blanket coat and mukluks with one hand on her hip and the other cupped around her chin. "How can we carry that much hay?"

Stephanie stood beside her grandmother-in-law. "We use the tipi poles. Attach two to the back of each wagon with the ends dragging on the ground. We tie on tarps of hay and pull it behind, and we should let the mules eat as much prairie grass as possible when we stop."

Chetan arrived. "We need to attach more animals when we send the next wagon. We barely got to the channel. They had to start swimming while the wagon was still on the riverbed. Also, the animals need to get out quicker. I'm practically freezing, and I was in the water only a minute."

Tom asked, "Will two extra per wagon be enough?"

"You figure it out." Bethany hurried her husband to the lodge.

"We should try eight and the lightest wagon," suggested Waya.

Eli calculated as they shuttled hay in the buffalo fur boat. "This still won't be enough."

Wrapped in furs, Tsula had watched and listened the entire day. She saw her opening. "We will sell you another stack of grass for ten blankets."

"One for each family," Luyu countered.

I won! Tsula serenely said, "That will be twelve."

Luyu wanted the people of the village to gain. "One person from each family must come to our wagon." She climbed into the wagon and passed blankets to Ke, who gave them to the villagers, who immediately hurried back to their warm homes.

The women had filled all twelve ground covers, and there was still hay to send across the Verdigris.

"Fill the hay wagon. I'll go over, wrap some in the tipi, and send back six tarps." Tom got in the boat.

On the far side, he and Roscoe spread the tipi over two poles, then went to work emptying hay. He tied the tipi closed with four tarpfuls inside.

Next, they filled the net under the wagon and then emptied some on the ground for the mules to eat. Roscoe got in the boat with the ground covers. Tom stayed beside the fire with the wagon and mules.

After they sent six more loads and filled the hay wagon, there remained only enough grass for the animals staying in the village to eat that evening and the next morning.

Noah remarked, "It is time to send the other wagons."

Chetan had taken the first wagon across. "I can gauge the ability of the animals to pull the wagon. I should take the second wagon and test using eight."

Dustu followed his father-in-law. "Crossing the river in a wagon sounds exciting. I will go with you."

"Me too," his twin informed them.

Waya put his hand on Adahy's shoulder. "We do not want to add more weight. You can come across with me."

Chetan imitated Roscoe. He made a slight tap on the rear of the lead mule. "Forward ho."

The mules, Redeemed and Rose, led the team into the river, followed by the donkeys: Honey, Smiley,

Goodbye Hideout

Chocolate, Spot, Big Jenny, and QuickSilver. They easily pulled the wagon. When they approached the channel, Chetan tapped Redeemed.

"Forward deep." He did the same to Rose. Neither understood the command. Suddenly, their front legs had no support. Redeemed didn't like it, but she swam. When Rose dropped, her head went under. Water filled her ears. She remembered when the Maumelle River had almost drowned her. She thrashed frantically.

Chetan called out, "Calm down," to no avail. Thinking he could soothe the mule, he again stripped off his outer clothes and jumped in.

The donkeys behind Redeemed and Rose saw those in front drop into the deep and started to swim before they reached the channel. That left the four behind with most of the burden, and they pushed Rose in the harness. She fought to get free and made it even harder for the others and herself.

Chetan called out and tried to get the panicked animal to focus on him. Then, she did. She saw something to step on to get out of the water. As she tried to climb him, Rose's sharp hooves pounded Chetan in the head and chest. He had no way to direct his body away. He blocked as much of the assault as possible with his arms until a powerful kick to his head knocked him out. As he floated away, Rose's hooves clobbered Chetan's legs.

Dustu realized his father-in-law's dire straits. He

jerked off his coat and the mukluks on his feet then dove in with the reins in his hand. He managed to grab Chetan before he reached the end of the leather straps. He flipped Chetan's face out of the water. *He is not breathing!* He wrapped the straps under Chetan's arms, then brought the ends back around and held them together. Dustu pulled the loose end of the reins up the attached portion. "Do not be dead!" Chetan's body drew closer to the wagon as Dustu drew up the leads again and again. They reached the wagon.

Holding the leather straps tightly around Chetan, Dustu climbed onto the wagon seat floor. He pulled in what he was afraid was only a body. He felt for a pulse in his father-in-law's neck. *Thank You, God!* He threw on his coat, shoes, and hat, and then started dressing Chetan.

By the time he had Chetan in dry clothes, the animals were climbing up the riverbank. Rose acted as if she had never felt a fear. Dustu flicked the reins hard. "Forward run!" The animals were tired, but they obeyed. "Halt!" He pulled the reins as they rolled up to Tom and the first wagon. "Chetan's hurt, and he was in the cold river again."

"What happened?"

"Help me get him into the boat." Tom and Dustu carried Chetan to the fur boat. "Rose panicked. He got in the water to calm her. She kicked and stomped him and pushed him under."

FOURTEEN

Nobody in the village had seen what had happened in the river, but Bethany saw Dustu and Tom carry Chetan's limp body to the boat. "Noah!" she screamed.

Her son came running. Bethany pulled the boat as fast as she could. "Pull with everything you're got. They put your father in the boat. I think he's dead."

Ke stood paralyzed. He didn't know what to do. He had always believed that nothing could hurt his father. He started to cry.

Sally pulled Ke to her side. "Your brother will help him."

"I hope so," Ke replied in a very shaky voice.

There was only room for two to pull the rope. "Mother, move. Eli, help!" As soon as he was at the shore, Noah and Eli hauled Chetan out of the boat. A long gash split Chetan's cheek. The side of his head was mangled hair and flesh. Noah remarked, "This is what my head must have looked like when Roy bashed it. Get my medical supplies."

Bethany ran to get a place ready while Noah and Eli carried Chetan to the lodge. Sally flew to the wagon and got Noah's medicine bag. When she ran into the lodge, Chetan's coat and shirt were already off. Bruises and lacerations covered his body. "He looks like he was in a horrible fight."

"The worst are the two on his head," Noah replied.

Chumani tried to go to her father. Ehawee stopped her. "Father needs you to stay away. Noah has to fix him."

The child continued trying to get around her sister. "Chumani help."

Ehawee picked her up and carried her out of the lodge. Diwali followed her. "I will take you to Sasa's lodge." At her home, he called out, "We need to take Chumani out of the lodge! Her father is hurt, and she is getting in the way."

"Come in." Sasa asked, "What happened?"

Diwali told her what little he knew.

At the river, Dustu arrived. Adahy looked at his brother, shivering violently with blue lips and ghostly pale skin. "What happened?" he asked as he hurried his brother to the lodge, now surrounded by people denied entry and knowledge of what was happening inside. They crowded Dustu. "Is he going to live?"

Dustu told them, "…. He looked bad when we put him in the boat." He turned to his brother. "How bad is it?"

Goodbye Hideout

"Bad," Adahy informed his brother. "Should I pull Tom over?"

"No. He said he will tend to the animals."

Hanataywee saw Dustu. She hadn't realized he was in trouble too. "Dustu, get over here!"

Ann gave instructions. "This may sound like I'm suggesting sex, but I'm not. You both have to get undressed. Hanataywee, press your body against Dustu. Wrap your arms and legs around him. Skin to skin contact is what will warm him. Both of you get between furs and press them as close around you as you can."

"Come." Hanataywee took her husband to their pallet on the floor.

So Hanataywee could warm his brother, Adahy repeated Dustu's story to the rest of the family.

"I'm going to shoot that mule." Ke walked toward his bed to get his bow and the two arrows he owned.

Noah continued to stitch the deep laceration on his father's head. He was glad his father was unconscious, and that Chetan had been in freezing water that had kept him from bleeding out. "Ke, Rose was scared. She didn't mean to hurt father."

"I don't care." He walked toward the door. Bethany wanted to shoot the mule too. She did not try to stop him.

Sally did. "Let's talk, then decide if we should shoot her."

As soon as Noah had cleaned all the wounds and

sewn all the places that needed stitches, he told his mother the same thing that Ann had said to Hanataywee. "Put your naked skin against him and roll him toward you, so your chests are together."

Ann already held another fur to put over them.

"Tell me the truth. Is he going to be all right?" Bethany asked through her tears.

"I think so, but I don't know. He's been unconscious for a long time. I don't know the amount of damage done to his brain, but I was hit hard too, and I'm fine."

Since their original plan would not work, the family talked about what had happened and what they should do. Roscoe said, "We have to stick to the schedule, or we'll be back to not having enough hay. I know my animals, and I got the first wagon across. I can take another wagon over."

Adahy looked at Waya. "I will stay with Dustu. If my brother dies, half of me will die with him!"

Roscoe asked, "Eli or Waya. Either of you willing to come?"

"I will, but no jumping in the water," Eli replied.

Knowing they were running out of daylight and still had two wagons to go, they left immediately.

Waya whispered to Luyu and pointed at what he wanted. "Get those two. They are very well made. We can use them as poles for a travois and as spears." He stood. "Noah, let us take the other wagon right behind them." The second two men left.

Goodbye Hideout

A moment later, Adahy ran to the river. "Noah, you need to stay. I cannot do anything for anybody here. I can help get this wagon across."

"Thank you, Adahy. This is one of the ways you show Ehawee how much you love her. You show her how much you love her family." Noah went back to the lodge.

As they got the animals, Roscoe told Waya as well as he could in what he had learned about the Cherokee language, "Stay beside me but slightly back. I will try to let Jumper and Blue know when it is going to get deep and signal to swim just before we reach the channel. You tell Honor and Justice, 'forward deep,' then 'forward swim.' Hopefully, they and all the others will see Jumper and Blue swimming and do the same. Do you understand?"

"I understand," Waya answered.

The last two wagons and the rest of the animals going to Fort Arbuckle started into the water. Everybody, except those in the lodge with Chetan and Dustu, stood on the riverbank to watch what would happen this time. The trip across went as planned. Roscoe knew when to give the command to swim. Waya did the same when he heard Roscoe. The mules swam when the water was deep enough but before the channel and never realized there was a sudden drop. When the mules pulled them out of the river and up the bank uneventfully, the villagers went back to their warm lodges. Roscoe and Waya joined the other two wagons.

"How is Chetan?" Tom asked.

Roscoe told him the bad news.

"What are we going to do now?" Tom rubbed a blanket over Chief to dry him as much as possible.

Roscoe dried Molly. "Some of us are still leaving in the morning with Coowescoowe. In the future, Rose should never be a lead mule. Especially during a river crossing. She needs to see what is going to happen as much as possible."

"I agree." Tom walked to the next mule.

Eli dried Shaggy, the furriest of the animals. "We all need to go back across, so we can decide what to do." He moved on to the next mule.

The five men dried the animals and then bunched them under the buffalo fur before they set up two animal tents.

Roscoe lashed the tipi poles to the back of the wagons. "I'll go over, but I'm coming back. We can't leave our animals and these wagons unprotected. I'll wrap up in my fur inside a pile of hay."

Tom informed him. "I'll come back with you."

Waya decided. "It will be better with more people together. I will come back too."

They put the animals in the tents not only to keep them warmer but also to prevent any of them from wandering, so they could get an early start in the morning. The men tied the door loosely closed and then found the boat already on their side.

"Did you pull the boat over?" Roscoe asked Tom.

Tom shook his head. It was dark. Across the river, a torch burned, but they couldn't see who held it. Tom went first, Adahy second, next Eli, then Waya, and last Roscoe. Each of them found Coowescoowe and Diwali waiting with a torch, which they lit with their own and then sent each man to the lodge with light.

Dustu was warm, his color was normal, and he sat with the rest of the family. Chetan was still unconscious. Yona served them the supper she had prepared. Bethany refused to leave Chetan. Noah brought her a plate of food.

During the meal, Luyu again negotiated with Yona. "I see you have plenty of spears. I will buy two of my choice for the rest of his honey, a ball of beeswax this big," Luyu shaped her hands into a sphere with the fingertips barely touching, "and five twists of tobacco."

"The spears belong to my husband." Yona looked at Coowescoowe.

"If you also give one of the big blankets, so Yona and I can sleep together under it."

Since they would have to give a gigantic three-point Hudson Bay wool blanket, Luyu brought the trade down to what she thought was fair. "Then, no tobacco."

"That will be fine."

After eating, with all the bedding they needed to spend a cold night outside, Tom, Waya, and Roscoe crossed to the wagons and then pulled out the blanket, the beeswax, and a bolt of duck cloth. Eli retrieved the boat loaded with the items they had agreed to trade.

The women brought out their sewing kits and made a stretcher with the two spears and the duck cloth. They decided Chetan should not make the more demanding trip but should stay on the east side of the river. Therefore, Noah, Ann, and Christopher would too. Everybody else would go on to Fort Arbuckle. Hanataywee and Ehawee agreed to take Chumani and Ke with them.

Ke, however, refused. "I will not leave my father!"

FIFTEEN

As they ate dried badger, squash, corn, and wild turnips cooked into a soup, Coowescoowe told them what he had decided during the night. "Both groups should circle north to the barley field. We set up the buffalo fur boat, and everybody comes over to help. We go to the next villages after the grain has been harvested and loaded."

Noah swallowed soup. "That would be much better. Diwali, Ann, and I would spend at least the whole day, if not more, trying to get the barley by ourselves. I was thinking about leaving it behind."

"Pop, Stephanie, Grams, and I talked it over. We think, Pop and I should take the wagons to Fort Gibson." Eli held his spoon halfway to his mouth.

Stephanie crumbled cornbread into her bowl. "Chetan will not get better care at Fort Gibson than he will from a son who is very knowledgeable and loves him very much. He should go to Fort Arbuckle and not be hauled around for weeks."

Ann turned and hugged her sister. Tears flowed from her eyes. "Thank you."

"I should have seen it from the beginning. I'm sorry for the past grief I caused." Stephanie held her sister.

"Everything is good." Ann kissed Stephanie's cheek. "The problem would be that neither of you would be able to talk with your guides. Waya, Dustu, or Adahy should go with either Tom or Eli."

Adahy immediately spoke up, "Ehawee, I should go," but was asking how she felt about it.

"Thank you. You always do the right thing." Ehawee kissed his cheek.

Noah held out one of their Lefaucheux revolvers. "Take this. Once I get Ann and Christopher across, I'll send you a box of bullets."

Bethany had mashed a portion of the breakfast food. After she had gotten Chetan's still unconscious body to swallow all of it, she went to the river. They lowered her husband into her lap as she sat in the branches covered with the furs they had sewn together. Noah pulled them across.

They headed west with all their remaining hay and the black bulge of the boat hanging from the rear of the wagon like a clinging bug shell.

Since the wagons were heavy, only Chetan rode. He lay on top of the stack of goose feather mattresses with only his face visible from under the warm buffalo hides. Both wrapped in insulating wool blankets, Chumani sat cuddled to Bethany. They rode a mule behind the wagon. Bethany assured her youngest child stayed warm, and she kept an eye on her husband. Noah carried Christopher in the sling across his chest. Ann walked beside him as Coowescoowe led them northwest toward the village of Adsila. When they were out of view of his home, he turned them due east.

Diwali knew a hidden path only a short way from the village that went to the barley field. Long before the rest of the family got there, Tom, Adahy, and Diwali parked one of the wagons parallel to the river then took the other and the animals to the field.

Diwali pulled out the bags his family used to harvest barley. The three men stripped seeds into the sacks that hung around their necks.

Coowescoowe arrived and parked across from the wagon on the east side. He angled it diagonally away from the river. The others parked the remaining four wagons in an arc. They trapped their animals beside the river to rest, drink, and eat the hay they dumped from the boat.

Roscoe wasn't sure that Ke wasn't still planning to kill Rose for injuring his father. Every hour that Chetan lay unconscious, Ke looked at the mule more menacingly. Coowescoowe had told him that the Hominy River would be wider than the Verdigris.

Roscoe wanted Rose to experience a good crossing and then leave her with the others who would not have to swim a single river. He held one end of a rope and rode Rose into the Verdigris.

Once the boat was back in service, everybody crossed except Bethany, who stayed with Chetan, a loaded revolver, and a wooden box filled with five hundred bullets. Coowescoowe led the others to the barley field where his son, Tom, and Adahy had bright red handkerchiefs tied over their mouths to keep from inhaling the dust of the dead plants. They had already filled one sack each, emptied those seeds into the wagon, and had started a second round.

Tom passed out handkerchiefs. Diwali handed them gathering bags. Diwali and Coowescoowe demonstrated how to move the barley head into the bag and then run a gloved hand down the stem, capturing the seeds that popped off.

Chumani wanted to help. Hanataywee tied a bag strap to make it short and hung it on her. The child quickly became bored. She went from person to person and demanded, "Carry me." Eli knew he was the strongest. He rigged up a way to safely strap the child to his back, then carried her napping body as he worked.

Like locusts, they stripped the plants as they moved across the field, devouring the seeds before them.

Goodbye Hideout

Coowescoowe noticed the animals closing in on barley growing outside the field. He drove them away. "You cannot let them eat dry grain. It will swell up inside them. Soak the barley for one finger of sun movement before they eat. Same for you. Drink first, then eat."

"Thank you for telling us." Noah went back to work.

It was well past noon when they arrived at the far end of the field for the last time. They had each filled their gathering sack many times. The seeds lay on blankets in the back of the wagon.

After they ate their mid-day meal, they tied up the wild barley. Diwali, Adahy, and Tom had to recover the distance they had added by going north. On top of that, they had the goats, sheep, and miniature donkeys. Travel would be slow, so they untied the rope from their wagon. Tom waved goodbye and left those who would be traveling on the other side of the river to get ready on their own.

Roscoe tied the rope to Honey. Across the river, Noah got into the wagon with his mother and father. "How is he?"

Ann joined them to nurse Christopher.

"Nothing looks infected. He's breathing well, and he doesn't have a fever."

Noah asked his mother, "Did you get any food into him?"

"I mixed acorn flour with honey and the yarrow

tea you made this morning. I got two cups into him. Let's pray." Bethany spoke her prayer. "God in heaven. Look down on this good man. See that we need him and want him. Grant us this request. Heal his body and his mind for Your glory. Amen."

"Amen," said Noah and Ann.

Roscoe, Eli, and Dustu pulled the fur boat back and forth until they had shuttled over all the barley, then pulled the boat out of the river and tied it like a bubble to the back of the wagon. Roscoe swam Honey across the river to take Rose's place. The rest of them scooped up the hay that still lay on the ground and stuffed it into a net under the wagon.

Even though they'd left after Diwali, Tom, and Adahy, they had lost less time. Their direction of travel was northwest, and they had only added a short distance by going east to the river.

SIXTEEN

The wagons were heavy, but the land was flat, and the animals had rested while they had harvested the barley. Therefore, they arrived at Adsila's village before the sun went down. Coowescoowe had them wait a short distance from the village, then went to speak with his friend. He returned an hour later. "You cannot stay here. I have asked everybody."

Noah spoke up. "Do you know Kangee?"

Coowescoowe assured him, "Of course, everybody does."

Noah retrieved Kangee's pipe and unwrapped it.

Coowescoowe sucked in his breath and recoiled. "How did you get that?"

"Kangee gave it to me. She said nobody would refuse to help us if we show them this pipe."

"I will talk with them again. Waya and Luyu, come with me and bring the pipe."

They were back in a quarter of the time. "We made arrangements for us. After we get the animals in their tents, we will quietly stay in the lodge assigned and not go outside until the morning when we will leave immediately. They will provide us a meal tonight and another in the morning. Kanuna said he will tell Waya how to go to the Red Fork, but none of them will take you."

Roscoe asked, "What are we trading?" so they could get what they needed.

"They will not accept anything because they have not agreed to let us stay. They are obligated to provide for us because of Kangee."

Just outside the village, they parked the wagons, watered the mules, and put up the animal tents that all had animal organizers installed. They filled the feedbags with hay, put each animal in its section, tied each closed, and then secured the flaps of the tents. Last, they put barley in their ten-gallon tubs and carried them to the assigned lodge.

As instructed, Waya knocked on the door. Their host allowed them to enter. All the women and children were gone, but food had been lain out. Only the warrior of the lodge remained. Kanuna told Waya, "Put all your beds in here, then eat." Noah and Dustu carried Chetan into the lodge on the stretcher. "You carry a dead man?"

Even though told not to say a word, Ke exclaimed, "My father is not dead!"

"What happened to him?" Kanuna inquired as he peered at Chetan's head.

Goodbye Hideout

Dustu explained, "He tried to calm a mule when we crossed a river. She panicked and tried to use him to get out of the water."

"How long has he been like this?"

Waya laid out his bedroll. "Since yesterday."

"He won't live," Kanuna informed them.

Ke ordered, "Do not say that! My brother is fixing him!"

Kanuna turned away. Ke sat beside his father and patted his hand. "Do not listen to him. You are going to be all right."

While the travelers forced upon him ate, Kanuna instructed Waya. "Go halfway to south of setting sun from one sunrise to sunset to Bird River. Do not cross. Follow downstream. Below joining of wide Hominy Creek where you see sandy ford, you will cross. Two fingers of sun, you in Osage Land. Travel toward setting sun between rivers until first sleep. Where south river ends, turn halfway south. Go between two river heads then straight to setting sun between two more heads. Turn south to Arkansas. If the water is red, walk upstream to the joining of the Red Fork. Short walk upstream from Red Fork are sand bars. There you cross only one narrow deep."

Waya spoke the absolute minimum. "I understand. We stay inside until morning, then we leave."

"Good." Kanuna left them.

SEVENTEEN

Tom and Diwali took a wide path around Diwali's village. They should have been far to the south, not just passing home. The temperature dropped as the sun neared the horizon. When they came to a stream of drinkable water, Diwali informed them, "We are far away from village."

Adahy asked, "Will they recognize you in the dark?"

"We should set up camp here. We need to get animals in tent before it is too cold."

Adahy started to unhitch the animals. "We do not need to go to any village. We know how to get to Fort Gibson."

Diwali protested. "The weather may get very cold again. If you need to get inside, you will not know where to find a village, and it would not be safe for you to just show up at a village."

Tom made the decision. "I hope we will be warm enough if we sleep together inside the buffalo furs and

Goodbye Hideout

blankets, but we need to get ready. Tomorrow, take us to the village before you go home."

In the morning, Tom, Adahy, Diwali, and all the animals were still alive. They rekindled the fire and prepared breakfast.

EIGHTEEN

In Kanuna's lodge, the family members inside the warm dwelling heard a knock on the door. Coowescoowe directed them, "Keep the white people back." Ann turned toward the corner to nurse her son. Stephanie put her brown fur hat over her blonde hair, lay on her bed, and faced away. Eli, Sally, Helen, and Roscoe quietly examined the stucco wall at the far side of the room.

Waya opened the door.

"I brought breakfast." Kanuna handed Luyu and Hanataywee baskets of food.

Waya said, "We need to feed our mules before we leave."

"Feed them after. Leave as soon as you eat. I advise you not to use Kangee's pipe again. It is not wise to make people think they have to fear Kangee."

Waya pointed out what he thought the pipe meant. "Did you consider that it could bring you good things if she knew you had helped the man she honored with her pipe?"

Goodbye Hideout

"What did you do for her?"

"I did not do anything, but one of us did."

"How I prove I helped you?"

"I will find out if you let us feed our animals right now. We must ration food."

"Feed them, but only real Cherokee outside." Kanuna took the empty baskets from the two women.

Nearby, Noah sat on the floor, but Waya hadn't asked him for the information. He was sure Waya had a reason. He said nothing.

"Until we are leaving, Dustu and I will be the only people outside, unless Coowescoowe helps us."

"Leave soon." Kanuna left the lodge.

Waya asked Noah, "How did you get the pipe?"

Noah only offered what he felt about the situation. "I do not think we should share why Kangee gave me the pipe and Kanuna hardly deserves a reward for the way we have been treated."

Coowescoowe interrupted. "I think he does. He went against the wishes of all the people out of respect for Kangee and because I am a friend."

"He can tell Kangee he helped a friend of Awan, but he should not ask anything about Awan."

Waya and his grandson carried hay and barley to the animals. Dustu asked, "Why do these people not want to help us? They could get good things."

"Because white men have forced the Cherokee off our lands, they do not see a reason to help us."

"But these people are not like that."

"Sometimes, people will not take the time to know an individual because they are blinded by what they already believe."

Dustu measured swollen barley into the next feedbag. "They only hurt themselves."

"I know," Waya agreed.

After putting out the feed, they returned to the lodge and ate breakfast. Bethany tipped a cup filled with a thin slurry of pemmican, rehydrated vegetables, and potatoes against Chetan's mouth. She gave him only a tiny amount so that it wouldn't choke him. Then, while Bethany ate, Ehawee fed her father. It was a slow process getting Chetan to swallow. Hanataywee took the next turn while her husband and Waya led the mules to the stream and took down the animal tents.

While they packed their bedding and got the space ready for Chetan, Noah cleaned his father's wounds with antiseptic wash, covered them with fresh cedar poultice, and then rewrapped Chetan's arms, legs, torso, and head like a mummy. He whispered to his father. "Listen to Ke, and get better because we love you." Chetan moved a finger. "Are you there?" Noah asked.

His father lay unmoving.

They carried him to the wagon. Ke got into the wagon with his father to continue feeding him the mush his body needed to heal and to be near him.

Goodbye Hideout

Bethany put Chumani in the harness they had made. She hung her youngest child on her back, facing away from her body, then put on the blanket coat she had modified to move a flap behind Chumani's head so that she could see. Stephanie protected Chumani's head, neck, shoulders, and face with a woven cover with holes for her eyes.

Ann put Christopher in the sling across her chest and wrapped her coat around them. Her son could look up at her from inside the warm coat. Ann saw people peeking at them from inside their lodges. "They think we are an enemy they are glad to get rid of."

Waya handed Coowescoowe the promised knife. "Thank you for everything."

"I am glad I could help. I am sorry nobody will take you on. I thought I had a stronger friendship than I do." Coowescoowe accepted the knife then left them to find their own way.

Helen walked beside Roscoe as Waya led them southwest with two wagons at the front, six mules in the middle, then the second two wagons with the people of the family walking around them on all sides.

NINETEEN

Kanuna sat in his lodge, thinking about the people who had spent a few hours in his home. *I do not understand why white people and Indians are willing to travel together in the middle of the winter. They are people my lifelong friend, Coowescoowe, asked me to help. They were women with children who loved men who loved them back. People trying to save the life of an injured man. If they do not find the place I sent them, the baby will freeze.* He stood up, "Fix me several days of food." He went to get his bow, arrows, and warm buffalo fur. His wife stood at the door with a bundle of food. Kanuna put on his warmest shoes, hat, and coat, all made of elk with long winter hair. "The baby does not deserve to freeze if they only find people who treat them the way we did and maybe not even let them stay inside."

"I understand. May the Great Spirit protect you and bring you home safely." Kanuna's wife handed him the bag.

Dustu watched their rear as they traveled.

Goodbye Hideout

"Kanuna is coming." Waya stood behind the rear wagon and watched the rider approach. Others lay hidden in the grass, hidden in the wagons, or standing in full view.

"Greetings, friend," Kanuna called out.

Waya asked, "Did we do something wrong?"

"You did not. I did. I treated my good friend and your family wrong. I hope to make it right by taking you to the next village and the Arkansas River if I need to."

"Then, welcome." Waya accepted the man's apology.

The people ready to protect their family came out of hiding. Kanuna saw that even the white women had been prepared to fight. He wondered if they just held weapons, or if they knew how to use them.

TWENTY

On the other side of the river, when Tom and Adahy were close to the village where they had hoped to spend the previous night, Diwali requested, "It will help get Nanpanta to take you if I can show him a knife. I am sure he will like it."

Adahy held out the reward. "This one is yours for helping us."

Diwali left the two men with the wagons. It didn't seem that Diwali had enough time to get to the village and ask Nanpanta to guide them before they were back. Nanpanta had nothing but the clothing he wore to protect him from the icy air.

"If you give Nanpanta his food this day, he shares what you eat in the next village tonight and what you eat tomorrow morning, and he gets one of these knives, he will take you."

Adahy answered, "That is acceptable. We will give him the knife when he leaves tomorrow."

TWENTY ONE

A jackrabbit in winter white popped into view. When an arrow skewered the animal, Kanuna saw that Sally did indeed know how to use a bow and arrow. He led them to a shallow lake for the mid-day break. Mallards fished in the waters teaming with their winter food. The whole group, minus Chetan, who was unconscious, and Stephanie, who was too pregnant to crawl on her belly, made their ways to the water. Helen crawled beside Roscoe to get a lesson in shooting one of the newly invented, French, twenty-round Lefaucheux revolvers they owned.

When fourteen feathered arrow ends stuck up from the grass, the people attacked. Their quarry died by arrow or pistol. Kanuna discovered ALL the women knew how to use their weapons. They started a fire, cleaned, and then roasted ducks and the rabbit, and prepared other food to go with the meat.

Ke sat beside his father in the wagon. "You should have seen me. I killed a duck. I am sure you would have killed many."

Maybe it was the smell of roasting duck or the love in his son's voice, or perhaps it was both. Chetan came into his mind. "You shot me a duck to eat?"

"Father!" Ke hugged his father's neck. "I was afraid I would never talk with you again. I am so glad you are back." He stuck his head out of the wagon. "Father is awake!"

The family gathered at the wagon. Bethany got in and hugged her husband. "Thank you, God." Then she told her husband, "I have prayed for you every second."

"What happened? Did we cross the river? Last thing I remember is getting the mules into the harness."

Dustu thought Chetan should know what had happened. "Do you not remember getting into the water to calm Rose?"

"No."

Dustu informed him, "Well, it did not work. She stomped you and almost drowned you."

"How did I get out of the river?"

"I pulled you back to the wagon."

"Thank you for saving me. I do not remember any of it," Chetan reached for his head, "but I sure feel my head, and everything else hurts too."

Noah ordered his father, "Don't touch it." Chetan put his hand back by his side. Noah asked, "Do you know who we are and who you are?"

Goodbye Hideout

"Of course, I am Chetan, and you are my family."

"Just trying to see how your brain is doing. Can you count?"

Chetan counted. When he got to forty-four, Noah stopped him. In English, he said, "You spoke in Quapaw. Can you count in English?" Chetan started over, stopped counting at twenty, and then still speaking English, "I hope I pass the test because I'm tired of thinking."

"You do. We'll bring you some food."

"I smell roasted duck. I sure am hungry."

Bethany kissed his forehead. "I'll get you some."

"No, I'll get him some of the duck **I** shot." Ke hurried out of the wagon.

Chetan asked, "Can you make me a pain killer?"

"I can't make willow tea. You'll start bleeding. I could sedate you, which may not be good when your brain was damaged so much. You were unconscious for two days. I already have cedar poultice on you."

The bandages wrapping him came to Chetan's attention. "So, that's why I'm tied up."

"I wish I could do more," Noah told his father.

"I know you do. It's all right."

Ke returned. "Hold this while I get in." He handed Noah the plate of food, then climbed into the wagon. Noah passed the food back to his brother.

Chetan told his youngest son, "Give me some of that duck you shot. I'm starving."

When darkness settled over the land, it found both groups welcomed into the home of the person, either Kanuna or Nanpanta wanted to be the next to help. Trading in both lodges was joyful that night. Kanuna wished they had been so kind.

Later, Luyu took Waya and spoke with Kanuna privately. "The people in your village did not want you to help us, but you gave us use of your lodge and two meals, and then you escorted us and found us a wonderful stopping place for the animals to eat without using our hay, which also had ducks for us to eat. We think you should have the items we usually trade." Luyu handed him a ten-foot piece of blue cloth folded around a sewing kit, a small spool of each color of thread, two sets of fishhooks and lines, and a package of apple seeds. On top sat a knife with its sharpening stone in their sheath.

"We were not kind. My family would not even stay in the lodge with you," Kanuna replied.

"The true and living God, the creator of the universe, forgives us when we do things wrong, then He even gives us good gifts that we do not deserve. We are His people. We do the same."

"Thank you." Kanuna put the items in his bag.

Still wrapped in bandages, Chetan stayed awake and helped formulate the plan to cross Hominy Creek and then travel four days to the Arkansas River at the Red Fork River confluence.

TWENTY TWO

Ann woke in the night. "Noah, we have to go. I dreamed I saw two men wearing long white robes and a large pendant on a chain hanging around their necks. They stood in front of me and said, 'Hurry to Fort Arbuckle. Go with all haste. Do not stop during the day. Do not stop during the night. You, your husband, and the child must leave immediately.' "

"It was just a dream," Noah told her.

"Then, don't come with me. Christopher and I are leaving now." Ann got out from under the fur.

Noah tried to reason with her. "You can't leave in the middle of the night and cross the river."

Everybody woke as Ann packed and argued. She told them the dream. "I know that a life depends on my speed."

The son of their host, Degotoga, who was supposed to escort them in the morning, spoke. "Father, if they are going tonight with just horses, you can take them across. I will take the rest of them with the wagons tomorrow."

Noah kept trying to reason with his wife, "Ann, it's not safe to take Christopher out in the middle of the night, especially across a creek," but he packed.

Ann wrapped Christopher in his warm, yellow buffalo fur blanket and put his matching hat on him. She slid him into the sling and put on her coat. "I need both of these." She grabbed two buffalo furs. "God will keep us safe." She walked out the door.

In the lodge, Sally said, "I'm not sure I even know what just happened."

"I guess we'll find out when we get to Fort Arbuckle," Stephanie replied. They tried to go back to sleep, but it was impossible.

Noah saddled Eyanosa and their mare, Zi. Degotoga put a horse blanket on his horse. He took them to a shallow crossing only wide enough for a horse then led them slowly and carefully across. "Wrap a fur around you. We will ride as fast as our horses can continue for days without stopping." He urged his horse to a slow canter.

Ann did not stop to allow Christopher to nurse. She let him have her breast from inside the sling as they rode. When the morning broke, they were fifteen miles farther south.

"We have to let the horses at least drink water," Noah insisted.

Ann didn't get off Zi. As soon as the horses lifted their heads from the water, Ann said, "Let's go."

TWENTY THREE

As Ann urged Zi back into a run, far to the east, Tom, Adahy, and Nanpanta left his village. Those first rays of light also lit the way for the rest of Ann's family as they forded Hominy Creek with Degotoga's son, Ahuli.

Once on their way, Chetan brought up a thought. "Since we don't have Christopher to keep warm, and because Ahuli is taking us all the way, we could travel farther and camp outside."

Sally, like the others, worried about Ann, Noah, and Christopher. "I want to get to Fort Arbuckle as soon as possible, and that would get us there faster, so I vote for Chetan's idea."

Nobody was against the plan. Therefore, they traveled well beyond the village, where Ahuli had initially planned to take them. They stopped with only enough time to check Chetan closely and get the animals into their tents with full feedbags. They cooked their meal after dark.

TWENTY FOUR

In the dark, Ann, Noah, and Degotoga tried to force their way through the grapevines that hung from the trees along the Arkansas River.

Degotoga called out, "I found a path wide enough for a wagon!"

Ann cantered over. "Lead on." They followed Degotoga and then saw the silhouette of the stockade around the buildings of the abandoned fort. Once inside the wall, Noah lit the torch with the matches he had thought to bring, even in the panic of their departure. They walked toward the door of the closest building. "It's not that one. Iiiitttt'ssssss," Ann looked around, "This one." She walked to a more protected building and opened the door.

Noah looked cautiously into the room. He saw a man lying on a pallet holding a book in his hand. "Friends here. May we enter?"

Ann pushed past him, went directly to the bed, and picked up the bundle beside him.

Goodbye Hideout

Noah and Degotoga walked over. Noah prodded the man. "Dead."

Ann handed the bundle to Degotoga and took off her coat.

Noah and Degotoga were shocked to see a baby wrapped in the blanket. "It cannot be!" Degotoga stated in disbelief.

Ann handed Christopher to Noah. "Give the baby to me." She took the baby back and put her nipple to its mouth. "I hope it's not too weak to nurse. It's so cold in here. It's a wonder the baby didn't freeze." The child barely sucked as it nursed.

Noah took the book from the dead man's hand. "To whoever finds us, I hope you got here in time to save our child. We named her Joy. Her mother died a week after giving birth. She never stopped bleeding, and I couldn't save her. I tried to feed Joy milk from the cow. She drank it but cried all the time. I went outside in the middle of the night to get wood for the fire. I didn't see the rattler in the warm wood by the door. Now, I'm dying, too. I have only minutes. God, please send somebody to save Joy. Tell her we lov— He wasn't able to finish writing," Noah told them.

Astonished by what had happened, Degotoga asked, "How did you know?"

"God sent His angels into my dream to answer that man's prayer to save his daughter."

Noah added, "What were the chances that a woman who could nurse Joy would be close enough?"

Degotoga believed. "Surely, the God who did this has given strong magic." He looked at Ann. *She holds magic stronger than any I thought was possible.*

Ann said, "Hello, Joy," to the little girl who didn't look at her new mother as she took in life-giving milk.

Noah opened the door. "We need to get some wood in here and get a fire going." He stepped back outside with the torch.

He and Degotoga came back with plenty of wood. Degotoga held a headless carcass. "He killed the snake that killed him." By the light of the torch, they looked around the room. Noah found a lantern with all the oil burned away and then the container of oil. They filled the lantern's tank, lit it, and then started a fire in the hearth.

Noah and Degotoga dragged the dead man's body to a different building then reconnoitered inside the fort. Before long, they returned. "We got the horses into the stable with the cow. There was hay and frozen water." They hung a tub of ice over the fire.

"Do you think they were planning to spend the winter here?" Ann asked.

"Probably." Noah lit another lantern he had discovered, then left. He returned. "Look what we found." He led in a golden, longhaired member of the previous family, wagging its tail so hard its whole body swayed. "Looks like our family is growing by the minute." He placed a bulging sack on the table.

Goodbye Hideout

Ann poured some of the melted water into the large tin pot on the floor beside the fire. "Must have been its water pot."

Degotoga dragged in another ten-gallon tub of ice and another sack. "Never in my life have I drunk milk. If you milk the cow, I will cut up this meat and these vegetables."

"All right. You two look after the babies."

"We'll watch them." Noah informed his wife, "The stable is in the corner to the right. I saw a milk bucket outside the cow's stall."

Ann put on her coat and carried a lantern out the door. Several minutes later, she returned with buckets of milk from the cow that had been very happy to be relieved after two days without milking. They drank warm milk while the stew cooked.

Ann changed Joy's diaper. Noah played with Christopher. "I read some of the journal left by Joy's parents. Her mother's name was Amanda, and her father was Mac. They were going west just like us. Back in Pennsylvania, Mac's father left everything to his older brother, so Mac came west. I don't know how they ended up here."

"May I hold Joy?" Degotoga requested after the baby's diaper was fresh.

Ann handed him the baby. "She's already stronger."

When the water had melted, Noah and Degotoga

carried the tubs to the horses and the cow. They were exhausted. Therefore, soon after eating, the enjoyment of holding and playing with Joy and Christopher ended in favor of sleep.

A few hours later, Ann heard a tiny cry. She instantly cuddled Joy closer. Joy took in the milk she needed to recover while Ann lay beside her and marveled at the wonder of the tiny, still living girl.

It wasn't long before Christopher also wanted to eat. Ann rolled over. Her son took his turn. Ann repeated the process twice during the night. She tried not to worry, but repeatedly checked to see if Joy was still breathing. She barely slept.

When the sun lit the corners of what was to be their winter home, Degotoga and Noah searched the fort more closely.

While Ann finally slept, part of her family approached with Ahuli. Far away, Tom gave Nanpanta the promised knife. Nanpanta started north at a slow run that he could keep up for the many hours it would take to return home. Adahy gave their host, Ayita, two red flannel shirts, a package of fishhooks and line, needles, spools of thread, apple seeds, and a knife like the one given to Nanpanta.

Tom and Adahy were told to ride a long day between the river heads, and they would be at Fort Gibson before the day was over. They left the village without an escort.

Goodbye Hideout

When Ann woke, she smelled the stew they had left beside the fire that had heated the room during the night. She opened her eyes and discovered that everybody was gone. She called out the door. "Noah?!"

From across the fort, she heard, "Be there shortly."

"You have the babies?"

"Yes."

Noah carried Christopher. Degotoga had Joy in a newly-made sling while they checked every nook and cranny with the new canine member of the family. They found the grave of Joy's mother. "We will dig a second grave beside her." Degotoga rocked Joy, who had started crying.

"Let us go. Come on, dog." Noah slapped the side of his leg to get the animal to follow them.

The second the five of them came into the room, Ann inquired, "How are the babies?"

The dog lay beside the fire.

"Joy is hungry." Degotoga got the baby out of the sling.

"She needs to make up for two days without eating. I've been reading the journal of her parents. We should give it to her when she's old enough." Ann took Joy. "How is Chris?"

"He messed his pants." Noah laid his son on his bedroll to perform the necessary task.

Ann ladled stew into bowls the men had found. "Joy is five days younger than Christopher. According to the journal, she was born on December 19th. Did these people have any paper? I want to draw her father."

"Not that we found, but I always bring my binder. I'll get it. While you do that, we'll set some traps and then dig a grave."

Degotoga said, "I could start a fire over there in that building, but him being frozen is keeping him from smelling."

"I will put Joy and Chris inside my coat. We will be warm enough, and if it does get too cold, I will come back over here. I wish I could have drawn her mother too."

They went off to perform their tasks. The hole was deep before Noah and Degotoga reached the body of Joy's mother. As the sun went down, they pulled her out of her grave. Degotoga and Noah entered the building, where Ann worked on making the likeness of Joy's father. Noah studied the drawing. "Looks exactly like him."

"But he looks dead, and I can't fix it."

"He is dead. Do you want me to work on making him look alive and happy while you feed the babies and cook?"

"Please do. I'll get a lantern."

"Ann, I hope you won't think we are horrible, but

we thought about what you said. Joy should know what her mother looked like. We dug her up. I don't think we'll make a ghost because we're doing this for her daughter. I'll draw her because she's not as nice as Mac."

"I want to see the mother of my daughter."

Noah put down the paper and pencil. "Be prepared." He led her to the building where they had put Amanda.

Ann looked at the body with a tangled, dirty mass of hair. The greenish skin by her ear was sloughing off her mud-smeared face. A worm protruded from her nose. "The poor woman. I'll clean her up after we eat."

"You are remarkable. That you would do that for her is very brave and noble." Noah held the lantern high as they walked through the eerie twilight past the building containing the dead body of Joy's father. "I should have Mac finished before dinner. I'll come over as soon as I'm done." Noah kissed Ann in the cold moonlight before she left him with the lantern and walked into the building where they were living. When he went to eat, he showed them the drawing.

Ann held it. "It looks just like him. I'm sure that is how he would have looked alive and happy."

Degotoga examined the drawing as he ate. "You have made a man on this paper. You have magic, very strong."

Ann said, "It's just a drawing."

"No. You drew him, but he was dead. Noah put the spirit of that man on the paper, and his medicine brought Chetan back from death. The spirits talk to you directly. You have power to see across distance and find Joy. You both have powerful medicine. You do not drain the power from each other. You add to each other."

Noah thought about what Degotoga said while they ate. "I can tell you where this power comes from. You can access the same power if you accept it."

"That power would destroy me."

Ann understood what Noah meant. "Not this power. The One who gives it loves us so much that He gives the ability to serve Him. One day, when the time comes, He will give all of us a new body that will live forever."

"Who is this one?"

Noah said, "His name is Jehovah. He is the one who created the earth, the heavens, and the stars. He is the one who put the breath of life into all living beings. He made the sun stop in the sky for a whole day while His people fought to take the land Jehovah wanted to give them. One time, He made the sun go backward in the sky for part of a day. He gave one of his servants, named Moses, the power to make the waters of a great sea stand up like walls on either side of a dry path. A whole nation of people walked between the water. After they crossed, Jehovah crashed the waters down over the people trying to keep them as slaves."

"Would a being so strong love a human?"

"He loved us so much that part of Him came to earth and became one of us. His human mother named Him Jesus. Jesus let the people of earth kill Him to allow Jehovah to forgive us for being so evil, but Jehovah did not let the people of earth have the body of His Son. After being dead in the grave for three days, Jehovah made Jesus alive again."

"That is a lie. Amanda will not come back to life."

"Not today, but at the end of time, she will, if she believed in Him. When Jehovah raised Jesus back into Heaven to live forever, five hundred people saw it."

"When did this happen?"

Ann said, "It was one thousand, eight hundred, and forty-one winters ago."

"So long. How do you know about this?"

"It was written by the people who saw what happened. To keep the knowledge alive, his followers have copied the book over and over." Noah walked to his pack and pulled out a Bible. "This has been copied into many languages, but Cherokee and Quapaw do not have this kind of language. This one is written in English."

"Then I cannot find out about this or become a servant of Jehovah."

Noah told him, "Go to the mission center north of

Fort Gibson. They will teach you about Jehovah. They will also teach you how to speak, read, and write English. Then you can read the Bible for yourself."

"I will find out about this. While I am here, you tell me about Jehovah and Jesus?"

Ann assured him, "We will."

Noah stood up. "But right now, we need to clean Amanda."

Degotoga wanted to watch how they put a person onto paper. "I can come and hold one of the babies. I will keep it warm for you."

"All right. I will clean the dishes and then use the water to clean Amanda." Just as Ann gathered the plates, Joy started to cry.

Noah picked up the baby. "Hello." He let Joy hold his finger. "Smile for father." He brought her close and kissed her ears, her forehead, and her cheeks. "Hello, daughter." After a few minutes, playing no longer made Joy happy. Noah carried their new baby to Ann. "You feed Joy. I'll wash the dishes."

Ann went to the chair that Noah and Degotoga had found in the barn loft. She hummed a hymn she had learned from Helen and held Joy's hand as she nursed. Before she was full, Christopher started crying. Noah tried to entertain him until he could take Joy.

"Bring Christopher. You burp this one." Ann passed over her daughter and then took her son.

Goodbye Hideout

Noah patted Joy's back. "They always want to eat at the same time. Do you think both of them are getting all the milk they need?"

"I think so. They both act satisfied."

Several minutes later, Degotoga carried Joy and the chair. Ann brought Chris and Noah's paper binder, pencils, and erasers. Noah had the dishwater. He put the tub on the floor and then leaned the body of Amanda over the edge. "Let me wash her. I don't think you should handle her then touch Joy or Christopher. After she's clean enough, I'll position her, then go back over to our building and wash well before I come back to draw her."

Ann didn't want to handle the body. She had only wanted to give the woman some dignity. "All right. If you don't mind." They watched while Noah very gently washed Amanda's hair and then turned her over and washed her face. He patted dry her face and hair then sat her up against the wall with the tub full of water to hold her up. He brushed the dirt off her dress and stood back.

Ann told him, "I think that's good enough. Go wash, and Degotoga, when Noah gets back, you should too. Bring all the lanterns over when you are clean."

After washing with lye soap and the fresh, warm water by the fire where they had eaten, Noah put on his blanket coat and wool hat, then wrapped up in a buffalo fur. He carried another hide and a lantern to light the way.

Inside the building that contained the body of Joy's mother, Noah put a buffalo hide on the floor. "Ann, you and the babies lie here." He put the other fur over them, then sat in the chair and started drawing.

Ann watched. "I'm so glad you're doing this. I'm pleased that I got to see what she looks like."

"Me too." Noah worked by lantern light. Frequently, he held a lantern close and studied Amanda's face.

When Degotoga returned with the other lantern and a third fur, Ann, Christopher, and Joy were asleep. He put the light on the floor to illuminate Amanda better. He held the other lantern behind Noah, so he could see the paper on which he was drawing. Degotoga watched the woman's image come alive on the paper.

Degotoga shivered. "It's too cold in here for us to be wet. Let me make a fire. It doesn't need to be cold in here now."

Noah handed him a lantern. "Check for snakes."

Soon, a fire warmed the room. Noah worked long into the night while Degotoga watched. Ann slept until a hungry baby woke her. She fed one and then the other the same as she had the night before. When Noah finished the drawing, he snuggled in beside Ann. Degotoga wrapped up alone.

Goodbye Hideout

They slept in the room with the body of Amanda, believing the spirits of the two dead people were grateful that someone had found Joy, loved their child, would raise her in a happy home, and one day give her the journal and drawings.

When the living woke, they went back to the other building to eat breakfast before they put Joy's father and mother to rest in the same grave. They covered them with earth one last time, read Psalm 23, asked God to take Joy's parents into Heaven, and to help Noah and Ann raise two babies at the same time. They washed again. The rest of the day, they gathered everything left by Joy's parents. Ann organized the supplies and milked the cow. Noah and Degotoga made the chair into a rocker with wood they had found in the barn, then started making a second cradleboard.

TWENTY FIVE

Three days after the barley harvest, just before nightfall, Tom and Adahy crossed the Neosho River at Fort Gibson. As planned, the men arranged for the animals to stay in the stable with food and water. Glad the animals were inside a warm shelter with plenty of food, Tom and Adahy left the fort to sleep in the cold.

When the sun went down the following day, all the tools Tom and Adahy had brought sat in the tent they had set up just outside the fort. Their wagons had their first coat of pitch on both the inside and the outside.

Far to their west, as the day ended, Ahuli and his charges arrived at the end of what should have been a four-day trip. There was still enough light for them to see the wagon path through the dense strip of trees that bordered the Arkansas River. They followed it to the closed gates of Fort Arbuckle. They hoped to find Ann, Noah, Degotoga, Christopher, and three horses locked safely inside the stockade.

"Your family is here!" They yelled together.

Goodbye Hideout

A few minutes later, Noah looked down at them from above the log wall. "We didn't expect you for another day. We'll open up." His face disappeared.

The gates creaked as Degotoga and Noah pushed them open. The dog barked, dashed back and forth beside the wagons, and wove between the legs of the entering animals. Noah called the dog to his side. "Meet the newest member of the family." He patted it on the head.

"Ann flew out here to save a dog?" asked Sally.

"And there is a cow," Degotoga informed them as Ann strolled across the courtyard.

It looks like she has a baby, but Noah has Christopher in his arms. Stephanie asked, "What do you have, Ann?"

"Meet the reason for our rapid trip," Ann moved the blanket away from a tiny face. "This is Joy."

Sally held out her arms. "Let ME hold her!"

"Where are her parents?" Luyu asked.

Degotoga pointed to the disturbed dirt with two markers.

"Oh, no!" Hanataywee exclaimed.

They closed and barred the gate then took the animals to the stable. Ann told them what she knew. "… The night I had the dream, a rattler bit her father. Poor child, she could barely nurse when we got here."

Ehawee took Joy. "She seems strong now."

"She has eaten non-stop since we got here," Ann informed them.

Roscoe glanced around the stable. "This is going to be a good hideout to spend the winter."

Chetan stood beside Bethany with Chumani on his hip. "And look at all the hay."

Eli had stocked a lot of hay at the store his father had owned. "It might have been enough for one cow. It's not enough for all the animals."

Ke looked down from the loft. "It's empty up here."

Dustu rubbed the dog behind its ears. "What is the dog's name?"

Degotoga said, "We read the journal. They always said 'the dog' when they wrote about him."

"You read it?" his son asked.

"They read it aloud. I listened."

"Come on. We will crowd into the warm building where we have been staying. We can figure out something else tomorrow." Noah exited the barn.

As they ate the evening meal, the dog begged. Hanataywee gave the hound a scrap of food. "Let's name him."

Roscoe swallowed. "What about Chester?"

Sally spoke up, "We should name him Goldie."

After many suggested then rejected names, Roscoe had an idea. "Let's all call for him. The one he goes to gets to name him."

"Great idea!" Stephanie asked, "May I have the bread?"

After the meal, they spread across the room and

called out the name of their choice. The dog hurried to his choice and nabbed the scrape of beef Dustu offered.

Ke frowned. "That's not fair!"

"Nobody stated any rules. Dustu was clever. We should let him name the dog." Noah looked around to see if anybody had further objections. Nobody did. "Tell us his name."

"Gihli," Dustu informed them.

As if he didn't already know, Hanataywee told her husband, "That is just dog in Cherokee."

"That book says, 'Dog' is who he is, but that word sounds hard. Gihli is better."

"I like it," Sally stepped out of the line.

Dustu asked, "Everybody agree?" Nobody spoke against the name. "Then Gihli it is."

Daily, Chetan used a lot of energy to heal. He felt exhausted. "We should rest. Can we unpack tomorrow?"

The others agreed. The following morning, Degotoga rolled up his bedding. "We go home. I am happy to know you. May the Great Spirit continue with you and bless you."

Luyu passed Helen the bacon. "Eat while I put together a bag to thank you for helping us."

"I will bring in wood for the fire." Degotoga put on the blanket coat they had been letting him wear.

"Be sure to check for snakes!" Ann called out.

Degotoga brought in logs and stoked up the fire. As usual, Sally and Roscoe worked together to prepare the meal. Helen enjoyed cooking with Sally. Even more so with Roscoe. She left the large area beside Sally open and stepped into the small space beside Roscoe. "May I help you?"

"I would love it." Roscoe did not widen the space between them.

The crying of Joy and Christopher filled the room. Both wanted food immediately. Ann held Christopher against her belly then lay Joy behind him to her other breast. "I hope they don't always want to eat at the same time." Ann looked into Christopher's eyes. "Good morning, my son." He reached up. His little hand touched her chin as she cooed at him.

Then, she looked at Joy. "Good morning, my daughter." As Joy's mother's life had ebbed away, she had been too weak to gaze into her daughter's eyes. As her father grieved for his wife, he had tried to feed their baby the cow's milk that she could barely digest. He had been worn to exhaustion by her crying and had not cuddled her. Then, Joy had spent two days wailing with no response.

Like the previous few days, she didn't look toward Ann's face. Ann moved Joy, so she would have to look up as she ate. She put her finger next to Joy's hand. The baby wrapped her tiny fingers around it. Ann drew the baby's hand toward her face to attract her attention. Ann talked to both of her children and took turns looking into their faces.

The family carried supplies to their designated places. Ke toted a sack of toasted pumpkin seeds. "I hate to unpack again. We will have to put it all right back into the wagons."

His father reminded him, "It won't be until spring, and it will be less because we will use a lot this winter."

Stephanie brought up a question. "How did Joy's parents get that hay here? There isn't a wagon."

Noah put down two parfleches of pemmican, then got the journal. He flipped through the pages and then read. "They left this morning with the horses and the wagon we traded for the supplies and hay we need to get through the winter. You should have seen the barge coming up the river with hay stacked a mile high. I was sure it would fall over, but they got it into the barn with no problem. Mac is going to trap this winter. In the spring, we will buy back our horses and the wagon with beaver pelts."

"Where can we get a barge? Dustu asked.

Chetan thought back to the times he had been in Fort Gibson. "I've never seen one at the Fort."

Roscoe had fed ten donkeys, ten mules, and four goats every winter for many years. He knew they needed more hay. "We need to get the animals to the fort before we run out of food. They can eat some prairie grass around here, but there won't be enough. It's not nutritious enough in the winter, and somebody will have to stay with the animals, so they don't wander away."

While they waited for breakfast, Degotoga and Ahuli helped unload. Degotoga noticed elk antlers as tall as Ahuli. He watched where they put them in case he decided to ask for them. He also saw flannel shirts, India rubber ponchos, tarps, Dutch ovens, knives, cloth, scissors, thread, fishhooks, fishing line, and tin eating sets, all kinds of food, packages of seeds, tobacco, and many other plants.

There was still a lot to unload when Helen put her head out the door. "Breakfast is ready." They put away whatever they had in their hands then sat on the floor, not even worn smooth before the fort had been abandoned. Still, the rough-hewn logs of the building where they ate did keep the cold out and the warm in.

TWENTY SIX

Eli thought about the animal food problem as they ate. *If we didn't need to get the animals to Fort Gibson, we could float the wagons down the river, fill them with hay and grain, and then pull them back like a barge. It would be much faster and easier.*

Hanataywee picked up a slice of the cheese left by Joy's parents. "Too bad you couldn't carry the animals in the wagons like boats and float them down the river to the fort."

Sally posed the question, "How many would it take to pull six wagons up the river?"

Roscoe said, "The wagons would be much lighter floating in the river. We wouldn't have to swap them out."

"Four each wagon should be enough, so twenty-four," Eli informed them.

Noah took Christopher, who was full. "If the animals can pull more weight, could we get enough hay in four wagons?"

Since Eli had contemplated the topic for several

days, he knew the answer. "No. It's not the weight; it's the volume. We need them all."

Dustu thought about it. "We already have animals at Fort Gibson. We only need to take eight more. If we went by river, I bet we could be there in a day. Another day to load everything, then seven days back. Do we have enough hay here for the rest of the animals for nine days?"

Noah had already counted the bales they had. "I think so. We can make the sedative, give it, then walk two mules into each wagon just before they should go to sleep."

Sally stood up. "I'll dig out what we need, but how will we get them both to lie down in the tight space?" She left the room.

Eli held his fork just shy of his mouth. "We stagger giving them the sedative, get the first one in and asleep, then bring in the other."

"We can probably get there today if we go now. It should be me, Dustu, Hanataywee, and Ehawee." Waya looked at his grandson to see if he had any objections.

Ehawee said, "I miss Adahy. I want to go."

Ahuli thought it would be fun to ride a wagon down the river. "We could help, so you would not have to drag the women around."

Ehawee looked at the boy. "I do not mind being dragged around."

Goodbye Hideout

Degotoga said, "We need to go home, but we can help finish unloading for more trade goods."

Waya swallowed. "Sounds good. We could use the help."

Sally came back into the one-room building. "I am ready to get started."

As mid-day approached, the wagon cover bows lay in the stable, and four empty wagons stood at the river's edge, ready to be loaded with eight soon-to-be-sleeping mules. Eight tipi poles lay on the ground beside the wagons. Each of the people leaving carried a moneybag. They gave the first four mules the sedative, then started eating dinner. Ten minutes later, they gave the doctored water to the other four. As soon as they finished the meal, they walked the first set of mules up the planks into the wagons.

Inside the building, Luyu spread a large sheet of duck cloth on the floor with trade items displayed. "Before we left your lodge, we gave your wife blue cloth, a sewing kit, six spools of thread, ten fish hooks, and a bundle of fishing line. We've given both of you a hunting knife and a flannel shirt. Here are the things we have. We want to let both of you pick ten things. One for each day you spent bringing us here, for helping us bring everything in from the wagons, and for you to get home. You can decide what you want after we go."

Degotoga squatted beside the blanket. "Agreed."

Lisa Gay

Degotoga and Ahuli shoved the first makeshift boat down the bank. Gihli jumped into the water then scrambled out. Noah, Chetan, and Roscoe waded into the frigid water and pushed Waya, Luyu, two sleeping mules, and two tipi poles into the deeper water. When they floated, Waya and Luyu stood up and turned the wagon downstream with the long poles.

Next into the river were Dustu and Hanataywee. Bethany and Ehawee piloted the third wagon. The last wagon carried Eli and Helen.

On the dry land, Stephanie called out, "Be careful!"

They waved goodbye and then hurried into the warm building. Ann was the oldest woman still at Fort Arbuckle. Therefore, she pulled the cloth of trade items close to the fire. She negotiated the trade while Stephanie and Sally held the babies.

Degotoga told his son, "You pick first."

"Can I have this coat I have been wearing?"

The coat had been Ann's when she had left Pine Bluff. *Joy's life is worth so much more than a coat.* "It is fine with me, and you can pick nine more items."

Ahuli picked out two packs of fishhooks and lines. He looked at his father. "These things are completely mine?"

Also looking at the items on the cloth, Degotoga squatted beside his son. "Yes, you earned them."

Goodbye Hideout

Next, Ahuli picked a one-point blanket. "If I do not take anything else, can I have one of those things you look through to see very far?"

Everybody knew they had several. All eyes turned to Noah. "I will get you one."

Ahuli took the spyglass from Noah. "This is a good trade. Take good care of Joy."

"We will. Thank you for caring about her," replied Ann.

Degotoga said, "I would also like to have a coat and a spyglass."

Since Noah had suspected that Degotoga would also want one, he had prepared. He took another spyglass from his pocket. Since it was Noah's coat Degotoga wore, he said, "You may have the coat."

"I would like this for my wife." He picked up a butcher knife. "If I don't take this already made coat, can I have enough blankets and thread, so my wife can make one for both of us and all our children?"

Ann thought about how much they would need then said, "All right." She put on Sally's coat.

Degotoga handed Noah his coat back. Noah followed Ann to the building where they had stored the blankets.

Ahuli thought about his father's request. Noah and Ann came back with two large two-point blankets, a couple of one-point blankets –all still in pairs– and two huge two-hundred-yard spools of stout, wool thread. Degotoga took the stack.

Ahuli slipped out of Ann's coat. "I want you to have your coat back. Mother can make me a coat with half of my blanket. I would like three more hunting knives for my brothers. What can I have for my little sister?"

Ann held up the corner of the duck cloth. "If you want to take some of this cloth, you can make a doll. I will cut some hair from a buffalo hide to stuff it. If you want to make it on your way home, I will give you two big needles, a small spool of thread of the color of your choice, and I will cut the pieces for you now."

Ahuli put the coat into Ann's hand. "It probably will not be good, but I will make it." He turned to his father. "What color thread should I get?"

"Pick the one you like."

Noah went back to the storage building to get the knives. Sally got her sewing kit to cut duck cloth into the shape of a doll.

Chetan said, "I'll trim buffalo hair from the boat. May I use a pair of scissors?"

Sally handed him the scissors from her sewing kit and then went to get Ann's.

Roscoe called out, "Bring me a pair. I'll help."

Sally came back with scissors, handed a pair to Roscoe, then cut the duck cloth with the other.

Stephanie held her arms all the way open. "Sally, cut a section this long for me." She took the cloth to the stack of food in the corner of the room.

Goodbye Hideout

"I cannot decide. I want to make the eyes black and the mouth red. Red eyes would look evil, and a black mouth would look dead."

Noah returned. He handed Ahuli the knives. "This is a very nice thing for you to do for your brothers. God sees it, and sometime in the future He will reward you."

Onto the cloth Sally had cut for her, Stephanie laid food for the two to eat on their way home. She fastened the diagonally opposite corners together and then tied the material beyond the knots into loops so that Degotoga could wear it like a backpack.

Meanwhile, Sally cut two large identical shapes of a body. She put them together, stuck two needles into and out of them, folded them, and then put them into a large red bandana with a small spool of black and another of red thread along with the two large spools of white thread they had already given to Degotoga.

Chetan and Roscoe came back with so much fur that Sally could fit only part of it on top of the doll-making materials inside the bandana. She tied the rest into a blue bandana, then cut another piece of duck cloth and made a pack for Ahuli to carry the knives and doll materials. He put it on his front side. Degotoga hefted his bag. "I do not have matches or a pot to cook this food, but I will take it home."

"Right." This time Stephanie put on her coat and left. She came back with a large dutch oven and a corked bottle of matches. "This is heavy."

"We can carry them." Degotoga slipped on the big pack, got on his horse, and then pulled his son up in front of him.

Noah told them, "May God get you home safely and bless you with happy and interesting lives."

"You too." Degotoga urged his horse forward.

As they rode away, Ahuli called out, "I will never forget you or the babies!"

TWENTY SEVEN

Chetan stood beside his youngest son as Degotoga and Ahuli rode away. "Ke, would you help me check the traps your brother and Degotoga set?"

Ke looked at this bandaged father. "Can you?"

"Just because a person hurts does not mean they do not have things to do. Dress warmly. We may be gone all day."

Noah knew his father didn't need to check traps. He remembered their father teaching him this lesson many years before. Chetan and Ke put on wool socks, mukluks, fur hats, blanket coats, and gloves, then got their bows and arrows. "To bring back what you find." Noah handed them duck cloth bags, a hatchet, and a rope.

On their way upriver, Ke swung from a dangling grapevine that hung from the trees around the fort. Its entwining branches laced through the trees in multiple directions and let loose a barrage of dried fox grapes. "Father, look!"

Chetan picked up several shriveled grapes. He popped them into his mouth.

Ke gathered some too. "We should shake out more and collect them."

"We will get some going home."

Ke carried a pocketful to eat on the way.

Ahead, Chetan saw a small stream. Noah had told him they had walked upstream a long way before they had seen turkey tracks and had set foot snares. Since he had not started at the mouth of the creek, Chetan didn't know if he was up or downstream of the traps.

As they walked toward the creek's source, Chetan's breath condensed in the cold air. He repositioned his scarf. "Cover your nose and mouth," he told his son. After two hours, Chetan decided he would turn back if he didn't see the traps soon.

"What is that?" Ke pointed at a massive pile of logs across the stream.

"A beaver dam. We will go very slowly and quietly. Maybe we will see some." Chetan crawled forward. Ke imitated his father.

SPLASH!

They froze until they heard a gnawing sound. Chetan moved his knee forward without rising, then slowly pushed his body forward. He paused a few minutes before moving again. When they had squirmed to the beaver dam, Chetan motioned for his son to come up beside him.

Goodbye Hideout

They silently observed the furry river dweller's large teeth gnaw a small tree. Another beaver chewed branches off a tree already lying beside the stream. It dragged the branch to a smooth, flattened path then hauled it into the pond.

Shortly afterward, a beaver's head popped out from under the water. It cautiously looked around but didn't see the humans in brown blanket coats. At the same entry point where the other had gone into the water, this one came out. It waddled to the tree and gnawed off a few more branches before its brother arrived back and dragged them away.

Chetan noticed a mudslide into the water that was closer to the beavers than the one the animals were using. Leaves lay in the track. He and Ke slowly made their way to the abandoned path. Chetan looked into the water. There lay the body of a beaver with its foot caught in a metal trap. He looked around the edges of the beaver pond then pointed.

Ke nodded and then pointed to yet another rejected entry point. Chetan stood up. The lookout on the dam slapped its broad, flat tail on the water. Beavers made a mad dash. Only seconds after the warning, every one of them swam safely under the surface.

Chetan reached into the murky water and pulled out the dead beaver. "They have good meat and fat like bears and bison, but this one has been dead too long. We can't eat it, but we can skin it and keep the fur. If Mac caught more, they'll be the same." Chetan released the latch and removed the carcasses. The trap lay impotent on the ground as they walked the pond's edge. They found another body where they saw the second abandoned entry point. The third possibility was on the other side of the creek.

"We can take these and go downstream. I saw a way across not too far back." Ke tried to pull the metal spike out of the ground. It didn't budge.

"It has to be in well enough that the beaver cannot pull it out." Chetan picked up a gnawed off branch and started digging.

Ke went to the first trap and did the same. Once they had retrieved the traps, they walked to the large stones and crossed. Near the final trap, ripples spread. A beaver swam back and forth. It stuck its nose out from under the water and inhaled. A trail of blood went from the water to a gnawed down tree.

"The spirit of the beaver does not want this one to die. It has struggled hard to live, and we have plenty of food."

"How can we free it?"

"I will pull it out of the water. We can use my coat to wrap up its feet and mouth. I will sit on it while you open the trap." Chetan took off his coat and pulled the chain. The beaver thrashed and thrashed as it tried to swim to the center of the pond.

Goodbye Hideout

Ke got behind his father and helped reel it in. "It is still very strong." Finally, they got the fat beaver as far onto the land as they could without getting too close.

"Drive a branch through the chain into the ground. We do not want it to get back to the water."

Ke turned to get a branch. The beaver rushed him. Chetan threw his coat over Ke's attacker, then quickly jerked the front over its head. He pushed it over with his foot, which rolled it into the coat. Even when the coat circled the animal a few times, its feet were barely secure. "Give me your coat."

Chetan whipped Ke's around the animal's free foot and sharp claws, straddled the ferocious river dweller, and then sat. The beaver squirmed frantically, but Chetan kept it under control.

Ke worked the mechanism that held the trap and popped it open. The beaver pulled its injured foot into the coat.

Chetan instructed, "Get a good grip on our coats. I will too. We don't want it to take them to its home."

"Is that where it lives? There, in the middle?"

"Yes."

"How does it get in?"

"The door is under the water."

"Clever." Ke wrapped the sleeve of his coat around one hand, and the sleeve of his father's around his other. "I have them."

"I'll jump off. When I tell you, pull the coats back." Chetan arranged his feet. "Now!" He jumped up.

The beaver felt the constraining material loosen and kicked frantically as the boy jerked the coats away. The freed animal scrambled toward the water as fast as its mangled foot allowed. It slid into the water, looked back at them, and then disappeared.

Ke put his finger through a hole. "Will it live?" He slid on his coat.

"The others will bring it food. It will stay in its den until it heals. I am sure Noah did not get to this pond. His traps must be the other way. Let us skin these two, and then we will go." Chetan put on his coat, with more holes than Ke's. He closed the trap, put it with the others, and then put his knife to a dead beaver. Ke skinned the other.

TWENTY EIGHT

Close to the river's bank, those still on the way to Fort Gibson propelled the wagons with tipi poles. They zoomed downstream twice as fast as the nine knots the water itself flowed. On the opposite side of the wide waterway, the Cimarron River that joined just above Fort Arbuckle refused to merge but flowed as a distinct red stream in the Arkansas River channel.

So far, the travelers had encountered no problems in the brown water on the north side of the river. Ahead, the land between the trees and the river disappeared. Trees leaned over their path. Waya held the pole straight out to the open side of the river and bent down. "Duck!" He hollered to those coming behind, "Move farther away from the shore!" then piloted the wagon operating as a boat away from the shore as little as possible.

As they progressed, branches hung closer and closer to the water. Waya knelt completely into the wagon to make it under another limb. "Oh, no!" He attempted to dodge the portion of the bank that had slid into the river. At eighteen knots, the wagon rammed the obstruction. Something snagged a wheel.

In the wagon behind him, Hanataywee tried to slow. She dragged her pole. Riding with her, Dustu stayed their course with his pole straight ahead. "Brace for the impact!" he warned. His pole slammed his grandfather's wagon, which broke it free. The underwater branch went with Waya and cleared a passageway for the wagons floating behind him.

Dustu and Hanataywee bounced sideways with too much momentum. Hanataywee jammed her pole straight down. It no longer touched the riverbed. "Catch us!" she screamed.

Bethany threw a rope as she passed. It fell short of Dustu's hand. Ehawee pulled it back as fast as she could.

Having observed everything ahead, Eli lay his pole on the wagon bed. "Grams, get the rope from Bethany." He tied his rope to the end of his pole. "Do you have their rope?" he asked his grandmother.

Helen reported, "I have it."

"Grams, lash our wagons together." Eli secured the free end of the rope he had attached to his pole.

Ehawee prayed. "God, help us save them."

Eli said, "Amen!"

Waya and Luyu struggled to push their wagon back upstream. They only succeeded in staying still as the other three wagons approached on the current. Waya stripped to his loincloth. "Tie this to our wagon." He jumped into the water with one side of the heavy hemp cord he had handed to his wife.

"Ready?" Eli asked for confirmation that the wagons were tied together.

Bethany and Helen answered at the same time, "Ready."

"Grams, push us out." Eli waited until he was close enough then hurled the pole like a spear. It carried the rope across the water.

Dustu caught it. He immediately tied on.

"Ready!" Hanataywee hollered.

Helen turned to Bethany and Ehawee. Bethany wasn't in the boat. Like Waya, she swam toward the shore, in the frigid water.

Bethany isn't going to allow the river to take them. Helen gave instructions to Ehawee. "Start pulling."

"I can't. I have to keep from going out with you." Ehawee jammed her pole into the muddy riverbed.

Dustu and Hanataywee's wagon reached the strong current. Just as Ehawee had predicted, the force of not one but now two wagons pulled Ehawee with them.

Fastened to Ehawee's wagon, Bethany's rope suddenly drew her away from the shore. Waya, having started much earlier, climbed out of the water, still holding his rope. He ran one circle around the closest tree. He had barely enough line or time to tie it off.

Luyu saw Bethany going the wrong way. She hollered, "Let go of the rope!"

Bethany released the rope still on the shore side of Luyu's wagon. Luyu grabbed the line, hauled it in quickly, and attached it to her wagon. She pulled her fingers out of the knot loop just as the rope snapped tight. Her wagon shot forward. She fell backward onto the sleeping mule. When the wagon stopped short, she tumbled forward. The mules slid with her. The people in the other wagons braced for the upcoming jolt.

Ehawee heard the pop as the line snapped tight. In chain reaction, Eli and Helen's wagon came to a sudden stop.

Blessedly, the tree refused to be jerked from the ground. Dustu and Hanataywee's wagon slammed to a halt. They pulled their wagon toward the shore as Eli and Helen drew them closer. Once there, they secured the line and got into Eli's wagon. The four dragged the two outer wagons to Ehawee.

Ehawee jumped over and threw her arms around Hanataywee. "God, thank you for saving my sister."

Together they tugged the wagons close to the river's edge. Eli notified Waya and Bethany, who shivered on the bank. "We're in shallow water. Get back in."

Goodbye Hideout

Waya tried to untie the rope, but the pull of the wagons kept the knot much too tight. "That's just as well. We need the wagons to stay in place, so we can get to you. We'll cut the rope at the wagon." He stepped into the Arkansas. "It seems colder than when I jumped in going to the shore."

"I think so too." Bethany shook as they waded into deeper and deeper water. They climbed into the closest wagon. Under their long blanket coats, they removed their wet garments, then put on dry clothes.

"Thank you. A person could not have a better husband." Luyu hugged Waya.

Hanataywee wrapped her arms around her mother. "We should not risk further catastrophe."

"We need to stay tied together." Ehawee stood pressed against her mother's back.

Luyu reassured her granddaughter, "We will."

"And stay close to the shore even though we have to fight past the branches," added Dustu as he helped warm Waya.

Once Waya and Bethany had warmed, everybody returned to his or her position. Even though he saw that they were, Eli asked, "Everybody ready?" He heard four confirmations, then cut and floated away from the rope, slithering in the water.

Waya studied the area. *Maybe I can find it going back to Fort Arbuckle.*

The fast travel in the substantial current had carried them beyond the entangling branches. The ride went smoothly for a long while. Just before it bent ninety degrees to the north, Waya realized the river didn't continue straight ahead. He stepped over the neck of a mule and hollered, "Everybody, get to the right side! You will have to dig in and push hard to keep from going into the middle of the river!"

Luyu got into a stable stance.

Waya jammed his tipi pole into the riverbed and pushed hard. Then, he ordered, "Now!"

Luyu crammed her pole down. The front of the wagon swung around. They moved away in the correct direction. Waya hollered, "The rear end is harder!"

Hanataywee and Dustu drove their poles into the mud of the river floor and push toward the rear. The wagon moved north but also out. Dustu spat out, "Not again! Back in and try again!"

Hanataywee did as instructed. Her husband did the same. The silt that had dropped on the slower inner side of the bend made the river shallow far out from the bank. The poles again sunk into the muck and moved them toward the shore.

Dustu knew Eli was strong, but Helen wasn't used to hard labor. He didn't know if she would be able to push hard enough. *I'll jump in and swim to a tree if I have to save them.* With the rope in his hand, he hurriedly maneuvered his wagon toward the shore.

Eli and Helen hadn't seen how Waya and Luyu

had gotten around the bend. Eli had watched Hanataywee and Dustu's maneuver and prepared to perform their actions. As Eli and Helen came around the corner, Helen pushed her post into the riverbed. The wagon rode over it. With all his strength, Eli pushed them back toward the shore. "Grab the pole if you see it on the other side."

Helen quickly stepped across the rear end of Ace. "I see it!" She knelt at the side. With both hands, she grasped her maneuvering rod. The muck tried to hold it, but she was determined not to fail again. As the wagon's rear swung away from the shore, it pulled the pole from the silt. Helen drew it around the back end of the wagon, jammed it into the mud, and pushed. "I'm sorry, Eli. I'm a worthless old woman."

"Grams, don't ever tell yourself that. You are excellent. Even a young woman who had lived in a city all her life probably wouldn't be able to handle that pole, let alone apply force. You just did. I think you're remarkable."

"Thank you for saying that, Eli. You are incredibly strong. By yourself, you kept us in place."

The wagon moved toward the shore.

Bethany and Ehawee got closer to the bank before they started the turn. The three leading wagons moving forward close to the shore, plus the lack of slack, held them in and practically slung the wagon around the curve.

They continued downriver.

When the sun was low, Waya feared Fort Gibson was still far away. He didn't want to be in the river in the dark. "Search for a good place to exit the river. We need a bank about as high as the side of the wagon, so the mules can step out onto the land. We also need trees close enough to tie on to them, and a slope where we can pull out the wagons."

Since it was safer to do so from the second boat, Dustu looked ahead through a spyglass for several seconds. Then he looked at their position to make sure they had stayed reasonably close to the bank. He pointed. "There. Get closer to the shore."

Waya again stripped to his breeches. When his wagon was almost at the exit, he jumped. In water up to his chest, he directed the wagon parallel to the bank.

Dustu brought in his wagon. He collided with the wagon ahead. The still significant force of the water, even at the riverbank, then bumped Eli's into Dustu's. Some of the mules stirred. Bethany's wagon rammed Eli's, which again jarred Dustu's. The third jolt woke a few animals.

Waya scrambled onto the land and tied his wagon to a tree. King raised his head. To get the animal to focus in the direction of the shore, Waya called, "King!" With Blue in the way, the mule struggled to find a place for his feet. King finally managed to get up and oriented. He popped onto the bank, out of the strange wobbly place.

They set up camp, prepared food and hot coffee, and took turns waiting beside the wagons to guide the mules to land as they woke.

TWENTY NINE

At Fort Arbuckle, Chetan and Ke stood at the gate. "We're back!"

Noah opened the small door in the large double gate. Ke carried in two fat pouches.

"What did you get, brother?" Noah asked.

Chetan entered the fort, dangling a gutted turkey by its feet. "You caught one. The other traps were all sprung. There were a lot of fresh tracks, so we set them again."

Ke peeled the pouch down from around one of the bundles he had set on the ground, then pulled out a pelt.

Noah took it from Ke's hand. "You must have found some of Mac's traps." He examined the tail. "Very nice. Take these to your aunts. They've been worried about you, and you must be freezing."

"Noah, our father is the greatest hunter ever. He wrestled a beaver, and he didn't even get hurt."

Noah watched his father, trying not to appear to

have any pain. "I'm looking forward to the story." Just before they stepped into the building that was their home, Noah sent Ke on a mission. "Ke, tell Roscoe to come home. He's in the barn."

Chetan went inside. Noah shut the door. "Let me see you. You shouldn't have been wrestling a beaver."

"It wasn't my plan. It just worked out that way."

Ann, Sally, and Stephanie all asked, "Beaver wrestling?"

"I'll let Ke tell the story. Please make me some of that willow tea. I hurt more than when I wrestled that mule."

They all laughed. Chetan held his side. "That hurts."

THIRTY

When the last mule woke, Eli was the only person awake. He called out to his favorite mule. "Ace, over here!"

Ace recognized the voice and sat up in the wagon.

"Come here," Eli called out again.

Ace got to his feet, saw the short step between him and his favorite person, and stepped onto the land.

Eli rubbed Ace behind the ears and stroked his neck. "Come on, boy." He led him to the others eating undergrowth on the side of camp opposite the river. It was only a couple of hours after they had tied the wagons against the bank when Eli lay down. He thought about Stephanie, Christopher, and Joy then fell asleep wondering about his baby that would join them in two months.

Luyu woke first. The others woke to the smell of cooking coffee and bacon. After a comforting breakfast, they stoked the fire into a hot blaze.

Goodbye Hideout

Hanataywee and Ehawee harnessed the first four mules before Dustu slid into the water. Waya passed him the wagon tongue.

While Dustu attached it, Eli led Jumper, Hector, Blue, and Redeemed a few yards in the cold river to the wagons.

Dustu hurried to the fire to get warm.

Waya untied the rope. He and the women kept a firm grip, so the current didn't drag away the wagon.

Eli said, "Throw the ropes into the wagon," then led the mules to the place they hoped they could exit the river.

Almost effortlessly, the animals pulled the dripping wagon up the riverbank. Eli immediately went to the fire. Hanataywee and Ehawee guided the mules to the staging area, unhooked them, and then brought them to the fire. Cold people and animals warmed themselves as the next group went for another wagon.

In the freezing water, Waya hooked up King, Ace, Gumdrop, and Glory. The riverbank was a little slippery. Still, the wagon went up the bank without a problem. Helen and Bethany got the wagon in position and brought the mules to the fire.

Since they were days ahead of schedule and didn't want people or animals to suffer hypothermia, they didn't start on the third wagon until all of them were thoroughly warmed.

Once again, they attempted the climb. As it had to, the dirt had gotten soaked. The mule's hooves slid. Waya slipped with them. "I was afraid of this."

"Maybe if we brought the wagon straight in instead of at an angle," Hanataywee suggested.

"We cannot go out very far, or we will have to fight the current." Dustu got into the water and directed the mules to back up. When they were just far enough to make a sufficient circle, they tried again.

Eli watched from the bank. "The water's current is going to catch the wagon when it turns. Move them fast." Before the wagon could slide down the hill or the current's force could engage, he hollered, "Forward run!" Hector and Blue were already on the dryer ground at the top of the bank. They couldn't transition into a run, but the formidable force with sound footing pulled out Jumper, Redeemed, and the wagon.

Eli rolled the wagon into the landside formation. "Let's get the mules warm again, then use all eight for the last wagon. We can have one team up here in a harness and attach them to the harness of the mules in the water when they get over to the exit. I do not think we can get the last one any other way."

"We should keep the four that just left the water up here." Waya unbuckled a harness strap.

Dustu unhooked the other. "I agree."

They took the cold animals to the bonfire.

Goodbye Hideout

When they were warm again, Eli led King, Ace, Gumdrop, and Glory into the water. Helen took the rest to the bank above the way out. Chilled too many times, Eli violently shivered as he secured the harness to the tongue.

Waya commanded, "Eli, get out of the water right now," then slid down the bank and led the mules toward the exit.

Luyu walked on the bank beside him. "Don't try to take them away from the bank."

Waya turned them sixty-degrees toward the exit before he dashed to the hot blaze with very blue lips.

The women backed Hector, Blue, Redeemed, and Jumper only far enough to connect them to the four in the river. "Forward Ho!" Luyu ordered.

On the drier land at the top, Hector and Redeemed tugged Blue and Jumper up the slippery mud. King and Ace drew the makeshift boat forward. When the wagon rose from the water onto its wheels, four mules walked on the level ground. Luyu smiled. *Good plan. No problems.*

The wheels arrived at the bank. The wagon suddenly stuck in the deeply churned mud at the river's edge. Glory's hooves went out from under her. She pulled Gumdrop down with her. Their yoke broke.

"Of course!" Luyu exclaimed. "Why did I think we wouldn't have a problem? Bethany, get the spare yoke. Helen and Ehawee, calm the mules already up top, AND NOBODY TELL THE MEN! They need to stay by the fire. Hanataywee, help me." Luyu slid down the mud.

Luyu's granddaughter removed the broken yoke. "There's blood. Glory is injured."

"Where?"

"I can't tell through all this mud. It can't be bad. She's getting up."

"Don't wash her off. The mud is keeping the wound from bleeding too much." Luyu helped Gumdrop to her feet and then ducked under the reins to get to Glory. "It's here. I don't think it's deep. If it were, the blood would be gushing. Still, let's get her up the bank and bring down Hector."

Hanataywee led Glory to the dry ground to their left. Once up, she traded the mules.

"It'll be harder now that we've stopped." Bethany followed her daughter with the yoke.

Luyu detached the broken one from the harness. The three women secured the yoke to Hector and Gumdrop.

Bethany spoke up. "I know the men need to warm up, but we need all of us."

"All right, get them."

Bethany and the men arrived. Eli went straight to Glory to make sure she didn't need immediate medical attention.

Goodbye Hideout

"Should some of us push?" Helen asked.

Eli was surprised by the question. "Absolutely not! What if the wagon rolls back?"

"Oh, right!" Helen asked herself *what was I thinking?* "It's just that Noah and Ann need us to make this work. I don't know how we're going to get this last wagon out."

"We all need this to work, Grams."

Dustu looked at the mules still harnessed. "We cannot have an uneven team. What if we take Redeemed out, tie a rope to both sides of the front yoke, and then attach it to her and us?"

"I can't think of anything better." Waya started unhitching the mule.

Once reconfigured, Eli called, "Forward, pull!" Every animal and person strained. Eli hollered, "PULL!" every few seconds. The wheels didn't move. "HALT!"

Helen offered a suggestion. "We need to roll back some and then try to come up where Glory did."

"Let's try." Eli commanded, "Backward, PUSH!" The animals bunched up. The wagon didn't move. "Us people have to push it out."

With two women on each side and the three men and Hanataywee pushing from the front, they again attempted the reversal. Eli instructed the mules to come with them. "Backward ho!"

SLURP. The wheels sucked out of the goop.

"Hurray!" exclaimed Helen.

Five feet out and lined up for a straight shot up but slightly to the left of the original track, Eli ordered, "Halt! Get back to the front."

They set up again. Eli requested, "GOD, HELP US!" then commanded, "FORWARD, PULL!" The wagon rolled. "PULL!" They moved faster. "PULL!" The wheels contacted the bank. "PULL!"

On dry, compacted earth, the left wheels' traction made the difference. The wagon came up and out. Helen placed her palms together under her chin. "Hallelujah!"

Eli remembered the mud they had slid down at Pine Bluff. He was already wet, and he had a fire to get warm. Eli sat in the mud, pushed off, and zipped down the bank into the freezing river. He jumped up. "Brrr!"

"You're crazy!" Dustu informed Eli.

"I was reliving an earlier time, but I think once is enough." He climbed the slippery bank. "Let's get the mules unhooked."

Waya handed Eli his bag of clothes. "We will let the fire burn down while we get warm."

When back at the fire, Eli took a cup of hot coffee. "I was thinking about seeing my father. I thought first he had to take all the tools and dynamite out of the wagon. Then it occurred to me that I hadn't taken into account the weight or the space taken up by them."

Waya frowned. "Now, we have to get not just

another yoke, but we will have to buy another wagon, more mules, and another harness as well."

"I do not think we will have a problem. We have always been able to get the military to give us everything we want." Hanataywee sipped her drink.

"That was Chetan and James. Not any of us, Tom, or Adahy," remarked Waya.

Ehawee agreed with her sister. "If they could do it, we can. Every time they helped, it was because there was something in it for them. We only have to figure out what that will be this time."

Eli poured himself more coffee. "Don't forget. Make sure nobody realizes that we're connected to Noah and Ann. Anybody else want some?"

Dustu held out his cup. "Maybe we can borrow a wagon, mules, and a harness."

Waya knew that wasn't going to happen. "They will not trust a bunch of Indians."

Luyu had overheard Chetan, Noah, and Ann's whispered conversation during the night in the lodge of Yona. "What if we buy two more wagons with mules and harnesses? We take all the grain we need and as much hay as we can get in the wagons, then go three days toward Fort Arbuckle. We unload the wagons we need to take back. The full wagons go on to Fort Arbuckle. The empty wagons go back to Fort Gibson. At Fort Arbuckle, unload the wagons, then go back to get what we left on the road. At Fort Gibson, we will sell back the two wagons, mules, and harnesses. We'll fill the others with as much hay as we can before we go to Fort Arbuckle. We'll probably all get to the hay on the road around the same time."

Eli swallowed the last of his coffee. "I will work on it while we travel. Everybody warm enough?"

"I am." Dustu stood up. They put out the fire, got the mules harnessed, then chopped through the grapevines and undergrowth to the road.

A short way farther, they saw the conjunction of the Verdigris, Neosho, and Arkansas Rivers.

Eli looked through the spyglass, "We traveled quite far yesterday. We could have gotten all the way." He passed the spyglass to Waya.

Waya looked at the massive amount of water flowing into the Arkansas. "We could not have crossed." He raised the flag to signal they wanted a ride.

THIRTY ONE

On the other side of the conjunction, Tom saw the flag. "It's too early for our family. I wonder who else is traveling in the middle of winter."

Every night he had slept outside the fort, Adahy had felt the sentiments against him. "We will see the people even though we will not know them. Maybe we should move out of view. Other people may not like me, either. Goats are more acceptable than I am."

"There is no real reason for anybody not to like you, and that is not why I agree that we should move. It is just to avoid any possibility of somebody who knows us, seeing us here. I will find out if it is all right to move behind the fort. Please get a small tarp from the store, then go back to our camp and lay it inside the wagon. We need to cover the pitch before we put anything back in."

"I will go."

"Try to avoid Ezra. I do not want him to know we are here either. "

Lisa Gay

Tom walked across the open courtyard just as Ezra came out of the barracks, saw Tom, and turned toward him. "Darn," Tom muttered under his breath.

"Hello, Tom. What are you doing here?" Ezra followed because he had important news.

"I came to cover our new wagons with pitch. Somebody is coming across the Neosho. I want to move out of view to the backside of the fort. Do you think there is any problem with that?"

Ezra opened a stall door and got two of the horses he knew were Tom's. "You can move to the backside of the fort, but first, I need to tell you that Joe Smith is dead."

"He is? What happened?" Tom asked as he retrieved more of his horses.

"We found him not far from the road when we were coming back. He was lying in his tent as frozen as can be. I figure it happened the night we left you. Now, you don't have to run away."

"It's good to know at least one person isn't chasing us anymore. Still, don't tell anybody you saw me and thanks for telling me about Joe Smith. At least Lola and Sebastian are safe. Too bad they don't know."

"Morris wrote a letter. He said he would send it to them from Spadra Bluff."

"Good. I've got to move my wagons. Remember; don't tell anybody you saw me." Tom left with all his horses. He and Adahy loaded up, hitched up, and pulled the wagons out of view.

Across the river, four almost empty wagons rode onto the ferry. The plan was for everybody to see an Indian family. Eli tried to look like an Indian as the ferry bobbed in the turbulence of the merging water. He couldn't resist and peeked through his spyglass across the river. He didn't see the wagons. *Oh no! They're not there!* He started to worry. The ride wasn't long, but it seemed to take forever. Eli was the first off. He hurried away to look for his father. Waya stepped off the wagon last. He handed the ferryman the fare.

Eli thought, *maybe they're inside, but that would be strange. The soldiers won't let them remain inside during the night.* He walked in through the same gates his father had hurried out of only a short time before. Eli went to the stable and glanced in. He didn't see the heads of any of their horses above the stall walls. He hurried back to his family. "They're not here. I'm going back and up the road to see if I can find them."

Waya stopped unhooking the harness. "You do not know which way they came. The land is too large for you to search."

"I've got to try. I'm taking Ace." Eli jumped on the mule bareback.

Luyu grabbed Ace's short mane. "If you go, then you won't be here either. Let's find out more first."

"What is there to find out? Our horses are not in the stable, and the wagons aren't here."

Ehawee feared for her husband. "I'm going with you."

Eli pulled her onto Ace behind him.

Fear coursed into Luyu's mind. She didn't want her granddaughter to leave even more than she didn't want Eli to leave. "Ehawee, you can't go off alone."

"I won't be alone. Eli will be with me."

Eli hurried Ace to the river before the ferryman had finished securing the ferry. "We have to go back."

"You should have stayed over there."

Eli dismounted. He stood a foot from the man's face and stared him down.

"There's going to be a fare for both ways." The ferryman untied the ropes and lowered the gate.

"Fine. Just take us." Eli led Ace onto the ferry. *Even with us getting here this fast, they should have already been here. If something happened to Pop, it would be my fault.* He stood on the ferry beside Ehawee and imagined the Cherokee skinning or scalping his father, a white man almost alone in their land.

Waya, Dustu, Luyu, Hanataywee, Helen, and Bethany took the other mules to the stable. Luyu spoke to the private who smelled like the manure he had just removed from the building. "We want to stable our mules for a day or two and buy them hay and grain."

"All the stalls are full. I'll have to find out if we can double them up."

Goodbye Hideout

Luyu looked at the stalls. "You may double ours, but the stalls look empty to me."

The soldier did not like to be questioned. "They're full of sheep and goats, and some horses are not in here at the moment."

"Really?" Luyu started toward the stall to see if they were their animals.

"What are you doing?" the private stepped between her and the stalls.

"I was going to see if they are the goats and sheep of some people we're trying to find."

"He's a white man. You wouldn't know him."

That's what I needed to know. "We'll bring our mules back later. Please find out if you'll be able to make space." She quickly informed the portion of her family beside the fort. "They're here somewhere. Find them." Luyu pulled the shotgun from the wagon. "I need to stop Eli and Ehawee."

Dustu discovered pitch in the grass. "Here!" he called out. They ran along the tracks of crushed grass. "Adahy! Tom! We need you now!" Dustu called as he ran the circle around the fort.

Adahy ran toward the familiar voice. "Brother!" He threw his arms around Dustu. "How did you get here so quickly? What's wrong?"

"You and Tom have to come to the river NOW! Eli and Ehawee are crossing back to the other side! They think you are in trouble!"

All of them ran.

CRACK!

They heard the report as Luyu fired the shotgun into the air over the river. Across the waters of the coursing Neosho, Eli, Ehawee, and the ferryman turned to look. A group of people ran toward the river waving their hands.

Eli pulled out his spyglass. "Where on earth were they?" He handed Ehawee the spyglass. "Take us back."

The ferryman snapped back. "I'm still charging for a trip both ways for one mule and two people."

"Fine." Eli was too happy to haggle about the charge.

The ferryman maneuvered the levers that controlled the paddle wheels and reversed the boat.

When they were close, Eli took the coins from his bag and handed them to the ferryman. "Sorry about the confusion. Much obliged for taking us out and back."

As soon as the ferryman lowered the gate, Eli and Ehawee hurried off. "Pop!" Eli hugged his father.

Ehawee fell into the arms of her husband. "Adahy!"

Tom enjoyed the embrace. "Come on, you two worriers." However, he was delighted to be with so much of his family again. "Tell us how you got here so fast."

Goodbye Hideout

"Let's get the animals into the stables. These mules haven't had anything to eat."

Tom said, "I'll bring the wagons around, so we can load them." Eli went with his father.

Ehawee also went to the wagons hidden behind the fort. "I've missed you," Ehawee whispered to her husband.

"Me too. A lot," he whispered back.

They brought the wagons around and joined with the others at the stable. Tom informed the stable hand, who didn't smell any better than the last time they had been in the stable, "You can double stall my animals to make room for these mules."

The private already had the stall doors open, the water buckets brimming, and the feed troughs full. "I figured as much. After we heard the shot, everybody saw you trying to get your friends to come back. I'll put the mules in first, so they can eat everything in the stalls and keep the horses in the aisle for now. I'll swap them around after the mules eat, and give the horses their food, then I'll double them up for you."

THIRTY TWO

Sergeant Timothy Anders came into the stable. "Colonel Howland demands to speak with the group firing the shotgun outside the fort."

Luyu said, "It was me. I'll come."

Eli didn't want Luyu to be under scrutiny. "It's my fault. I got on the ferry. I'll go."

Sergeant Anders ordered them, "Every one of you, come with me."

The ten of them followed across the courtyard. Tom trudged along. *This is the end of nobody knowing we were here. How are we ever going to be safe?*

Ezra watched Sergeant Anders escort Chetan's family. He thought about which of them the colonel would know, then he thought about which of them Anders would know. Ezra realized he was the only one who knew who they were. *Should I report what I know to Colonel Howland? I did promise Tom I'd keep his secret. I'll see what happens.*

Sergeant Anders knocked on Colonel Howland's office door. "I've brought them, sir."

Goodbye Hideout

The voice behind the door said, "Bring them in."

Six Indians and four white people went into the commander's office. The colonel looked at the five men and five women. He knew what went on in Indian Territory, especially right beside his fort.

"Thank you, Sergeant Anders. Stay just outside." When the door closed, the colonel started the interrogation. "Which one of you discharged a firearm beside this fort?"

Luyu spoke up. "I fired a shotgun to get the attention of some of our family out on the ferry."

"How many times have you fired a shotgun?" Colonel Howland's gaze bored holes into the woman he questioned.

Luyu thought it was obvious how many times she had fired the gun. "I shot it once."

"I mean, ever in your life." The colonel attempted to intimidate the woman with an intense stare and scowl.

"Once."

The colonel thrust his chest out. "So, you thought it was safe to fire a shotgun beside my fort when you know nothing about how to do that?"

Waya interjected, "I told her to shoot it."

Colonel Howland stood up, put his hands on the desktop, and leaned toward Waya. "Unless I am asking you to speak, don't talk. Do all of you understand?" His penetrating stare drilled into each of their minds.

Every one of them nodded his or her head in the affirmative and spoke only two words, "Yes, sir."

The colonel stood only a few feet in front of Luyu and repeated the question. "Did you think it was safe to discharge a shotgun knowing nothing about how to do it?"

Luyu showed no concern for the overpowering presence of the commander of Fort Gibson. "I would never use a weapon, knowing nothing."

The colonel walked before the line of people in his office as he sized them up. He walked back to the woman who stated she had shot the gun. He turned inches from her face. "You just said that was the only time you ever shot a shotgun."

Luyu believed she understood what the colonel was driving at. "Yes, sir. I did say that was the only time I fired a shotgun, but some things are the same between weapons. Unless you intend to kill, you make sure you are not pointing your loaded weapon in a direction where there is any possibility to hit something by mistake. I knew the shotgun was loaded. I knew you only have to pull the trigger with this type of gun. I purposefully shot toward the empty river where I knew the distance across is farther than the shot can travel. I knew it was the only thing loud enough for my family to hear, and I knew that the possibility of problems or injury to my family would be much higher if I let them go than if I got them to come back."

Goodbye Hideout

"I think you were trying to signal others to attack."

"I was signaling others but not to attack. I would be very stupid if I tried to get a war party to attack by firing a gun that would make everybody look just before people tried to run to the only gate in the light of day. They would all be shot by your men as they ran across the field. If any of them did make it that far, which I doubt, the gate would have been closed long before they got near it."

"Humm." Colonel Howland thought for a moment. He pointed at the two of them who had been there for days covering their wagons with pitch. "So, other than putting pitch on your wagons, why are you here?"

Tom wanted everybody to think they were leaving the area immediately. After years of negotiating for his store, Tom knew how to end up with everybody getting a fair deal. He led the conversation away from the shooting of the shotgun toward a sale. "We want to buy a large amount of grain and hay."

"How much?"

Eli already had their hay and grain requirements figured out. "Eleven hundred bales of hay. If your animal grain comes in fifty-pound sacks, we need eighty-one sacks. A week later, one-hundred and forty-four more bales of hay. In the end, we want to sell the two wagons we just coated in pitch and two four-horse-harnesses."

"Why on earth do you think we would sell that much?"

Since the colonel was talking to Eli, Eli answered, "Because you have traded with and helped our family before, and we have helped you. It wouldn't make sense to allow one of your men to warn us, then destroy us yourself by not allowing us to buy the hay and grain we need to leave when we have to go."

"So you must be the family of Noah Swift Hawk and Ann Williams. How exactly are you related?" The colonel kept his eyes trained directly on Eli.

"I am married to a sister of Ann."

The colonel turned to Tom. "And you?"

"I'm Eli's father and a longtime friend of the Williams family."

The colonel looked at Adahy, who answered, "I'm married to a sister of Noah."

"Next," the colonel ordered the young female.

"I'm the wife of Adahy, the sister of Noah, and daughter of Bethany and Chetan."

Dustu looked at his wife. "I'm married to Hanataywee. She is one of Noah's sisters." He then looked at Adahy. "Adahy is my twin brother."

"I can see that," stated the colonel.

Hanataywee pointed at Bethany. "She is my mother. Noah is my brother. Ehawee is my sister. Dustu is my husband."

Goodbye Hideout

Waya spoke next. "I'm the grandfather of those two men, but I raised them as sons, and I'm married to Noah's grandmother."

Helen stated her position in the family. "Tom is my son. Eli is my grandson."

Bethany stood beside Helen. "I'm Noah's mother. These are my daughters. Chetan is my husband."

Luyu said, "Chetan is my son. Noah is my grandson. These people are my family by birth or by marriage."

The colonel walked to his desk. "How are Chetan, James, and the others in the village?"

Tom spoke up. "Everybody in the village was fine when we left, but a mule badly injured Chetan after we left."

"Is he going to recover?" Colonel Howland didn't allow his concern to display in his voice.

"I don't know." Tom looked at those who had been with Chetan more recently.

Luyu thought maybe this was a way to get the army to help them again. "We hope so, sir. He regained consciousness after two very long days. Noah is taking care of him. Nothing seems infected yet, but he has many injuries, bad ones to his head, and dozens of stitches. He'll have many scars when he heals."

The colonel sat in his chair behind the desk. "What did he do to make a mule that mad?"

Dustu explained.

"Talk with the quartermaster, Sergeant McCormick. I'll issue the authorization to sell twelve hundred and fifty bales of hay and four thousand and fifty pounds of grain depending on our supply. I will also approve our purchase of the harnesses and the two wagons you just covered with tar. I will send it over later today. Now, to the matter of shooting the shotgun beside the fort. You will all spend a very long time in the stockade if there is another discharge of a firearm anywhere around this fort by any of you. Then how will you leave Indian Territory?"

Luyu stated her compliance. "Yes, sir. I promise I will not shoot the shotgun or any other weapon around the fort ever again."

The colonel continued as he sat behind his large, sturdy walnut desk. "I'm assuming you didn't bring Chetan here to get a medic to look at him because you're running from Joe Smith. The man is dead. You can let me send help."

Bethany stated the situation. "Just because nobody is coming right now, that doesn't mean nobody will later. I will not give anybody a chance to harm anybody in my family, so we are leaving. Even so, if I thought Chetan would get better care here, I would bring him, but my son is as good, if not better than any other doctor."

"I'll issue an authorization for various

medications. Talk with the medic. Tell him Chetan's condition. Get the medications you need and tell Chetan I wish him a speedy and complete recovery. Tell James that I send my regards."

Tom informed the colonel, "We won't see James."

"I thought he was part of your family."

"He is the uncle of the Williams girls. He is their father's brother. He has a life here that he wants to keep."

The colonel returned to the matter that had caused the meeting. "You are ALL under orders to tell everybody who asks about this meeting that you were told sternly not to discharge a firearm or use any weapon while near this fort. You will NOT say anything else about our conversation. Give my regards to the rest of your family. You are dismissed."

Tom said, "Thank you, Colonel Howland." They left the building. Bethany and Eli went to speak with the army medical staff. The rest went to the store to buy the trade goods and personal items they wanted.

Tom handed the private on duty his list of items to trade: a large bolt of red flannel, another of calico cotton material, thread, scissors, awls, butcher knives, hunting knives, thimbles, buttons, red flannel shirts, bottles of matches, and blankets of various sizes.

For the family's use, they got: green coffee beans, pressed tea blocks, cinnamon sticks, whole nutmegs, cloves, peppercorns, a spice grinder, a smoked ham, a wheel of cheese, ten pounds of dried compressed vegetables, five pounds of dried potatoes cubes, fifty pounds of bacon, two dozen eggs, and a pound of peppermint sticks.

On the non-food side, they purchased lantern oil, linseed oil, and two decks of playing cards. They left the store with their packages under their arms.

Hanataywee smelled baking bread and remembered the stories about éclairs, danishes, and fresh bread. "I want to go to the bakery, but we should all go together." They ended up back at their wagons with ten éclairs and five loaves of bread.

When Bethany and Eli joined them, everything was packed. Bethany added the medical supplies.

They put up the tent Tom and Adahy had taken down when they had hidden. Inside it, they put together a meal. Eli took a bite of ham, chewed slowly, and savored the salty taste. "Food sure tastes good when you haven't eaten for a whole day."

"I wonder if it's the same for mules," Adahy inquired as he enjoyed the meal.

"Are you ready for your treat?" Hanataywee offered the box of éclairs to her husband.

"Yes, I am." Dustu bit into the pastry. The custard oozed out the far end. He informed the others. "Find the hole, and start eating at that end." He licked the chocolate frosting and custard off his fingers.

Tom lay back to rest for a second. Soon his eyes closed. While the others slept, Adahy sat beside them and played a made-up solitary game with a deck of cards. An hour passed before Tom woke. "I will see if the colonel sent the authorizations yet."

"I will go with you." Adahy stacked the cards.

"Come on." The two of them went into the store. "May I speak with the quartermaster?" Tom asked.

"If you want to know if the papers have arrived, they did. Sergeant McCormick went to find out how much hay and oats we have. You can wait for him to return or go to the stable."

"Thank you," Tom replied. He and Adahy left the store.

Sergeant McCormick and the foul-smelling private stood in the loft, counting bales. The sergeant saw Tom and the Indian who had been with him since they had arrived. "Hold on for a few minutes."

"Sure." Tom thought about helping but decided if it were him, he would want to verify the numbers himself. He waited while Sergeant McCormick wrote numbers on his sheet, talked with his helper, and then climbed down the ladder. The sergeant walked to Tom. "Right now, we can sell you all the oats you want, but we can only sell you five hundred bales of hay. In two weeks, we can have the rest."

So he could estimate a fair price, Tom inquired, "Will you be going to Fort Smith for the rest?"

"Yes. We'll discuss the arrangements on the way to the store." Sergeant McCormick walked beside

Tom, but relegated Adahy to following. "The grain is thirty cents for a fifty-pound sack, and the forty-pound compressed hay bales are fifty each."

Tom didn't haggle. "Will it be the same price for the next set of bales?"

"You're also going to have to pay for the hay it takes to feed the sixteen mules, and for the rations it takes for the men to take the wagons down to Fort Smith and back to get the hay."

Tom quickly figured one hundred and five bales of hay plus thirty-six meals. "So that would be sixty-five extra dollars."

"Right."

The men and mules will have eaten the same amount of food if they stay in the fort or if they go to Fort Smith and back. I should talk about this with the family. "I'll let you know." At the tent, he explained the situation.

Dustu remembered the story from the book Joy's parents had written. "Joy's parents got somebody to bring hay on a boat. Can we do that?"

"Who is Joy?" Tom asked.

Eli realized they hadn't told his father about anything that had happened while they had been apart. "Ann found a baby named Joy."

Tom thought, *unbelievable.* "How did she find a baby, and how could she know its name?"

Eli told the story.

"So we have a new member of the family. I'm

looking forward to meeting her." Tom switched back to the original topic. "Let me see if there's a steamboat we can hire at Fort Smith."

Tom didn't want to influence his negotiations with Sergeant McCormick, so he went to the barracks and spoke to the man who opened the door. "Would you direct me to Private Knuckles?"

"He's on duty in the mess hall." The man pointed.

"Thank you." Tom walked away. He found Ezra washing pots.

"Hello, Tom. Does the colonel know who you are?"

"Yes, with a lot of details. Do you know if there's a steamboat at Fort Smith? We want to rent one to take hay up the river."

"Edwin, Robert, Morris, Matt, and their sons hired the steamboat to take them to Maumelle. The ship's captain said he was going to stay in Little Rock this winter."

"So, there is NO boat that could go upriver?"

Ezra continued washing. "I don't think so."

"Thanks, Ezra. And thank you for not telling the colonel, but we told him exactly who we are."

"Good luck and safe travels."

Tom returned to his family. "There is no boat."

Luyu stated her opinion. "I say we buy the five hundred bales of hay and the grain and go home. Even if we float the wagons to Fort Smith, it's going to take more hay to come back, and we won't be able to carry it all home if we sell the wagons."

Waya spoke next. "We can do what we originally planned. We're not adding that much time because we got here so quickly, and we can get to Fort Smith quickly as well."

Eli looked up from a paper full of numbers and columns. "I figured out the least amount of time to get the most hay to Fort Arbuckle. Two people take twelve horses, one small wagon carrying thirty-nine bales of hay and their personal supplies to Fort Smith.

"Everybody else takes all the rest of the animals, the other five wagons, four hundred and sixty-one bales of hay and all the grain to Fort Arbuckle. Noah, Ann, Chetan, Ke, and Chumani stay there.

"The other ten of us float the five wagons and ten mules down the river and take them out at the same place we did today, then build a fire and wait for the mules to wake up.

"We cross on the ferry the next day. We sedate the mules again, put them in the wagons, and get back into the river. We get out at Fort Smith and load them with as much hay as we can carry, and they will sell.

"We'll buy two more mules at Fort Smith, then we all go home. Did you already pay for feed for all these animals for five more days?"

Adahy said, "We have paid for feed for six more days for four goats, four sheep, the two little donkeys, and twenty-four mules and horses."

Goodbye Hideout

Eli figured for a minute. "After the feed for all the animals today, we'll own seventy-three bales of hay and one hundred and thirty-two pounds of grain. We'll use eighty-two pounds of grain going to Fort Smith, and take the rest to Fort Arbuckle on the first trip."

Waya said, "It's Cherokee land between here and Fort Smith. It would be best if at least one other person and I take the mules and the wagon."

Luyu said, "I can go with you."

"Very good."

Tom stood up. "I'll go buy the grain and hay. Bring the wagons to the stables." At the store, Tom informed Sergeant McCormick of their decision. He counted out two hundred eighty-two dollars and forty cents.

Sergeant McCormick took the money, locked it in the safe, and then went with Tom to make sure the private on duty closely monitored the transfer. "They've bought five hundred seventy-three bales of hay and eighty-four sacks of grain."

Tom reminded him, "Plus thirty-two more pounds of grain."

"Right. Let them load it, but you count what they take." The Sergeant left them to the hard work.

Lieutenant Olson saw McCormick coming toward him but waited for him to knock before opening the door of the command building.

Sergeant McCormick stood at attention outside the building. "I request an audience with the colonel."

Lieutenant Olson spoke through the door into the inner room. "Colonel, Sergeant McCormick is here again."

"Send him in."

"Colonel, they don't want us to go to Fort Smith to get the rest. We still ought to get more. We don't absolutely need to, but it's better to have more than less in case it's a cold winter."

"Do you want to go yourself?"

"No, it's too cold."

"I'll ask for volunteers. What will they need?"

"Four wagons, four men, sixteen mules, and supplies for two weeks. Maybe they could also trade some of the buffalo meat for other supplies."

"Olson, issue a requisition for the supplies Sergeant McCormick specifies. Assemble all the men in the barracks after you've written the requisition."

Later, Ezra Knuckles, Ham Blanders, and Morgan Finch walked into the stable with Sergeant Tim Anders. Anders handed over the paper from Colonel Howland. "Kenneth, we have a requisition for mules, wagons, and mule food."

"You'll have to get it yourself or wait. I have to count the hay we just sold."

Tom stopped swinging bales toward the ramp, taking the hay to the ground. "May I ask where you're going?"

Goodbye Hideout

Sergeant Tim Anders gave the official answer, "I can't tell you. It's a military mission."

Waya whispered to his wife, "Tell them we're going to Fort Smith, and they can come with us if they're going that way." He went back to moving hay to the wagons. Luyu passed on the message.

Tim issued orders to his men, "Get the mules and harnesses. Take one of the wagons to the store and get these supplies." He handed Ham the list. He thought it would be better for Ham to get supplies since his nose was still recovering from his fight with Joe Smith. "You two help me load hay and grain."

Tim, Ezra, and Morgan loaded the small amount of hay and grain they needed, then left.

Bethany passed Luyu a bale of hay. "You should leave now. They're probably going to Fort Smith. It would be better if you went with them."

"We shouldn't leave before the hay is loaded."

"We can load the hay. You and Waya go now."

Luyu found Waya stacking hay. "Bethany says we should leave now so we can go to Fort Smith with Sergeant Anders."

Tom heard Luyu. "I agree, but hold on for a minute."

Waya rolled the tarp over the sides of the stack of hay, then climbed off the wagon.

Tom came back with one of their twenty-round Lefaucheux revolvers and four belts of bullets. "Take this. You never know what might happen."

"All right." Waya took the gun and ammunition.

"See you in eight days." Tom knew his mother wasn't used to working this hard. "Ma, come tie down this tarp." He took her place so that she could do the less strenuous job.

THIRTY THREE

Waya and Luyu found Sergeant Anders and his men examining their wagon a short way down the road. "Hello. Can we help you?" Luyu asked.

Ezra introduced his friends to each other. "You two might have seen us when Sergeant Anders made arrangements for Waya's village to trade with Fort Gibson for your vegetables."

"I'm sorry. I only noticed Waya those days."

Waya thought *how nice it is to have a wife who is very happy to have me as her husband.*

Sergeant Anders motioned for Waya and Luyu to follow. When they were out of hearing of the other soldiers, he explained his unrelated problem. "A month ago, Colonel Howland received information that there was trouble between the Creek and Choctaw. I went down there to find out if there was a problem, but it was so cold we barely did more than keep from freezing to death.

"I want to check again. If I have you two with me, I figure I can leave the road and cut across Cherokee land. We can ride most of the border. We have three weeks before your family gets to Fort Smith. Since this is a military mission, I will requisition your six wagons full of hay at the military cost to pay you for helping."

"Let me talk with my husband." Luyu translated Tim's request and offer.

"We only have eight days, not three weeks. We could get there just in time, but he would not have much time to look for anything. These soldiers have been good to us. Let me think about this."

Waya paced for several minutes. "Sergeant Anders needs to tell Ezra to wait to get the hay until after our family arrives and rests one night. It will take many hours to load ten wagons, so they should spend the night after loading and start back the next day. That would take ten days. We could be there by then. If not, we can catch up with them on the road back to Fort Gibson.

"Anders can tell his men he wants to check one more time. He does not have to say he did not check well the first time. I will help him look. I will find out what is happening better than his men could. They don't know what to see."

Luyu waved Sergeant Anders over. She told him what Waya suggested. "...and so you tell your men to take our wagon with yours. They don't need all these mules to pull empty wagons. We will take three."

Goodbye Hideout

Tim thought it over. "We'll walk back. I'll tell Colonel Howland that I just discovered I should recheck the border. I'll requisition three horses and more supplies. We'll cross the Arkansas on the ferry."

Luyu told Waya about the slight change, then informed Sergeant Anders, "We agree."

Anders issued new orders to Ezra, Ham, and Morgan. "Continue to Fort Smith with our original orders and all these wagons and animals. Upon arrival, stable the animals, then report immediately to Colonel Habersham and give him the request for hay. Don't make the purchase. Enjoy yourselves as good soldiers, and wait for me. I'm putting Ezra in charge while we're separated."

"Yes, sir." Ezra saluted his commanding officer. "Let's move this wagon train forward." He was thrilled to have again been selected to lead a mission. Even though they were his good friends, this time, he was responsible for an assignment with real soldiers.

THIRTY FOUR

While the others tied the tarps over the wagons in the stable at Fort Gibson, Tom went to talk with the ferryman. "We have five wagons, four goats, four sheep, twenty horses, and eight people to cross the Neosho and Verdigris Rivers."

"Today?" The ferryman had just brought them over that morning. Then he had taken the man, the blue-eyed girl, and a mule partway out and then back. Now, they wanted two more trips to get them all to the other side.

"Yes. Today."

"Two dollars per wagon, five cents for each sheep or goat, twenty-five cents for each mule, donkey, or horse, and fifty cents per person. My horses are tired. Your animals do the work, and those will ride for free."

"All right."

"Are you ready now?"

"We will be at the dock in a few minutes."

Goodbye Hideout

"Ferryman Orville King at your service." The man, yet again, went to get the boat ready.

Tom walked back to the stable.

The ferry gate was down when they arrived. Helen and Hanataywee drove two wagons onto the ferry, set the brakes, then brought Chocolate and Blanco down the ramp into the treadmill slots on the right. Tom and Dustu herded the sheep, goats, Little Jack, Little Jenny, Spot, Honey, Smiley, and QuickSilver into the ferry pen. Tom put Big Jenny and Shaggy into place on the left, facing the opposite direction from Chocolate and Blanco.

Orville hooked the work mules into the harnesses. Dustu held the reins of Chocolate and Blanco as if the animals were about to pull a wagon. Tom stood behind Shaggy and Big Jenny, but Hanataywee and Helen sat on the wagons. All held the reins of their team.

Tom called out, "Forward ho!" He and Dustu tapped the rear of the donkeys in front of them. Helen and Hanataywee pulled back on the reins of the mules attached to the wagons, silently telling them to stop. The animals in the slots walked forward on the treadmill that ran the paddle wheels. The ferry moved away from the boardwalk into the current that pushed them downstream.

Orville pulled a lever that changed the gears in the mechanism below. The upstream paddlewheels turned slower than the downstream paddle. They traveled at an angle across the confluence of the rivers. A large eddy of turbulence rocked the ferry. Tom and Dustu grabbed the rail. Big Jenny and Shaggy faltered and then walked erratically, which caused the boat to turn downstream.

Orville called out instructions to the women. "Walk in front of them. They should focus on you and be all right."

Helen got off the wagon and did so. It didn't solve the problem. The donkeys seemed confused as they walked forward but saw themselves moving backward.

"Stop them. Lady, you stop too. Put these on those two." Orville pointed at Big Jenny and Shaggy. He threw two sets of blinders onto the deck. Desperately trying to keep the ferry from capsizing in the swirling water, he worked the levers.

Dustu and Tom pulled back the reins. Hanataywee jumped off the wagon, ran across the deck, grabbed the blinders, and dashed to the faltering donkeys. Big Jenny staggered and fell against the rail. Hanataywee handed a set of blinders to Tom. He put them on Big Jenny's head as Hanataywee put the other on Shaggy, blocking the mules' view to the sides. All the animals then saw was Helen in front of them.

Orville needed to get power to the ferry wheels

fast. "Forward, ho!" he commanded. "You too, lady! Walk in place again!"

The donkeys walked on the treadmill. Big Jenny and Shaggy oriented on Helen and immediately understood how to walk again.

Orville changed the gearing and turned them more directly upriver. Not only did they recover the distance the current had taken them downstream while the donkeys had floundered, but they also moved toward the far shore. Finally, they arrived at the dock.

Hanataywee and Helen drove the wagons off before they removed the penned animals. Tom paid the fare, then he and Dustu switched the donkeys. Spot, Honey, Smiley, and QuickSilver got into the ferry slots with the blinders already on. The donkeys, relieved from service, happily left the traces. Tom walked in place before Smiley and QuickSilver as they rode the empty ferry back to Fort Gibson.

"What happened?" Adahy asked when they pulled up to the dock.

Orville explained, "The donkeys got confused by walking forward but moving backward. I had to train mine not to get disoriented."

The second trip went smoothly. As previously planned and to generate goodwill, after removing their mules, Dustu and Tom helped Orville get his horses into the slots to take the ferry home. "We'll be back in about seven days and want to go back across."

Orville exclaimed, "Why on earth do you need to go back and forth?"

Tom told the truth. "We're getting hay and grain for the winter."

"I'll keep a lookout for the flag." Orville's horses moved the ferry into the river. *These people are going to make this a very profitable winter.*

THIRTY FIVE

Lieutenant Olson knocked on the colonel's door. "Sergeant Anders is here to speak with you, sir."

The colonel scowled. *He disobeyed a direct order.* "Send him in."

Sergeant Anders knew the colonel did not like his orders to be countermanded and knew to show his respect immediately upon entering Colonel Howland's presence. He stood erect and saluted crisply. "Sir, I have new intelligence to report."

"Olson, step outside and close the door."

Olson did as commanded.

"I spoke with that Cherokee after leaving here and believe we should recheck the Creek-Choctaw border. Privates Knuckle, Blanders, and Finch are continuing the mission to Fort Smith. I will rejoin them after reconnoitering the border. I can hire the services of two Indian scouts and pay them with the opportunity to purchase supplies at Fort Smith at the military rate. Plus, I'll need rations for three for two weeks, authorization to transport us across the

Arkansas on the ferry, and the use of three horses and three knapsacks."

"Get Olson." He pulled a sheet of paper out of his desk, opened the ink well, and picked up a quill.

Tim Anders opened the door. Olson sat in the chair at the desk across the room. "Colonel Howland wants you to come in."

The colonel issued new orders. "Anders, complete your mission, as we discussed. Olson, write a requisition for the use of three horses, three knapsacks, a trip across the Arkansas on the ferry for three people and three horses, and the standard issue of supplies for three soldiers for two weeks."

Olson went to his desk and wrote the order while the colonel wrote a letter. He went back into the room with the requisition as Colonel Howland melted sealing wax over an envelope's flap. The colonel pressed his seal into the wax, took the paper from Olson, and signed the requisition while the resin hardened. After a few seconds, he handed Sergeant Anders the letter addressed to Colonel Josiah Habersham and the order to issue the supplies he had requested.

"You are both dismissed."

Olson and Anders replied in unison, "Yes, sir." They turned crisply and headed to the door.

The colonel ordered, "Close the door going out."

Tim Anders, Waya, and Luyu were waiting at the

Goodbye Hideout

landing when the ferry docked. Sergeant Anders handed Orville the order to transport them across the Arkansas River.

"Get on. I'll be right back." Several minutes later, after getting permission to be off station for the night, Orville returned. He didn't want to lose control of the boat in the strong current they would encounter as they crossed, not the smaller Neosho and Verdigris river confluence, but the Arkansas River itself. He kept his horses in the traces to power the ferry.

They made the voyage uneventfully. Tim, Waya, and Luyu disembarked and headed to the border between the Cherokee and the Creek.

Knowing there was no reason to spend unnecessary time on that part of the trip, they cantered at a slow lope for a couple of hours. They stopped for only half an hour to let the horses rest and graze on the sparse prairie grass, then loped along for another couple hours before stopping for the mid-day break at Polecat Creek. Luyu rummaged through the sack to see what they could eat. The horses again rested and ate prairie grass.

After they resumed travel, they quickly rode to another large river. Waya stated, "We made it to the Goo-al-pah River."

Tim said, "You mean the Canadian River?"

Luyu corrected him. "That's what you call it, but it's the Goo-al-pah."

They set up camp. Waya went to the river to fish. Luyu searched the woods for downed branches to make a fire. She heard a low growl, dropped the load of wood, and then picked up the most substantial stick. "Waya!" she screamed at the top of her lungs.

Waya dropped the pole and ran. He heard the growling as he dashed into the woods with the drawn and fully loaded Lefaucheux revolver.

Enormous gray bodies, drooling saliva surrounded Luyu. She circled, swinging the branch fiercely. The animals had a well-established plan of attack. One of the wolves jumped toward Luyu's back. The force of the rotation of her body added power to the impact on its head. It yelped, staggered, and then fell over dead.

Another darted toward what it thought would be an easy meal. Luyu slammed it away with the branch. It quickly circled back and sunk its teeth into her left hand. She hit its skull, but it was too close to strike hard. The hungry carnivore jerked her to her knees. Luyu saw another coming at her from the opposite direction. *The wolf spirit doesn't want me to take Waya away.*

The revolver's report rang out. The ripping teeth dropped from her hand. She turned and clubbed the wolf attacking on her other side. The second round from the revolver dropped it.

With the third slug, Waya shot the one rushing

him. The animal attackers didn't know Waya's name was wolf, and he wasn't of their pack anyway. Therefore, as Waya fought, the wolves focused on the new adversary. Others continued the attack on Luyu.

Tim rode in on his horse and shot a vicious carnivore when it knocked Luyu to the ground.

Waya twisted, downed the one closest to him, then took out the snarling canine over Luyu. She jumped up and whacked wolves with the branch.

Tim shot two more attackers. The last of them ran into the woods. Tim dashed after them on his horse.

Waya ran to Luyu and swept her into his arms. "I will never let a wolf or anything else take you away from me." He raised her bitten and ripped hand as Luyu shook with fear and adrenaline. He did too. "It's a wonder that you were still able to grip the branch."

Tim returned. "I shot every last one of them."

Luyu tried to relieve her anxiety. "I know a good recipe for wolf barbeque, but I am pretty sure we do not have any of the ingredients except the wolf."

The others laughed.

"We still need this." Waya picked up the branches Luyu had dropped. Tim kept his eyes open for any further attackers as Waya and Luyu gathered wood.

In camp, Tim got the first aid kit, handed it to Waya, and then started building a fire.

Waya again held Luyu's hand. "Move your fingers one at a time."

After being courageous when fighting but now

safe, Luyu cried. "The wolf spirit does not want me to have you. They tried to eat me because I am taking you away from Cherokee land."

Waya put his arms around his wife. "They were just hungry animals that saw something they thought they could eat. Besides, my home was the mountains back east. They should not have tried to eat such a powerful woman. You crushed the skull of the first one you hit."

Luyu's tears flowed. "I do not want to cry. I am afraid."

"My wild dove, you have been through a terrifying experience. You are allowed to cry." Waya held Luyu in his lap for several minutes as she released her fear in the form of tears. "Stay here, but let me take care of your hand."

Luyu held out her hand.

"This will hurt." Waya poured whiskey over both sides of her hand then carefully positioned some gauze over her ripped flesh and wrapped it in a bandage.

Once they had a roaring fire, Tim asked, "Do you want the wolf bodies?"

Luyu growled, "I'm going to skin every one of them and use their hides to line our new tipi. Any wolf that tries to eat me will become my house." She stood up. "Let's get them."

They laid the wolf carcasses across their horses,

took them to their camp, dumped them, and then went back for more. Before dark, they had gathered twenty dead wolves.

They skinned the rest while the one that had bitten Luyu roasted. Eating it didn't help her. Every time she closed her eyes, she saw drooling fangs attacking her.

The next five days, Luyu stuck to Waya as he searched the river, spied on the Creek villages on their side of the Goo-al-pah, and looked across the river into Choctaw lands through the spyglass.

All they saw was peaceful family life, no accumulation of horses, no buildup of arrows, bullets, guns, or other weapons of any kind. There wasn't any appearance of preparation to flee or move quickly. "Luyu, tell Tim there are no hostilities brewing. There is no reason to search for days. If problems were coming, all the villages would be preparing. We are not even halfway to Fort Smith, and I want somebody to look at your hand."

Luyu transmitted Waya's belief.

"We can move quickly, but keep looking."

The next day, Waya was glad they had stayed beside the river. "Cedars! I need to get some to make medicine for your hand."

Luyu's hand was severely inflamed. Tim was worried too. "Let's set up, so you can make it right away."

THIRTY SIX

Five wagons approached Fort Arbuckle. Roscoe peered through his telescope and then rang out the proper signal on the bell. Ann remained with the cooking cedar and the babies, but Stephanie hurried out the door.

Chumani hadn't been getting as much attention as Christopher and Joy. She had reverted to infantile behavior, one of which was insisting that she be carried. Therefore, Sally carried her across the courtyard on her hip.

Noah, Roscoe, Ke, and Chetan opened the massive door. Roscoe called out, "Welcome home!"

Eli had Stephanie in his arms seconds after walking through the gate. "I've missed you. How are you and the baby?"

"Worn out. Even with all of us here, Chumani has kept us running."

Chumani called out 'mother' in Quapaw. "Ida."

Sally lowered the child to the ground.

Bethany ran to her daughter. She knew after

Goodbye Hideout

being gone for seven days that Chumani needed to know how much her mother loved her. She picked up her youngest child.

Chumani hugged her mother's neck. "Ida."

"I missed you so much." Bethany held her daughter close.

Chumani kept her arms around her mother's neck and her head on her shoulder. Chetan stood with his arms around them. He kissed his wife's cheek. "Where are mother and Waya?"

Chumani put her hands on either side of Bethany's face. "Ida" She hugged her mother's neck again.

Bethany explained. "Luyu and Waya took one wagon and twelve mules to Fort Smith. We have to leave tomorrow to meet them there."

"You better let me go. Chumani needs to be with you. Fathers aren't as good as mothers in the eyes of little girls."

Bethany carried Chumani as they herded the goats and sheep into the pen, then unhitched the horses and got them into the stalls. They put out food and water, but left the wagons loaded and went inside.

The turkey Chetan had brought home from Noah's traps, stewed with dried vegetables. It smelled heavenly. Bread, baked that morning, sat on the table in anticipation of the family's return.

Bethany told Ann, "I love Chris and Joy, but Chetan tells me I need to give all my attention to Chumani. I hope that's all right with you."

"I agree. I know how much Chumani missed you. So did I." Ann hugged Bethany.

Tom explained what they needed to do. "...and we need to carry three horses in two of the wagons to make all the six animal teams we need."

Roscoe gave his opinion. "Maybe we should buy two at Fort Smith. Otherwise, we're always going to be short two animals."

Dustu thought about the river trip they had just made. "It was hard enough to move around with two sleeping mules. Three would be about impossible."

Noah agreed. "We have the money. I would like to get horses. We can breed them."

Everybody agreed, then spent the rest of the evening telling each other what had happened while they were apart. Ke was very proud of his father's skills and his part in containing a dangerous, squirming beaver. He told the story with much animation and waving of his hands.

That same evening Ezra, Ham, and Morgan arrived at Fort Smith. They left the wagons and animals at the stable and reported to Colonel Habersham.

THIRTY SEVEN

Waya hoped the cedar had helped. He washed his wife's hand in warm water and soap. He and Tim examined the injury in the morning light. In English, Waya reported, "Not better."

"And it hurts more." Luyu was exhausted. She had barely slept. When she did sleep, she woke screaming or trembling with fear. She was tense and anxious all the time.

Tim looked at her hand. He believed it was his fault. If he had done his job the first time he went to check on the relationship between the Creek and Choctaw, they wouldn't have been in the woods with hungry wolves. "We'll go fast."

Waya put a fresh batch of cedar in the bandage on Luyu's hand. He packaged the rest of the prepared medicine and many branch tips. They stopped following the river and spent no time scouring the countryside for problems. Instead, they made a beeline to Fort Smith.

THIRTY EIGHT

Chetan helped unload. Noah carried heavy blacksmith tools beside his father. "You shouldn't work so hard. You're still recovering."

"I'm fine." Chetan wanted to do his share. He continued to move hay into the loft.

Noah saw his father hurting. At mid-day, he served willow tea to everybody. He did the same at supper.

As they lay on their feather-mattress bed on the floor, Noah told Ann, "I should go. Not my father."

"I agree. It's a hard trip, and we don't even know what the river is like beyond Fort Gibson. We'll be fine locked inside this fort while you're gone. Although being here didn't stop your father from wrestling that beaver."

"I know, but it's almost certain that it will be too much if he floats a wagon down the river."

Ann also knew Noah didn't want to be left behind with the wounded and pregnant again. "I hope your father will agree to stay here."

Goodbye Hideout

Hours before morning broke, so that the animals could wake up at Fort Gibson, Sally dropped fumewort and Valerian into boiling water. When the brew was ready, Noah joined her. They went to the barn, gave the animals the sedative, and got them into the wagons. After everybody was awake, Noah spoke with his father. "I want to go. I hate being left out of the excitement."

Chetan was happy to stay at Fort Arbuckle. The hard work of the previous day had left him barely able to move. He knew he would be a hindrance.

Noah understood that Chetan wanted to be invincible in the eyes of Ke. He went to talk with Bethany. "Mother, you know how father pushes himself to be an example for Ke. I want to take Ke with me, so Father can rest."

Bethany had just been thinking about that very thing, but she wasn't sure she should let Ke go into a dangerous situation. "Ke could fall into the river and drown."

"I'll keep him safe, and besides, he is going to be floating in wagons on rivers when we cross the country."

"You are right." *That's not good.* "Ask your father. If he agrees, Ke can go."

Noah went back to his father. "I want to take Ke with me. Mother agreed to let me."

"She did? All right. Take very good care of him."

"I will. Do you want to tell him, or can I?"

"You may ask him if he wants to go."

"Tell Sally to put the rest of the sedative into canteens to take with us." Noah went in search of his brother. He found him tying a bag of folded tarps to the inside of one of the wagons. "Ke, do you want to come with us?"

"Really? Can I?"

"I've asked Mother and Father. They said you may come, but you have to do everything I tell you."

"I will. I promise." Ke ran off to pack. He ran into the room where Ann was feeding Joy. "Guess what, Aunt Ann?"

Ke looked very excited. Ann figured she knew why. "You're going to Fort Smith."

"Yes! I have to get ready." Ke went to his bed. He rolled up his blankets, pillow, and extra clothes inside his buffalo fur. He tied it up, then grabbed his bow and the quiver with his original two and three new arrows that he and Chetan had recently made using stiff turkey wing feathers as fletching.

"Be careful," Ann called out as Ke flew out the door.

"I will!"

After a few minutes, Ann laid Joy on the bed and then wrapped up both babies. She put on her blanket coat, winter shoes, hat, scarf, and gloves, and then carried her children out the door.

Goodbye Hideout

Noah kissed Chris, "See you again soon, my son." He kissed Joy. "See you again soon, my daughter." He kissed Ann. "See you again soon, my wife. I love all of you."

"We love you too. Be careful."

Eli kissed Stephanie. "I love you. Don't have that baby until I get back."

Stephanie assured Eli, "I won't."

Tom lay a harness on top of the sleeping mules. Eli pushed the wagon as far out as he could without getting into the water, then got in. Bethany and Chetan forced the wagon farther into the river.

Chumani tried to follow her mother into the water.

Stephanie caught the child by the hand. Chumani screamed, "Ida! Me go!" She struggled to get to her mother, but Stephanie held her tight.

Eli waved as he floated away. "See you soon, with lots of hay."

This time, Gihli didn't jump in the water. He stood on the bank and barked.

Dustu and Hanataywee pushed the next wagon, two mules, and a harness to the edge of the river, then jumped in. Just as they had with the first wagon, Chetan and Bethany took over. The water was up to the top of their thighs before the wagon floated. They did the same for Adahy and Ehawee in the third wagon. Roscoe and Helen rolled in next.

Ke sat in the last wagon as Noah and Sally pushed it to the water. Sally climbed in, then Noah gave a hard push and jumped on. Bethany and Chetan shoved them away. Chetan reminded his oldest son, "Remember what you said you would do."

"I will do what I promised. That's just as important to me as it is to you."

Ke waved. "You don't have to worry. I'll be careful."

Happy to be on another adventure, Noah waved goodbye as well. Ann didn't do so. Her arms were full of tiny children. "Come on, you two. You need to get out of those wet clothes and get warm."

Chumani insisted that Bethany carry her. Even though she got wet, she refused to be put down. Chetan, Stephanie, Ann, Christopher, Joy, and Gihli walked with them back to the warm fire, a pot of hot coffee, and hot willow tea for Chetan's aching body.

Goodbye Hideout

THIRTY NINE

The wagons zipped along as they directed them with tipi poles. The underwater branches failed to grab them since the navigators knew their locations, and they had cleared the path during the first trip. The sun was just past its zenith when they got to their riverside exit above the ferry.

Tom and Eli jumped out and directed their wagon to the shore where they could tie it. The others did the same. When all the wagons were secured, they started the soon-to-be-much-needed fire, cooked a hot dinner, and waited for the mules to wake up.

As soon as all the mules were on the land, Roscoe and Helen walked to the ferry landing and raised the flag. The others executed Noah's plan to use ropes and pulleys to get the wagons out of the river without getting the mules into the water.

When the ferry arrived to pick them up, five wagons each pulled by two dry mules in harnesses designed to hold four or six waited at the landing.

Orville didn't notice that the wagons were damp. "You must not be staying very far away."

Noah spoke a true statement. "It would appear that way."

Ke wished he could tell the man all about the ride down the river. Even though it went much better than the first trip, navigating the bend where the river turned north had been challenging and exciting. Ke was under orders not to say anything about how they got there, the location of their winter hideout, or where they were going. Ke decided it would be best not to say anything, in case he made a mistake.

Roscoe informed Orville, "We all want to go across at the same time."

"You can't fit."

Tom, however, was an expert packer. "Yes, we can."

"Since the wagons are empty and light, if you can safely fit everything on, I'll take you all in one trip. I'd like that better anyway, but it won't cost less." He sat back to watch.

They pulled the first wagon on and positioned it diagonally across the front. Eli unhooked Brandy and Starlight, the mules he had bought in Dover, and put them in the pen. Everybody then pushed the wagon into position straight across at the front. They pulled the next two wagons on side-by-side, unharnessed Honor, Justice, Beauty, and Dollie and penned them.

Goodbye Hideout

After they disconnected the tongues of the wagons, they pushed them forward until they touched the front wagon. The last two wagons they pulled halfway on with mules 7 and 8, the two mules that Sally had bought in Little Rock but still hadn't named, and Glory and Gumdrop. Once the mules were contained and the wagon tongues removed, they pushed the last two in the rest of the way. The eleven passengers climbed into the wagons since there was no room on the deck for them to stand.

Orville attempted to close the gate. It clicked into place with under an inch of extra space. He sat in the operator's chair. "I surely didn't believe it was possible. Forward ho." His horses walked, the paddle wheels rotated, and they moved away from the dock.

Ke was impressed. In Quapaw, he said, "It is just like you told us. The horses are walking on water."

Orville and his horses had made the trip many times. The ferry rode the turbulent waters where the three large rivers crashed together. Through the spyglass, Ke looked at the fort across the river. It looked a lot like Fort Arbuckle, but he was excited to go into a real fort with real soldiers. He thought they would all be like Tim Anders, Ezra Knuckles, Morgan Finch, and Ham Blanders.

After they got everything off the ferry, Roscoe paid Orville the fare. They rode beside the river until they found a place they could get back into the water.

Noah told Ke, "Remember the story we told when we first came to the village? Some of the soldiers don't like us. Roscoe, Sally, and I are not going into the fort. I want you to stay out here with us."

Ke complained, "But I want to go into a real fort."

"You said you would do what I tell you."

Ke threw his body down on the dry, winter grass. Noah left him there. Out of hearing of Ke, Eli said, "He can come with me if you want to let him. I promise I will protect him."

Noah knew Ke was disappointed, and Eli had brought Ann, Stephanie, and Sally to him at Pine Bluff. "All right. I want to walk up to the mission and see if I can get some Bibles. We'll tell him he can go with you. Come with me."

Noah went back to his brother, still on the ground not helping. "Ke."

"What?" Ke snapped.

That irritated Noah. "Talk to me respectfully."

"I am sorry. What do you want?"

"Eli said you may go with him. You have to stay right beside him and do exactly what he tells you. Do you agree to do that?"

Ke jumped up. "I do. Thank you, Tahatankohana." He hugged his brother.

Roscoe, Sally, and Noah headed off to the mission. Everybody else entered Fort Gibson dressed in mukluks, fur hats, gloves, and blanket coats. Helen,

Goodbye Hideout

Dustu, Adahy, Hanataywee, and Ehawee took the animals to the stable, bought them hay and oats, and left instructions with the private on duty not to give them any water. They then walked to the forest across the field around the fort to look for firewood.

Tom, Eli, and Ke went to the store. Ke stood beside Eli and watched Tom ask for something unusual. "Have you ever thought about the profit to be gained by selling the same item over and over?"

"How could I do that? Once I sell something, it's gone. I don't have it to sell again."

"You could sell it, get it back after a short time and refund some of the money, and then sell it again for a short time, and get it back again over and over. If you did that a lot of times, you could earn more than you could by selling it once."

"How would I get it back?"

"For example, you sell me a cooking set for full price. If I don't bring it back, it's just like I bought it, but if I do bring it back, you give me back most of the money, but not all of it. You keep the difference. Want to try it?"

"All right. The cooking set costs twenty dollars. How much would I give you when you return it?"

"Nineteen dollars and fifty cents."

"How about I give you nineteen dollars?"

"Deal. You'll see how good a plan this is. I'd like to do the same with five eating sets, but I want to buy three dozen eggs, two pounds of bacon, four ounces of roasted ground coffee, two dozen brown sugar cubes, four tins of butter, a small jar of strawberry preserves, a gallon of milk, and a bar of soap."

The private came back with the requested items. Tom paid the man. "I'll be back in about an hour."

As they walked to the bakery, Tom told Ke, "It's not that I don't want to pay for the cooking utensils. It's that I don't want to have them going down the river. I only want it to cook us some food right now."

Ke said, "I understand. It's a good plan. May I try one of those éclairs and a danish?"

Eli turned to his father. "Pop, we'll go to the bakery. We'll meet you back at the wagons."

Ke smelled the aroma in the air. "I like the smell of cooking bread."

Eli opened the door. Ke entered first. They walked to the counter. Eli turned to Ke. "I do too." He was still looking at Ke when he said, "Eleven éclairs, eleven danishes, and four loaves of bread." The man didn't move. Eli looked at him, "Excuse me. Eleven éclairs, eleven danishes, and four loaves of bread!"

"I don't hear people who would rather talk to Indian children than the white person they should be talking to."

Eli informed the man, "I was talking to you."

"You're not talking to me if you're not looking at me."

Goodbye Hideout

Eli looked directly into the man's eyes. "Please sell me eleven éclairs, eleven danishes, and four loaves of fresh bread."

"Are you saying you think I'm going to try to sell you stale bread?"

"I didn't mean I thought you would sell me stale bread. I was just thinking about how tasty fresh bread will be, so I said fresh bread. Are you purposefully trying to find offense with everything?"

The man said, "Since you're an Indian lover, maybe I am." Ke backed up and stood behind Eli. He peeked around the side of Eli at the man behind the counter.

"How would you want this Indian lover to ask for the éclairs, danishes, and bread?"

"It doesn't matter. I don't have enough to sell you."

Eli could see that there was more than enough. "What can you sell me, sir?"

"Sir is good. I'll sell you either the éclairs or the danishes and two loaves of bread."

Eli asked, "Ke, which would you rather try?"

In a little voice, he said, "Éclairs."

"Sir, please sell me eleven éclairs and two loaves of bread."

The baker took the pastries off the tray with tongs and then smashed them into a paper bag. He handed Eli the bag.

Lisa Gay

Eli passed the éclairs to Ke, paid the man, and then took the second bag with the bread. At the door, he stopped, let Ke step outside, then turned, and said, "A man like you who has no real knowledge of the Indians, or how to behave civilly, shouldn't be out here. You're polluting the land." Eli wanted to have the last word. He stepped through the door.

The man came out and yelled, "You're the one polluting the land, Indian lover!"

Eli positioned Ke in front of him, so he was between him and the man. "Ignore him." They kept walking. "I don't know if any piece of food is worth dealing with a person like that."

Ke asked, "Does Ezra think about me like that?"

"Of course not. Ezra has a brain in his head and a heart in his chest. That man is an empty shell."

Tom put his purchase in the wagon and then went back into the fort to get water. He saw Eli and Ke walking his way with only one small bag and a single larger one. They joined Tom and walked together to the well. Eli lowered the water bucket.

Ke told Tom what had happened. "That man in the bakery doesn't like Eli because he loves me, and he hates me, but he doesn't even know me."

Tom instructed Ke, "Ignore what he says or does. He's an ignorant person. Just be careful to stay out of his way."

Eli poured water into the pots and put the lids on.

Goodbye Hideout

"Let's go. We should get back on the river as soon as possible."

They left the fort as the others came across the field with wood. They arrived together and started the fire.

From behind the fort walls, Colonel Howland watched them through his spyglass.

While they cooked eggs, bacon, and coffee, Ke told them about the baker. They cut the two loaves of bread into eleven pieces, slathered on butter and strawberry jam, then poured milk into the tin cups that Tom had rented.

Adahy told Ke, "They treated me that way too. I could do the same and say I hate all white people because of the way some of the people in that fort behave, but I know Eli, Ann, Sally, Stephanie, Tom, Helen, and Roscoe. You have to judge each person by his or her own actions. A whole village of our people acted the same way. As if all white people are horrible, and they didn't want to help us. They were wrong too."

"You're right. I won't let it bother me."

That wasn't what Adahy meant. "I didn't say it shouldn't bother you. It is wrong, and it doesn't make you feel good. Just don't judge everybody by the way some people act. Let's try something your brother would do. Let's pray for that baker."

Ke asked, "May I say the prayer?"

Tom was quick to say, "Of course."

"God, I think you made all us humans on this earth. You made us look different, but you love us all. Help us love each other, especially help that baker. And help me not hate him back. Amen."

"Amen." Adahy put his arm across Ke's shoulder. "You are a good person. I liked your prayer very much. I want God to help me too."

By the time Noah, Roscoe, and Sally returned, the food in the rented frying pan was ready, and the big rented pot was full of hot water. Using the rented dinnerware, they ate every bite of the fried eggs, bacon, bread, butter, and jam, and drank all the milk and sweetened coffee in rented cups.

Noah, Sally, and Roscoe cleaned the cooking set and dishes with hot water and the bar of soap while the others went back to the stable with the canteens of sedative they had made that morning. They divided the sleeping potion into ten pails and then filled them halfway with water. After half the mules drank all their sedative, they refilled the water buckets with plain water until the mules didn't want more.

Five minutes after the first five mules consumed the sedative, they did the same with the other five. They had only twenty minutes from the time the animals drank the sedative before they would be asleep. They immediately took the mules to the river and led the first set into the wagons. The mules had learned to go into a wagon and lay down. They were in position only minutes before they were out.

The family got the second group set. When the mules were ready, the rented cooking kit and dishes had been scrubbed soot-free with sand and then washed with soap. Tom rinsed everything again with fresh water from the fort's well before he took them back to the store. "I should have asked to buy and return a dish drying towel."

Sergeant McCormick walked in from the back room. "Private Donnelley tells me you're buying and then returning a cooking kit and dishes."

"Yes, sir. I'll dry them if you let me use a towel."

McCormick examined each item as Tom dried it. "You did a good job cleaning everything. All of this looks as if it has never been used. So, we keep a dollar and get everything back?"

"That's my suggestion."

"Give him the nineteen dollars, Donnelley." Sergeant McCormick walked to the shelf with the cooking kit. "It's been a pleasure doing business with you." He put it beside the others, then the eating kits too.

"Likewise." Tom put the nineteen dollars back into his bag, then hurried back to the river.

Approximately two hours after they had come out of the river east of the Verdigris and Neosho River confluence, they were ready to enter the Arkansas

River on the southeast side of Fort Gibson. Dustu and Hanataywee went first. They pushed the wagon down a bank steeper than the entry at Fort Arbuckle. The water was already deep enough to float when they rolled in. Adahy and Ehawee went next. Noah, Sally, and Ke rode the third wagon down the bank into the river. Behind them, Roscoe and Helen entered. Tom got into the last wagon before Eli pushed it over the edge of the bank and jumped on. They splashed into the water.

The first four groups already controlled their wagons with their poles. Tom had his hands on one end of his pole and the other end in the riverbed, keeping them by the shore. Eli picked up the pole laying in the small space beside the mules. They tied the five wagons together and then floated out of Colonel Howland's view. Colonel Howland went to find out everything they had done while in the fort.

FORTY

Luyu cradled her swollen, beet red hand. "Getting to Fort Smith isn't going to help. It's already too bad. Cut it off, or that wolf will have killed me anyway."

Waya refused. "No. It is only a couple more hours. White medicine may save it."

Luyu's wrist and arm throbbed. "It hurts too much." Twice she filled her tin cup with willow tea and gulped it down. They continued to Fort Smith. It wasn't long before her blood, thinned by the drink, drained out the tooth holes and rips. She passed out and leaned precariously. Waya jumped off his horse, climbed on behind Luyu, and held her.

Tim tied the reins of Waya's horse to the back of his saddle. He hoped Waya would understand. "She's unconscious. We can ride faster."

Waya nodded. "Go faster."

Tim wanted the horses to be able to make the

217

remaining fifteen miles straight through. He led them at a fast canter.

Waya watched Luyu's blood drip over his leg and then roll down the horse's side. *Maybe that is better. The poison may go out with the blood. Edwin used maggots and spider webs to save Robert. He also said he opened the wound, cleaned out the pus, and poured whiskey in. When we get to Fort Smith, we can get those things. Running away may have killed my wild dove. I will track down and kill that assassin and that judge too.*

FORTY ONE

Even though the river was not as wide, the people floating in the wagons could see the deeper water flowed much faster after the addition of the Verdigris and Neosho Rivers.

Ahead, a sand bar came into view. Dustu poled toward what looked like the deepest passage without getting into the main channel. Askew, the wagon arrived at the bank of sand and gravel. The wheels scraped as they floated over sideways. He yelled, "Come at this same place but directly on!"

Adahy and Ehawee had almost gotten straight before they arrived. Their wheels scrapped away more of the obstruction. So that they would hear the instructions, Adahy turned to direct his voice toward those yet to cross. The wagon behind was already perfectly lined up to shoot the gap.

Noah and Sally quickly crossed over the bank lowered by the first two wagons. The following wagon had no problem either, but the last got dangerously close to the channel.

"Come where we did! You'll lose control out there!" yelled Roscoe.

Tom and Eli tried to get there. Just as the first wagon had, they hit askew. Both being strong men, they muscled the wagon up the incline. Once over, the caravan poled closer to the river's edge. They floated over several sand and gravel banks without contact. Suddenly, Dustu saw a significant change in the water's color. "High sand bar ahead!"

The shallows over coarse gravel extended to the deep channel. *We are not going to float over that.* Before he made contact, he hollered, "We will be on our wheels!" When the wagon came to a sudden stop, Dustu slammed his head against the front of the wagon, and Hanataywee toppled onto a mule. Dustu scrambled to his feet. "Are you hurt?"

"No, and I did not hurt Brandy either."

The wagons behind approached as a knot formed on Dustu's forehead. "We need to get out of the way. Can you push?"

"You are hurt!" Hanataywee dug in her pole.

"I'll be fine." Dustu pushed with all his might. The wagon rolled slightly. They pulled up the poles and tried again, but barely made any headway. "Go around!" Dustu hollered as Adahy and Ehawee barreled down on them.

"But we will jerk the rear of your wagon."

Before it was too late, Dustu screamed, "Go around!"

Goodbye Hideout

Adahy poled away from the shore. They dropped their poles and held on in case they didn't make it over either.

They didn't. Two side-by-side wagons now blocked the way. The four people in them made minuscule progress. Adahy jumped into the open space at the rear of his brother's wagon. "Maybe if we push together." The three pushed.

"It is not enough. I will come over." Ehawee joined them.

Ke spoke what Noah already knew. "We shouldn't go farther out. We'll end up in the channel and out of control."

Sally moved to the front of the wagon. "If we don't hit them too hard, maybe we'd push them over without busting up." She and Noah shoved their poles into the river bottom in front of them. They didn't slow much.

Ke asked, "What can I do to help?"

Noah ordered, "Get behind the mules and lie on the wagon bed. Brace for the impact. Do it now!"

Ke immediately obeyed.

Noah spoke to Sally. "We don't want to be thrown forward. Drop backward and cover your head when I tell you." They continued slowing.

Dustu, Hanataywee, Adahy, and Ehawee pushed forward and up. The first wagon made it to the top, but the gravel bar still held them. Adahy called out,

"The front wheels are over!" They tried one more push. The rear wheels arrived at the top.

"Sally, put your pole across the bow. Push it forward, so it touches their wagon. Hold on tight." He did the same. Upon contact, the poles shot backward out of their hands, slammed into the back of the wagon, and then dropped. The front wagon rolled down the far side of the gravel bar. Noah, Ke, and Sally's wagon took its place beside the empty wagon.

Noah called out, "Ke, are you injured?!"

"Just a busted lip."

"Let me see."

Ke sat up. "The pole dropped on my head and slammed my face against the wagon."

"Come up here." Noah looked at Ke's bloody, torn lip. It was nothing more than what Ke had reported, and they needed to get over the gravel bar. It was going to be even more difficult for them. There had been four adults working together to get the previous wagon over. *If they can get their wagon going fast enough, maybe they can pull over the empty wagon.*

Noah looked into the water. Like the first sand bar they had crossed, the wagon that had gone over had scraped away gravel. He yelled. "Go as fast as you can!"

Those ahead took off.

"Ke, get to the front. I don't want you at the back if the next wagon hits us. Sally, come to the back and help me push."

Goodbye Hideout

They hurried to the rear, picked up the poles that blessedly hadn't flown out of the wagon, dug in, and shoved.

Unobserved, the first boat pulled the lighter one across the underwater gravel. Just as Noah and Sally pulled up their poles to push again, Ke stopped watching the wagons approaching from the rear and looked toward the front. He saw the rope rapidly skimming across the water as the slack disappeared. "Prepare to be jerked!"

The wagon shot forward. Noah's and Sally's legs scraped across the backboards that pulled at the mukluks on their feet. Their faces slapped the freezing water. The poles went with them.

Ke had no way to get to his brother or sister-in-law. "Help them!" he screamed.

Dustu, Adahy, Hanataywee, and Ehawee turned. They didn't see the people being swept along below the surface of the swift water. Noah and Sally swirled over the gravel bar behind their freed wagon. In the deeper water beyond, less water pressure controlled them. They shot to the surface.

Noah saw Sally nearby. "Are you all right?"

"I think so. Are you? Did Ke fall in?"

"I'm all right," Noah answered, and then yelled, "Ke!"

"I'm in the boat!"

"Thank You, God." Noah pointed outward. "There go the poles! We need to get them before the channel catches them!" Hampered by their heavy blanket coats, they swam farther away from safety; into the life-threatening, icy water.

Helen and Roscoe had seen Sally and Noah slam into the water, and Roscoe knew the power of coldness. "They'll have only minutes before they'll be incapacitated. Push as fast as you can. We cannot get stuck."

Prepared with as much momentum as possible, they slowly rolled over the bank of gravel significantly lowered by the three wagons that had gone before. Roscoe poled toward the swimmers. "Sally is much smaller. We have to get her first."

"Sally, head to the wagon!" Noah ordered.

"I'm almost there. I can get it." Sally continued away from salvation.

The rope between the approaching wagon and the one behind it pulled tight. Roscoe and Helen's wagon stopped. Roscoe jerked the rope to no avail. "We can't get there!"

Tom and Eli were stronger by far and approached the obstacle with much more force. They went right over and then moved outward as fast as they could.

Sally reached a floating pole. "Got it!" She fought her coat and the fast-moving water, but got herself and the poling rod turned. A wagon once again rapidly approached her. She was exhausted, and the cold sucked away her ability to think. *I'll just wait for them.* She draped her arms over the pole and allowed herself to float with the current.

Roscoe grabbed the girl. Helen retrieved the pole. Noah got to the boat just as Sally's limp body slipped into the wagon. Helen reached out for his pole as Roscoe released Sally. "Get her to the other side of the wagon, quickly." Helen dragged Sally over the mules as Roscoe hauled in Noah.

"I'm so cold," Sally's teeth clattered loudly.

Helen jerked off her coat. "Undress and lay on Beauty."

Helen held the wet coat around her while Sally removed her freezing clothes and lay belly down on Beauty. Helen took off her dry coat and laid it over Sally, who wrapped her arms around her mule because she needed the warmth but also because she loved the animal.

Noah lay on the other mule with Roscoe's coat over him. The dry folks held the wet coats over the edge and wrung the water back into the river. Helen slipped one on. "Thank God wool keeps you warm even when it's wet." She noticed Sally's bare feet. "Your mukluks must have gotten lost in the river."

Sally focused on her feet. "I didn't even realize it. I just thought my feet were as cold as the rest of me."

Noah realized his were gone. "Me too. I've had way too much cold water in my life, and this river also took my hat."

Roscoe and Helen took off their footwear, put the wool blanket inserts on Sally and Noah, then put their mukluks back on.

As they floated down the river, Eli poled toward the shore, and Tom drew Roscoe, Helen, Noah, and Sally closer with the rope tied between them. Dustu and Adahy pulled in the wagon vacated by Adahy and Ehawee. Ke pulled his boat toward his brother. When they all came together, Ke jumped into the boat with Noah. He knelt beside his brother, still shivering under the coat. "I'm sorry I didn't warn you in time."

From under the coat, Noah assured his worried brother. "It's not your fault. I'm the one who told them to go fast. I should have been paying attention."

Adahy held up a fur hat. "We saw this floating past. Ehawee grabbed it."

Roscoe took it. "This one belongs to Noah. It's a wonder it was still floating. Must have landed just right to trap an air pocket."

Noah peeked out from under the coat to verify if it was indeed his hat. "Good. That one came from Pine Bluff. I would hate to lose it. I'm sorry you lost yours, Sally."

"I'm glad we only lost a hat and some shoes."

The wagons floated close together at the speed of the current. They used the poles only to stay close to the river's edge. Helen prayed, "Please get us to Fort Smith without any more problems."

Goodbye Hideout

"Amen!" said Ke.

Ehawee knew it was worse for Helen to be in the wet coat then it would be for her. "Helen, give me that wet coat. You take mine." Ehawee slid the spare clothes she had brought over what she already wore.

"Use my extra clothes too," Adahy told her.

Ehawee did so before she put on the wet coat.

"Here's mine." Eli took off his coat and exchanged it for Roscoe's wet one. He removed his mukluks before donning both his own and his father's extra dry clothes. He pulled off his wool blanket inserts that Noah and Ann had given him at Pine Bluff. "Put these on Noah's feet."

Tom ordered, "Stop. I'll give him mine since you'll have on a wet coat."

Ke put the second set of foot covering on Noah, who still lay on Dollie under the dry coat.

Hanataywee took off her inserts. "Ke, get these on Sally." Ke walked to the other end of the wagon, got them, then put them on Sally.

Noah knew they were losing a lot of time, but he and Sally could not yet move away from the bodies of Beauty and Dollie. When he finally did feel heated enough, he asked Sally, "Are you warm yet?"

"No. I'm still freezing cold."

"Ke, do you think you can help me with our wagon?" Noah asked.

"Let me try." Ke put a pole in the water, pushed

against the river bottom, and then brought it forward through the water. "I can do it."

"Sally, stay as long as you need to. Ke, get my clothes. Everybody, go back to your positions."

Ke retrieved Noah's bag.

"Give us Sally's for when she's warm enough," Helen requested.

Noah dressed, then stood up and held out the coat that had helped warm him. "Roscoe, take yours back. Thank you so much for letting me use it, but I need to wear Eli's. It's bigger." They swapped coats. Noah climbed in with Ke.

Dustu and Hanataywee sat in the lead wagon. "Everybody ready?" Dustu asked.

When they all affirmed that they were, they pushed forward again. Far downriver, Adahy and Ehawee's wagon got caught in a submerged tree. Dustu and Noah joined him in the wagon. They broke the branches with the poles, freed the wheel, returned to their wagons, and then rapidly poled forward.

Only a short way on, Eli and Tom snagged a branch. As strong as they were, they couldn't get loose. The other four men joined them. Together they pushed the wagon from the large branch that held the wagon. They floated sideways immediately into a different branch of the same tree. Smooth as silk, the branch slid between the spokes of the back left wheel.

Ke plopped onto the floor of the wagon and put his hands against both sides of his face. "Not again!"

Goodbye Hideout

They took turns peering at the problem under the freezing water.

Sally hugged her mule. "Thank you for your warmth. I love you, my Beauty." She dressed, came out from under the coat, and put it on.

The women stayed out of the way in Helen's wagon and watched the highly irritated men, who had very little room to maneuver because of the mules.

Hanataywee loved all three of her new sisters, but she especially loved Sally. They had spent many hours mapping the fields and the forest with the other young women in their village. She put her hat on Sally's still damp head. "You need this, my sister."

Sally hugged her. "Thank you."

Hanataywee pulled up her hood, then slipped her arm across Sally's back to continue to warm her.

Sally kissed Hanataywee's cheek, then turned and kissed Ehawee's too. "Helen, come here." Sally kissed her as well. "I love all of you. Thank you for saving me." The four women held each other.

In the stuck wagon, Tom stated what they all hated but knew had to be done. "We have to break the wheel."

"All right. When I tell you, push the back end around." Eli shoved the pole into the wheel and pushed down until two spokes snapped. He broke another set and then did it a third time. With the spokes out, he positioned the pole into the rim to use the wagon's side as a fulcrum. "Ready? One, two three." Eli and Tom pushed with all their might. The rim broke. "Push!"

The other men did so. The back end of the wagon moved off the branch, swung around, and became the front, but they were free.

Eli declared, "We can't keep doing this."

Helen thought *that's a silly remark.* "I don't see how we have any choice but to keep doing this however many times the Lord allows us to get stuck."

Eli sighed. "I know."

They barely made any progress as they attempted to see what was under the water and fought past snag after snag for miles.

Twenty-eight miles downstream from Fort Gibson, they reached Greenleaf's Creek and floated beyond the last obstruction. Adahy told Dustu, "We need to get there before the sun goes down. Keep a sharp lookout ahead."

FORTY TWO

At Fort Smith, Tim took Luyu and Waya straight to the infirmary. "She's a military scout. Help her. I'm going to Colonel Habersham to get authorization."

Tim ran to the command building and requested an audience. He did not ask. He got right to the point and told the colonel, "Sergeant Timothy Anders reporting, sir. I have an injured Indian scout hired by Colonel Howland. She needs immediate treatment. Authorize it."

"What was the mission?"

"We had a report of trouble between the Creek and Choctaw. We were reconnoitering. She doesn't have time for me to dally."

"What on earth would make you think there was trouble between the Creek and Choctaw?"

"Colonel Howland told me he received a report of trouble. Colonel Habersham, time is essential."

"All right. It will be quicker if I go than to write it up."

"Thank you." They hurried to the infirmary.

Lisa Gay

The doctor had cut the bandage off Luyu's hand. "I tried to find out what happened. He just says, 'wolves bite.' If wolves bit her, they would have eaten her."

Tim confirmed what Waya had reported. "A wolf did bite her. She clubbed a few. Waya and I shot most of them."

"This infection is terrible. We need to cut off the lower part of this woman's arm."

The colonel approved. "Take whatever steps are necessary."

The doctor opened a drawer and took out a saw.

Waya saw it. He stepped between the doctor and his wife. "No."

Tim hoped Waya would understand his words. "It needs to be done."

"No." Waya left the revolver in its holster but drew his long knife. "Do something else."

"Nothing else will work." The doctor tried to get to Luyu again.

Waya refused to let him pass. "No!" He waved the knife and begged, "Help! Do not cut!"

As the sun set, Waya still refused to allow the doctor to butcher his wife. Her hand dangled beside the stretcher. Blood and pus dripped onto the floor from her fingertips that dangled beside the stretcher.

Waya made a decision. *Maybe we need the God my new family talks about.* He spoke in Cherokee. "Living God, if you are real, save my wild dove."

FORTY THREE

Dustu took the spyglass from his eye. "I see the fort. I will look for a way out of the river."

They were almost at the fort and had not found a suitable place to exit. Not only did those on the river see the fort, the sentry saw them. He sounded an alarm. A soldier ran past the infirmary. "To stations!"

Tim demanded information. "Private, stop!"

The soldier knew a commanding officer when he heard one. He obeyed.

Tim asked, "What's happening?"

"Indians are attacking from the river."

Tim asked for verification, "Somebody's coming on the river?"

Waya called out, "Tim, family on river."

Tim ran out the door, issuing commands. "Do not shoot anybody! I know them!"

Colonel Josiah Habersham demanded answers while hot on the sergeant's heels. "First, you bring an armed Indian into the infirmary, and we have a standoff at knifepoint with that warrior keeping the woman from getting treatment. Now, you want me to give boatloads of Indians access to the dock? I don't know you. Why should I trust you?"

"My men are already here and reported to you with a request from Colonel Howland. Privates Ezra Knuckles and —"

"Ezra Knuckles. He did speak with me." He bellowed out, "Bring Knuckles! Now!"

Already knowing some of what was happening by questioning the soldier sent to fetch him, Ezra climbed the ladder behind the fort wall and spoke to the colonel. "Give me your spyglass."

This was the second man who had issued him an order. He didn't like it, but he handed the private the requested device. "That's Dustu and Hanataywee. I see Adahy. There's Sally. She is so beautiful."

The colonel said, "I noticed."

Ezra continued to report what he saw. "So that's how they got here so quickly. They're using their wagons as boats. They are NOT a threat. They only want to buy hay and probably supplies."

"Sergeant Anders, you and Knuckles go to the landing. Get them out of the river, and bring them to me."

"Yes, sir. Thank you, sir." Tim motioned to Ezra. They hurried away. "Take all the rest of them to the colonel after they are out of the river." He said the only name by which he knew Noah. "Tahatankohana needs to get to the infirmary immediately."

Ezra had learned that Tahatankohana's other name was Noah Swift Hawk and that he should never share that information. "What's wrong with him?"

"It's not Tahatankohana. It's Luyu. She's in the infirmary about to die."

"Oh, no!" Ezra ran.

Dustu called out, "I see Ezra and another soldier running toward us!"

Colonel Habersham watched Tim issue commands to those at the Arkansas. "Follow Ezra to the landing. He will get your wagons out. Tahatankohana, swim over. Luyu needs you immediately."

The colonel saw everybody do exactly what the sergeant wanted. Even he had done so.

Noah responded to the name his father had given him. "Sally, guard Ke." He voluntarily dove into the freezing water. Tim pulled him up the bank by his hand. "What's wrong?" Tahatankohana inquired.

"I'm afraid you're too late. Waya won't let the doctor cut off her arm." Tim dashed away.

Tahatankohana raced beside him. "Why does he want to cut off her arm?"

"It's horribly infected from a wolf bite."

"A wolf bite?" Tahatankohana ran into the infirmary.

FORTY FOUR

Waya saw Tahatankohana. He put his knife into its sheath and spoke in Cherokee. "Wolves attacked her. One bit her hand and pulled her down. I shot it, but its poison is in her. Help her!"

Tahatankohana examined her hand and arm. The pink line left by the infection showed that it had been farther up her arm than the red streak he saw. He looked at the puss and blood on the floor. "She needs to bleed more." Luyu's hand was so swollen that the bite holes had stretched open, but they were filled with congealed blood. Tahatankohana drew his knife. "Whiskey now."

The doctor opened his desk drawer and handed Tahatankohana a bottle.

Tahatankohana saw a bedpan. "Is that clean?"

"Yes." The doctor handed him the pan.

"Get somebody to put on India rubber gloves and clean that up." Tahatankohana held the blade over the pan. He poured whiskey over it and his hands then put the knife tip to one of the tooth punctures. He poked it in and twisted. Blood flowed. He did the same to all the holes on both sides of her hand.

Above the red, he circled her arm with his hands, squeezed, and then drew his hands toward the floor. Blood and yellow goop flowed out the holes.

While a private cleaned the floor, Tahatankohana drew the infection from Luyu. Pus and blood flowed into the pan that Waya held under her hand.

FORTY FIVE

The rest of the family floated past the fort. Ezra, joined by Ham and Morgan, walked along the shore and told them what little they knew about Luyu. Ezra asked about the animals in the wagons. "Is it a family secret how you put the mules to sleep?"

"It's not a secret. We put a sedative in their water." Roscoe poled his wagon to the dock.

Helen stepped onto the wooden boards. "We need to buy a replacement wheel to get that one out. Where is the wainwright?"

Bruce, a soldier stationed at Fort Smith, hooked the first wagon to the winch the army used to pull boats out of the river. "Which wheel?"

Eli pointed down. "The back left of this wagon."

"We can get it out. I'll be back soon." Bruce walked away. A short time later, he returned with a mule hooked to the trailer they used to carry boats away for repair. Four of the wagons already stood on the land. "Attach your wagon and winch the front onto the trailer." He looked into Eli's eyes. "Take off the right front wheel." He pointed at Adahy. "You remove the other one."

Eli opened the toolbox attached to the side of the wagon, removed the appropriate tools, and carefully climbed on the trailer to the front wheel.

Adahy remained in the wagon. Ke stood beside him. They watched Eli push the wrench toward the rear of the wagon and loosen the nut that held the wheel. He turned the last rotation very slowly and carefully, so the nut did not drop into the river. He passed the wrench to Adahy.

Ke held out his hand. Eli placed the nut in it. Since the front of the wagon rested on the trailer, Eli simply pulled the wheel off then navigated the trailer, rolling the wheel beside it.

Adahy lay on the dock. He carefully removed the nut and then tried to pull off the second wheel. "Not enough room." He handed the wrench and nut to Ke.

Bruce went over, looked, and then told Eli, "Lead Beatrice forward and slightly to the right. I'll tell you when to stop." He turned back to Adahy. "Get ahold of that side." They walked the dock as the wagon moved. "Halt." He motioned with his hands. "Pull it in, then straight up." The two of them pulled the wheel onto the dock. "I'll go crank the winch."

The soldier turned the handle. The bottom of the wagon scraped the trailer. Tom, Roscoe, and Eli simultaneously called out, "Stop!"

Tom continued the instructions, "Back the trailer into the water until the wagon floats. Then we can pull it on without damaging the bottom."

Bruce ordered the mule, "Backward ho." The wagon rolled on its one intact wheel.

Tom called out, "Halt!"

The mule stopped at his command. They winched the wagon on to the rear wheels. The soldier ordered, "Get them off."

Ke handed Ehawee the two nuts. "I want to try."

Bruce held up his hand with his palm out. "We don't have time to mess with the boy."

Ehawee spoke up. "Let him try for a minute."

Ke put the wrench on the nut and pushed. Nothing happened, so he changed his angle and shoved with both hands. The fastener didn't budge.

"We're wasting time." Bruce fidgeted impatiently.

Ke told Ehawee, "Get me a hammer." She opened the toolbox lid and retrieved the sledgehammer. Ke put the wrench on the nut, so it was vertical, then swung the hammer.

CLANG.

The wrench flew into the river, but Ke saw it land. He handed Adahy the hammer, took off his mukluks, and then dropped into the shallow water. He reached down and picked up the wrench. He quickly waded out, hurried along the dock, put the wrench on the nut, and then pushed. The nut turned. He looked at the soldier. "I told you I could do it."

Goodbye Hideout

Adahy praised his young brother-in-law. "Very good thinking."

Ke rotated the last turn with his hand around the nut. It dropped off the bolt. "Oh, no!" He stood up.

Hanataywee exclaimed, "Don't tell me you dropped it."

"All right, I won't." Ke opened his hand and revealed where it had landed.

Adahy smiled. "You are a bad boy. Give it to Ehawee. I will help you pull off the wheel."

Ke handed the nut to his sister. Dustu took the wrench. "I'll get the last one." He stepped into the wagon.

Sally saw somebody headed their way. "Here comes another soldier."

Adahy and Dustu wiggled the remains of the broken wheel from the wagon. "Ready," Dustu informed Bruce, who stood at the winch.

The soldier cranked the wagon the rest of the way onto the trailer. As Beatrice pulled the damaged wagon out of the water, the newly arrived soldier informed those who had just ridden the wagons down the river, "Colonel Habersham wants to see all of you."

Sally thought *it works better if a woman refuses orders.* "We have sedated mules we must attend to."

"Privates Knuckles, Finch, and Blanders will handle the mules. Come with me."

Bruce remained on guard duty at the dock. The soldiers from Fort Gibson remained at the river to attend to the mules when they woke. Everybody who had arrived in the wagons reported to the commanding officer.

Goodbye Hideout

FORTY SIX

Even though she didn't believe they would have any problem, Sally positioned herself and Ke beside Helen, Hanataywee, and Ehawee. The five men formed a perimeter around them.

Ke watched his family make almost unnoticeable signals as they followed their escort. *We are not just a family. We are a band of warriors. We can carry out a plan without talking. I am going to learn how to be part of it.*

In the infirmary, Tahatankohana opened Luyu's wounds again, stroked her arm, and forced out more infection. He lifted her hand to the stretcher for a few minutes and then repeated the procedure over and over.

The doctor watched the red streaks in Luyu's arm fade and drop away from her heart.

Waya caressed his wife's face and hair. "Do not die," he ordered her many times.

In the command building, the colonel questioned the rest of the family. Hanataywee translated between

Dustu, Adahy, and the colonel. The colonel knew Cherokee, but he let them believe he did not.

Ke heard his family tell the truth, but not add information beyond what was necessary. They did not reveal anything about their winter hideout.

Colonel Habersham knew that Indians would use women and children as a camouflage for their intentions. However, these men stood in a configuration to protect the women and the child, not to sacrifice them. He spoke to Ke last. "Where do you live?"

"My home is between Spring River and the mountains by Five Mile Creek."

"Why did you come here?"

"My family tells stories about trips to Fort Gibson. I wanted to have an exciting adventure and a story to tell. Also, I want to help my family get the hay we need."

"How does a child speak English so well?"

"My parents taught me English from the beginning of my life. I also know Quapaw and Cherokee."

"Who are you're parents?"

"Bethany and Chetan. Those are my sisters." Ke pointed to Hanataywee and Ehawee.

Bethany is a white woman's name. "Is your mother a captured white woman?"

"She is a white woman, but she was not captured.

Goodbye Hideout

My father saved her after her parents died. She wanted my father to keep her."

"Why did you come to Fort Smith for hay?"

"We couldn't buy enough at Fort Gibson."

The colonel thought *that explains why Colonel Howland asked for hay.*

"Who is the woman in the infirmary?"

"She is my grandmother. What happened? Will she be all right?"

"She has an infection from a wolf bite. I doubt if she will live. The man with her won't let the doctor treat her."

"Let us see her." Ke begged, "Please."

Colonel Habersham heard the child's concern for his grandmother. Nobody spoke anything indicating subterfuge, and the women had translated accurately. He decided they actually were a family of half-breeds needing hay. "You're dismissed." He ordered the man he had earlier summoned to the outer room. "Sergeant Anders, take them to the infirmary."

Tim tried to prepare them as they walked. "She's unconscious. You won't be able to talk with her."

Tom thought it was bizarre that Waya was preventing treatment that Luyu needed. "Why won't Waya let the doctor take care of her?"

"The doctor wants to cut off her arm."

Dustu let out a sigh of relief. "No wonder! I knew grandfather wouldn't do anything to hurt Luyu. He loves her." They went into the room where Luyu lay on a gurney. "Is she going to be all right?"

Tahatankohana told them what he hoped. "I think so. The infection was up to there. Now, it's down to here."

The doctor spoke to Tahatankohana. "Do you want to take a break and let me do that for a while?"

Waya glared at the doctor. "You, no touch!"

"I'm glad you were right, and I'm glad you stopped me, but I was trying to help."

Tahatankohana told Waya in Cherokee. "If the infection had gotten to her heart, it would have killed her. He was trying to do the right thing. He wants to help."

Waya circled to the side of the bed where Tahatankohana stood. "I will do it. Not him. You get warm."

"All right." Tahatankohana turned to his family. "She needs a lot of water to replace the blood. If those marks start to go up her arm again, get me immediately."

They weren't going to let him help, so the doctor said, "Come with me." He took Tahatankohana to a hot bath. Since Tahatankohana had no more dry clothes, Eli went with them to give his brother-in-law one of the three sets he had on. Eli bathed too.

Roscoe, Helen, and Sally went to the store and bought food, heavy wool socks, a replacement hat and mukluks for Sally, and mukluks for Tahatankohana, which Roscoe tried on to make sure they would fit.

Tim joined them as they went back to the infirmary. "The colonel said all of you may stay in the infirmary tonight, but we have to lock you in and post a guard."

Sally replied, "Good grief. You know that's not necessary."

"I've slept around this family night after night and people from your village as well. I know you won't hurt anybody, but Luyu needs to be in the infirmary, and that's the only way to do it."

"I understand and am much obliged. I'm sure you made this possible." Sally kissed his cheek.

Tim knew the protection would more likely be needed the other way around. "We'll stay there to make sure nobody bothers you."

Helen pointed out another problem. "We need to check on the mules, and we don't have our bedding in there. Can we go to the stable?"

"They're closing the gates now, and there are plenty of beds, blankets, and pillows in the infirmary. We better go straight there. Ham, Morgan, and Ezra will let you know the status of your wagons and mules when they get here."

Helen felt satisfied. "You know what's best. I trust you and them."

They hurried to the infirmary with baskets of

food for the night and the morning. The soldiers posted to guard the fort from the people in the infirmary locked the doors from the outside immediately after they entered. At Sergeant Anders' request, the doctor showed them to the hospital ward. A man lay in a bed. As the doctor showed them the location of the bedding, he told them, "I'll move my patient."

Sally asked, "What's wrong with him?"

"Broke his jaw. I wired it up."

"You don't have to move him. He won't bother us, and we'll fix him something good he can eat with his mouth mostly shut."

"Wait here. I'll ask." The doctor walked across the room and spoke to the man. He pointed at Sally and Helen, standing by the door. The soldier looked at the beautiful young woman. He nodded his head. The doctor waved them over.

"This young man is Gad Mead."

Gad held out his hand to Sally.

The doctor said, "I don't know your names."

Sally shook the man's hand and made a tiny curtsey. "Sally."

Gad extended his hand to the other woman.

"Helen."

Sally told Gad her plan. "We will fix you a very nutritious good tasting meal. We'll bring it to you when it is ready. Do you read?"

"No, ma'am."

Goodbye Hideout

"Do you like to hear stories?"

"I would love to hear you read a story."

"Very good. Doctor…." Sally waited for the man to fill in the blank.

After a few seconds, he said, "Artrell Seibel."

"Doctor Seibel, what books do you have? What can we use to cook a meal?"

Doctor Seibel didn't want to entrust the care of his patient to people he didn't know, and it would be delightful to look at beautiful women for a while. "You can use the woodstove, but I'll have to accompany you and care for my patient in the hospital ward with the rest of you this evening."

Sally permitted him. "We would love for you to join us. Please show us the books and then the stove."

There were storybooks with the doctor's manuals. Everybody in the family had already read or heard every book they owned at least once. Sally was very interested in something new. "I don't suppose you would let us buy any or all of these. Would you?"

"I've read every one of them many times, but at least it's something to read. I've even read my manuals repeatedly."

"If we send some different books back to you, would you sell these?"

"How would I know you'll send your books?"

"You don't, but I give you my word that I will get eight books to you for these five." She took all five fiction books off the shelf. "And three others if you will. My whole family would so appreciate new books. I'm sure a man who enjoys reading understands the allure of a new story. My brother will be interested in your medical books. If you've read them repeatedly, you must know the information already. Would you consider a sale or trade of medical books for the other three?"

The refined behavior of the girl, who less than an hour before had maneuvered a wagon that had been made into a boat, surprised the doctor.

Helen was taken aback as well. She had never seen Sally behave so daintily. Helen watched the doctor happily help the charming, sweet, gorgeous young woman. She let Sally steer the interaction.

"I'll think about your request. Tonight, you can read one of those books to us in the hospital ward."

"Thank you for considering my proposal, Artrell. Please show us where we can prepare the meal."

The stove was very similar to the one of her youth. Sally thought about the stove that had been destroyed when the Butterfield Gang had burned her home to the ground. That made her consider the fact that Hank and Roy Butterfield's mother, their sister, and Judge Atwood were close. Sally put down the baskets. "Thank you. You have been very helpful and pleasant."

Tahatankohana went back to Luyu and set up a

schedule for taking turns massaging the blood and infection down Luyu's arm and out her hand during the night. Since it was possible to have one, the rest of them took turns bathing and looking at the books.

The doctor, Gad, most of the family, and the four soldiers who were their friends, gathered in the hospital ward. Sally, Helen, and Roscoe brought in supper. They pulled chairs and the hospital food trays together then sat beside Gad and Luyu.

Waya quickly made his request. "May I say the prayer before the meal?"

They all bowed their heads and waited for Waya to speak. "Hanataywee, will you translate what I say?"

"Of course." He spoke a thought in Cherokee, then paused and allowed Hanataywee to repeat it in English. "Living God, You are the true Great Spirit. You are not a piece of wood somebody carved that sits powerless. You make things happen. Before we know what to ask, You have placed the possibility for the answer into existence.

"You do not stop every bad thing that might happen. Wolves attacked Luyu. One bit her. They put fear and infection into my wild dove. I asked You to be real and to save her. I believed You had a plan, so I protected my wife's arm. I had to wait for You.

"You started the solution when You made her hand bleed before we got here, and You were already bringing Tahatankohana on the waters of the

Arkansas. You caused him to leave his injured father, two babies, his wife, and pregnant sister. You gave them a very safe place, so he could leave.

"You arranged everything just like You arrange a beautiful sunset where colors, sky, clouds, plants, animals, and earth flow together in perfect harmony. You brought Luyu to this safe place where she can be cared for, where we can all be around her in a warm, dry, safe place where we can cook, sleep in warm beds with warm blankets and soft pillows, and even take a bath. Not only did You answer my prayer to save my wife, but also You did it with so much love.

"I give my heart to You. I want You to live in me just as You did in the people we read about in the book they call the Bible. I will serve You all the rest of my life. Amen."

"Amen," replied all the others.

Hanataywee hugged Waya tight. "Welcome to eternal life with this family, our God, and all the saints from the ages. I am very happy."

Everybody hugged Waya and told him how happy they were that he had asked God to be the master of his life. Dustu and Adahy thought about what their grandfather had said. They still didn't know how much they believed. Gad sat in the chair beside Sally and thought about Waya's words.

Sally gave Gad a cup of warm willow tea, then thick pemmican soup with rehydrated dried vegetables and potatoes. After that, a mixture of cornmeal, milk, and honey. He worked to spoon the food through the small space between his teeth. Last, he drank hot coffee with milk and sugar. "I feel so much better." He didn't know that Sally had given him a painkiller.

Sally opened the book <u>Paul Clifford</u> written by Edward Bulwer-Lytton. She read, "It was a dark and stormy night; the rain fell in torrents...." Hanataywee softly repeated the story for Dustu, Adahy, and Waya.

After a few hours, the doctor insisted it was enough. Each person got into one of the not wholly comfortable hospital beds and slept, only waking the next person when it was their turn to work on Luyu's arm.

FORTY SEVEN

The next day, when Tahatankohana went to look at Luyu, he found her awake. After barely sleeping for five days, her body had insisted she sleep for eighteen hours.

"I guess we're at Fort Smith. I see Waya had his way and saved my hand. I told him to cut it off, but he wouldn't."

Tahatankohana joked with his grandmother. "If you're upset about that, I can still do it."

"No, I'll keep it since I can, but it sure hurts."

"I should not give you willow tea. We drained a lot of blood out of you. You need to keep the rest, and you need to drink a lot of water." Tahatankohana poured some into a cup and handed it to his grandmother.

She gulped it down and held out the cup for more. "I am very thirsty."

Tahatankohana refilled her cup twice before he looked over her arm and hand. The infection in her

Goodbye Hideout

arm was barely visible. He couldn't see puss in the lesions, but her wrist and hand were still swollen and fiery red. "Much better, but we still need to get cedar on your hand. That will help with the pain and infection."

"Waya brought some."

Waya heard his wife and woke up. "My wild dove, Tahatankohana saved you!"

"You did, too. Thank you for not listening to me about my hand."

Tahatankohana asked, "Where is the cedar? I'll get it."

"It was with the horses. I have no idea where they put them."

"All right." Tahatankohana went to see what he smelled cooking. At the stove, Roscoe and Helen stood very close, stirring something in a pot. "What are you cooking up?" They jumped apart. Tahatankohana smiled. "No worries. Your secret is safe with me."

Roscoe denied everything. "We don't have any secrets."

A blush colored Helen's cheeks. She looked lovely. "All right. You don't have a secret. What are you cooking?"

"Something Helen calls goulash. It can be eaten by Gad too."

"It smells wonderful. How long?"

"Ten minutes. Tell everybody to get ready."

"I'm on my way." Tahatankohana's footsteps echoed in the empty hall as he walked back to the large room filled with beds, people, and windows.

The orange of sunrise bathed everything in a warm, soft light. Gad watched the people in the room. Ke sat up, rubbed his eyes, and then looked at the bed where they had put his grandmother. He called out in Quapaw, "Ikka!" He jumped out of bed, hurried to his grandmother, and hugged her. "I was so worried."

Luyu hugged him back. "Me too."

"Were you terribly scared?"

Waya knew how tormented Luyu was by the memories and dreams. He stopped Ke. "Luyu doesn't need to think about it."

"It's all right. Maybe it will help to talk about it. Yes, Ke, I was very scared when I was fighting them and after. I thought skinning all of them would make me feel triumphant. I even ate the one that bit me, but I'm still scared. I see them when I close my eyes. The pain keeps me thinking about them all the time." She realized she hadn't felt scared that morning. "Although it doesn't seem so bad while I'm in here."

"You are very brave and strong to fight wolves. How many were there?"

"Twenty, but I only killed one. I crushed its skull. My own wolf and Tim killed all the rest and saved me. Now, tell me what happened to your lip."

Goodbye Hideout

Ke told the story of their trip down the river, including the pole landing on his head.

The Indian men still lay in the narrow beds with their wives. Gad swore he saw the love in the eyes of those women when they looked at their husbands. In the orange morning light, the scene of family love was serene and inviting. Gad wondered *why did I ever want the life of a soldier at the edge of nowhere?*

Sally hugged Luyu with as much affection as Ke had. Gad thought *if these people love each other regardless of ethnic differences, everybody could. There's no real reason for all the hate between the Indians and us.*

"Breakfast will be ready soon." Tahatankohana's words broke the spell that held Gad.

Suddenly, Sergeant Anders, who had been in the same room all the time, broke into the scene. "I want to do something to help heal Luyu's hand. I'll find the cedar." He strode to the infirmary's door and knocked. The guard outside turned. Sergeant Anders issued orders to the private, "It's daylight. Open the door."

"When I see them open the gate, I'll open the door."

"Then just let me out and lock it back." The soldier opened the door, let his superior officer out, and then bolted the rest of them in. Tim walked to the barn. Just as the soldier on duty in the stable came in, he found Waya's pack. "Private, give unlimited water and double grain to all the horses and mules my men brought, the three horses I brought yesterday, and the ten mules that were in the wagons." He handed the private the fee.

"I'll get right on it, Sergeant."

Tim hefted the pack. He hurried past the creaking gates as Fort Smith opened to the world. "Private, open the door. The gate is open."

His assignment to guard the fort from the Indians in the infirmary ended when the gates opened. "Yes, sir, Sergeant." The guard unlocked the door, handed Tim the key, and then left.

"Your pack. I believe it has the cedar." Tim put it beside Waya. Waya and Luyu both ate from the bowl in Waya's hand.

Luyu cradled her hand in her lap. "Thank you."

Tim looked at Sally, sitting beside Gad. Gad laughed at himself as he tried to mash food between his teeth. The food flew away from him with the laughter. Sally laughed with him. Gad looked happy as a lark. He didn't appear to be suffering at all.

Tim scooped goulash from the pot. When Luyu finished eating, Waya set the bowl down, took the pack, and went to the stove. He added enough water to moisten the cedar he had cooked on the trail and then rewarmed it. He took the warmed cedar to Luyu. "Tahatankohana, look at Luyu before I wrap it."

Tahatankohana examined her hand. "Wait a

minute." He walked away. "Roscoe and Sally, come here. I want to do something different. What do you think? We could soak Luyu's hand in whiskey, or I was thinking about that anti-parasite medicine. Maybe we should soak her hand in that and get her to drink it too. If it kills parasites in your intestines, maybe it will kill the infection in her blood."

Sally replied, "Whiskey would burn like fire. I don't know what the parasite medicine would feel like in an open wound, but we know drinking it is a good thing. If we are going to make it, we should make enough for everybody but maybe not Hanataywee or Ehawee since they're pregnant."

Roscoe added his opinion. "I like the parasite medicine idea, and we should use maggots too. We may be able to find some behind the kitchen. Let's tell Luyu what we're thinking."

The three of them returned to Luyu and Waya. "Grandmother, if we can get them, we want to make medicine from walnut husks, cloves, and mugwort. You'll soak your hand, and you should also drink some. We also think we should find maggots to eat the rotten flesh."

Luyu looked at Waya. Waya answered, "I will put the cedar on her hand until its ready."

Tahatankohana sat beside his grandmother. "You can talk to me anytime you want."

Luyu knew her grandson meant what he said, "I know."

Tahatankohana remained while he ate goulash. "I'll go see what I can get."

At the store, he bought cloves and whiskey. When he got back to the infirmary, everybody was prepared to leave. "Doctor, do you know if there is a walnut tree around here?

Gad spoke up. "I do. I'll show you if Sally will ride with me and continue reading <u>Paul Clifford</u>."

The doctor nixed Gad's request. "You shouldn't go anywhere. Your jaw is wired shut."

"It's my jaw, Doc, not my feet. I plan to listen. I won't be talking."

Ke didn't want to miss the story. "I want to go."

"Maybe I should go. I can't help load hay, but I can pick up walnuts," Luyu sat at the edge of the bed.

Waya refused. "No. You need to stay near the infirmary."

Hanataywee stated her idea. "All the rest of us women could go if you men can load the wagons without us."

The men all said, "Of course, we can load wagons without you."

Gad looked at the doctor for permission to leave the infirmary.

"All right. Show them the tree."

As they walked to the stable, Tahatankohana told Ke what he knew Ke wasn't going to like, "I promised to keep my eye on you. You need to stay here."

Goodbye Hideout

Ke complained. "I'm going to miss the story."

"You promised to do what I tell you. Help me get the mules in the harnesses."

Ke kicked the dirt.

Hanataywee thought Ke should be allowed to enjoy himself. "I can watch over Ke as well as you. Let him come with me. I'll make Ke my top priority."

"Because you were willing to stay, and because you agreed to do what I told you even though you didn't want to and because I know you will do what your sister says, I'll let you go."

Ke quickly climbed into the wagon. "Thank you."

Tim, Waya, and Luyu went to speak with Colonel Habersham. "I have a letter from Colonel Howland." Tim handed the colonel the sealed letter that he believed was the request to sell at cost whatever supplies his two Indian scouts wanted.

Colonel Habersham opened the envelope and read the letter. "What is it that you want?"

Luyu remembered that Wakanda had asked for everything. "Six hundred bales of hay, three hundred and fifty pounds of oats, two horses, one wagon wheel, two weeks of food, cooking and eating kits, and traveling supplies for thirteen people."

Waya held up Luyu's hand. "Medicine."

The colonel turned to Sergeant Anders. He held the letter Ezra Knuckles had delivered days before. "You want five hundred bales of hay and rations for four for seven days. It's a six day trip."

"Delays may arise."

"I want two detailed copies of your survey of the Creek — Choctaw border from all of you. Wait outside my office. Send in my aide."

Luyu said, "I will write in English what my husband tells me. He can't write."

"That will be acceptable."

"Thank you, sir."

Waya knew the last words Luyu had said. He did the same. "Thank you, sir."

"Yes, sir. I will send him to you." Tim saluted and then turned. Waya and Luyu saluted and rotated just as crisply, then followed Sergeant Anders.

Tim told the man in the outer room, "Colonel Habersham wants you."

The man picked up a box holding paper, a quill, ink, and a blotter, then went into the colonel's office and closed the door. A few minutes later, he came out. He handed a paper to Tim that authorized the transfer of five hundred bales of army hay to Fort Gibson transported there by Sergeant Anders and his men and authorization to issue seven days of rations for four soldiers. The paper he handed to Luyu said to sell six hundred bales of hay at one cent a pound and three hundred and fifty pounds of rolled oats at twenty cents per fifty-pound sack. Sell no more than two horses from the sellable stock at fifteen dollars each. One wagon wheel is to be sold for twenty

Goodbye Hideout

dollars, up to three cooking kits for six at fifteen dollars each, whatever food and miscellaneous supplies they wanted at cost and medicine as prescribed by Doctor Seibel at cost.

Luyu read the paper. "Thank you."

She followed Tim out of the command center toward the hay depot outside of the fort but then saw everybody at the river. Gad sat in the driver's seat of a wagon with Ke, Helen, Sally, Ehawee, and Hanataywee in the back. Sally held the open book. Roscoe and Tom backed a team of mules to the wagon. Eli, Tahatankohana, Dustu, and Adahy stood beside the wagon, speaking to Gad. Luyu changed direction. "I'm going to the river first."

"You don't know where to get the hay. I'll go with you." Tim went with Luyu and Waya.

Gad, Ke, and the women rode away, waving goodbye before Luyu, Waya, and Tim got to them. They could see that all four of the women had a Lefaucheux revolver in the gun belt around their waists. Luyu knew they would have a box of bullets in the wagon as well. Gad had his service rifle and an ammo belt.

FORTY EIGHT

Luyu spoke to her family in Cherokee. "I have very good news. Oh, no! You already bought a wheel. How much did you pay?"

Tahatankohana answered, "Twenty-five dollars."

"I had no idea Colonel Habersham would write an authorization for us to get everything we want at cost." She turned to Tim. "Can we get the difference of money back for the things we already bought?"

Tim answered, "You can, but those are private businesses. It will make them unhappy after they already sold the items at their own rates."

Tahatankohana agreed. "We planned to spend this much. Let's be generous about the few things we already bought."

Luyu issued instructions. "All right. One of you, go with Tim to the hay depot. I want Tahatankohana to go with me to talk to the doctor about medicine."

Roscoe offered, "I'll go with Tim, then come back."

Goodbye Hideout

Luyu handed Roscoe the letter from Colonel Habersham. "I almost died getting this, and I'm not completely healed yet either. Make sure you get this price."

Roscoe took the authorization. "I will."

Eli pulled a wagon jack out of the toolbox on the wagon. "We'll probably be ready to go when you get back."

Luyu slipped her healthy hand into Waya's. "The doctor does not seem comfortable around you because you protected me so well."

"You will be with Tahatankohana. I will help here." He picked up the wagon jack.

Tahatankohana walked beside Luyu. "Grandmother, I wasn't able to get mugwort at the store. I bought whiskey to kill the infection. It will hurt."

"I will do that if I need to, but I noticed other Indians are living in the town. Let me see what I can do after we talk with the doctor."

Lisa Gay

FORTY NINE

As if it echoed the peace that Waya, Luyu, and Tim had found when they had scouted the border between the Choctaw and Creek Indians, only silence met Tahatankohana and Luyu in the infirmary. Tahatankohana knocked on Doctor Seibel's office door as Luyu announced who was knocking. "It's Luyu. I'm the one with the infected hand."

Doctor Seibel opened the door. "I know who you are. Come in." He stepped back to allow Luyu and Tahatankohana to enter. "Have you come to complain about my attempt to remove the infected limb?"

Tahatankohana assured him, "Absolutely not. An army doctor treating battle injuries would have to do exactly that. He would have to perform the fastest, most efficient way to save as many lives as possible. He wouldn't have time to invest in a slow and chancy procedure. I prayed I wouldn't have to amputate and tried to prepare my mind to do it if I didn't see quick progress. It takes a fearless man to do such a thing. I took the coward's way out."

Goodbye Hideout

The doctor's countenance lifted. The man was right. He didn't need to feel horrible about having wanted to remove the woman's arm. He'd had to amputate a leg in the past. He knew it was a hard thing to do even when a soldier had an advanced infection of gangrene. "What can I do for you?"

"Colonel Habersham issued authorization to buy medicine for my hand at cost. It's on the same paper Roscoe is using to buy the hay. We wanted to come now to give you time to put together what we need. We will bring the letter over later and show it to you."

"Do you have anything in particular in mind?" He looked at the man who obviously had medical knowledge and probably already had something in mind.

"We'll need a large supply of gauze, bandages, sutures, and suture needles. I would like to have a scalpel, forceps, a lance, retractors, clamps for blood vessels, surgical scissors, hemostats, ligature needles, injection needles, and a medical book about blood veins."

Doctor Seibel had thought they would ask for laudanum. He was pleased that they only wanted things they needed and not the opiate. "I'll put it together and calculate the price. Tahatankohana, come over here and look at these books."

"I'll leave you to look at books." Luyu headed to the door.

Tahatankohana asked the doctor. "Do you have any protective gloves?"

"No, but the store sells all kinds of gloves. I can write a medical order for gloves. That way, you can get them at cost."

Tahatankohana instructed his grandmother. "Wait for the doctor to write the order. You need to keep your hand very clean. Buy gloves that are the best for keeping dirt out and so comfortable that you will wear them all the time."

"I will." She took the prescription for gloves, but went first to speak with the people most likely to have the mugwort they needed.

The doctor returned to the topic of the books. "Your sister wants to trade books or buy books. She wants my five fiction books and any three you want, and she said she'd send me eight fiction books in return if I won't just sell these books." The doctor took a book off the shelf. "I have two of How to set up and run a field hospital. Would that interest you?"

"Maybe. Show me what you're willing to let me have, and I'll pick." The doctor laid out a copy of Primitive Physic by John Wesley and Contribution to Physiological and Pathological Anatomy by John Godman.

"I have An Introduction to the Surgery of Arteries by John Bell. I want to keep it, but I'll let you look at it."

Goodbye Hideout

Tahatankohana flipped through the book. "I'll buy paper at the store and copy the arteries book. If you're willing to trade, I'd like the other three and the books Sally wants. I'll make sure you get ours."

"I doubt I'll get your books, but I'll take the chance to get something new."

"Wonderful. I promise we'll get the books to you. I'll be right back." He hurried to the store, bought two quires of paper, several pencils and erasers, and a new binder, then rushed to the wagons. "I have a chance to copy a medical book. If you allow me to not help load the hay, I will unload it all when we get home."

Eli said, "Fine with me."

"Go on." Tom pushed the last wheel onto the wagon.

Dustu held the nut he was about to screw on. He waved Tahatankohana off. "Go copy while you can."

"I appreciate it." Tahatankohana dashed back to the infirmary and started through the book to determine the order of the drawings he wanted to copy. He numbered strips of paper and inserted them at the pages he wanted to reproduce in the order of importance.

FIFTY

At the river, all five wagons were ready to roll on wheels. When the people saw Roscoe coming, they instructed the mules to go.

Roscoe stopped and waited. "I would like your opinion about my idea. Tim needs to start with five hundred bales of hay, but that is too much weight, and when they get to Fort Gibson, they won't have five hundred bales of hay because their horses will eat some of it on the way."

Dustu didn't get what Roscoe was driving at. "What does that have to do with us?"

The question Dustu asked let Roscoe bring up what he wanted to propose. "I'm glad you asked. I have the idea that we could make an offer to Sergeant Anders. If he asks for a hundred thirty-two more bales of hay and two hundred and fifty more pounds of grain, which is what his and our animals will eat between here and Fort Gibson, then we will carry it and the extra two thousand pounds of hay his mules can't pull.

Goodbye Hideout

"As we go, we'll be taking hay and grain from the wagons, making them lighter every day. When we get to Fort Gibson, Sergeant Anders will be able to deliver the whole five hundred bales of hay. They unload from our wagons the hay we carried for them. We'll have used up all the extra hay and grain. We go on with all our animals and wagons and get home with five hundred and twenty bales of hay and two hundred pounds of grain."

Eli figured in his head. "Or we could let Anders ask for only four hundred and fifty bales of hay and one hundred pounds of grain. The two smaller wagons would be empty when we get to Fort Gibson. We could sell them and the harnesses because we can carry the four hundred and fifty bales of hay left on the other four wagons. We get home with three hundred and seventy bales of hay and six pounds of grain. We already have enough grain, and we'll have fed our mules for twelve days. We won't need as much hay at Fort Arbuckle. If we do it this way, we won't have to go back to Fort Gibson to sell the wagons."

Roscoe countered, "We need all the hay we can get, but we could get two hundred pounds less of grain and make the load twenty pounds lighter per wagon. Each day each wagon would have eighty-eight pounds less of hay and twenty-four pounds less of grain. You know, if Sally gets those books, she's going to have to go back to Fort Gibson and ask them to take the books to Doctor Seibel the next time somebody goes to Fort Smith or comes from Fort Smith. We could even get no grain here and buy three sacks at Fort Gibson to make it lighter by thirty-five pounds per wagon on the way to Fort Gibson."

Eli started another alternate, "Or we could–"

They were at the hay depot. Tom stopped his son. "You don't need to debate what we'll buy right now. The amount of hay and grain Sergeant Anders adds would be the same either way. We just need to find out if he will do it, then we can figure out what we'll get."

"Right. I see they're already loading their hay. I'll go ask." Roscoe went over. "Sergeant Anders, sir. I had a thought. Since you are supposed to deliver five hundred bales of hay to Colonel Howland, we'll carry two thousand pounds of your hay and the extra hay and grain your animals will eat on the way if you will also get the hay and grain ours will eat going to Fort Gibson, and we'll carry that too."

The Sergeant hadn't thought about that. Was he supposed to get five hundred bales or deliver five hundred bales? He didn't want to make a quick decision. "I'll think about it. I'll find out if I can get more. If I decide that is what I want to do, I'll let you know."

Roscoe went back to his family. "He'll let us

know. We shouldn't buy any hay or grain until we know. Let's buy the other supplies."

Waya led a wagon out of the barn. Roscoe called out to Sergeant Anders, "We're going to the store. Be back before very long."

Luyu joined them in the road, wearing thin, white silk gloves. "Waya, where are the wolf hides?"

"In the barn."

Luyu told the others, "We'll meet you back at the barn. I'm going to trade a wolf hide for some mugwort. I have three women who will trade a basket of mugwort for a fur. They didn't want to, but I showed them my hand and told them why I needed it. They agreed."

Waya walked away with his wife. "I'll carry them for you. Show me which you want to trade. We need to get salt to put on those we keep. Maybe we can trade another for the salt. How many do you want to keep?"

"Let me ask the others if they want any of them. For now, let's take four." Luyu was getting only one basket of mugwort from each woman. She picked the smallest furs.

I want Luyu to go to Tahatankohana. He will look at her hand. As they walked, Waya suggested, "After we get the plants, I will ask the others if they want a hide. You ask Tahatankohana if he wants one."

Waya carried a wolf hide into the store. The

shopkeeper saw it. "May I look at your fur?" He held out his hand. Waya handed it to him. "Very furry, but it needs to be tanned immediately. Are you selling this?"

Waya didn't know what the man was asking. He shrugged his shoulders.

The shopkeeper was accustomed to working with Indians who did not speak English. He drew the fur to his chest, and held out a five dollar coin. "I want it."

Waya took the coin and then looked at his family, who had been staying out of it. "You want one?"

In Quapaw, Roscoe asked, "How many can you sell?"

"Wife trade three. Store man buy one. You want one?"

Dustu and Adahy understood what their grandfather asked. "Can we both have one?"

Waya answered, "Yes. You come first."

Eli held out his hand to the shop owner. "May I look at yours?" He took it. "The whole head is attached with the skull still intact. That means the brain is in there. I'd like one. What about you, Pop?"

Tom liked to work with his son, and it was a nice pelt. "Sure."

Roscoe counted on his fingers then spoke. "If we all get one, and you already traded three and sold one, that is all of them. How many does Luyu want?"

"She come here soon. You ask. I buy salt." Waya held out the coin. "Salt," he said in English.

Goodbye Hideout

"All right." The man came back with four sacks of salt totaling one hundred pounds.

Waya put the salt in the wagon, started toward the fort, and then met Luyu. "Everybody wants a wolf pelt. I traded one for salt."

"We can be a pack of wolf skinwalkers."

"Did Tahatankohana look at your hand?"

"Yes, he said to bring the mugwort to him. He wants me to go back and soak my hand in whiskey. He said it looks redder than this morning."

"You go. I look for maggots." He returned to the store, where they were packing the supplies into a wagon. "Roscoe, help find maggots. Hand bad."

Roscoe put an arm full of empty ammo belts into the wagon. "We will go to the barn as soon as we find some maggots." He motioned for Waya to follow.

FIFTY ONE

Since the doctor knew them, and the state of Luyu's hand, Roscoe and Waya walked side by side into the infirmary. The doctor's office door stood open. Tahatankohana sat at the desk with Doctor Seibel looking over his shoulder.

Luyu sat in a chair, holding her hand in a deep bowl of whiskey. Pain contorted her face as she suffered the burning of the alcohol in the wounds of her hand. Waya saw that Luyu was suffering. He went to her. "What can I do to help you?"

"Find maggots, so I can do something other than this."

Roscoe spoke up. "Doctor Seibel, do you think it would be possible for us to search for and gather maggots at the kitchen?"

It was fascinating to watch Tahatankohana draw a copy of the illustrations, but Doctor Seibel knew he wasn't helping. He could help gather the needed medical treatment. "We'll go together." The three men hurried off.

Goodbye Hideout

It wasn't long before Tahatankohana stood up, walked to Luyu, and squatted beside her. He removed her hand from the bowl, examined it, and then released her from the torture. "That's enough for now."

Luyu set the bowl on the floor then walked over to see how the drawing was coming. Tahatankohana was halfway done copying the illustration of a hand with its tendons and arteries. He drew only a single line designating the book held between the fingers in the engraving of Charles Bell.

"I can copy the explanations of the drawing?"

"I would appreciate that very much."

Luyu took a sheet of paper and picked up a pencil. So as not to interfere with her grandson, she sat to the left of Tahatankohana. She copied the explanation written on the page opposite of the drawing. She finished long before Tahatankohana was done with the drawing. "Is there a part in the other book that goes with this picture that I can copy?"

"Yes. It's long, but there is a lot of information and commentary I don't need."

"I'll start." Luyu opened the accompanying book by John Bell, the brother of Charles Bell. She found the section and started writing.

Tahatankohana wanted to provide the best possible care for Luyu and believed they would both benefit if he heard everything. "Read it aloud. I'll tell you to copy it or not." As Luyu read a paragraph, Tahatankohana told her yes or no.

Tahatankohana had completed the hand illustration and had started drawing an arm when the doctor triumphantly returned. He gave Tahatankohana the report. "We found a few, and we put out some food where it may encourage more to hatch. Waya and Roscoe went to the barn to help load hay."

Tahatankohana took the larval flies, dropped them in the whiskey, swirled them in the bowl, and then scooped them out. Luyu didn't want to see the maggots on her. She looked away as Tahatankohana put the three creatures on the worst parts of her palm. They tickled as they squirmed until they found their food and started eating the putrid flesh. Luyu took out another sheet of paper to write the explanation of the arm picture.

Dr. Seibel offered, "I can do that if you want to continue what you were copying."

"All right." Luyu handed the doctor her pencil and a sheet of paper. She picked up reading where she had left off in the section about hands. The three of them transcribed drawings and words.

Goodbye Hideout

FIFTY TWO

When Roscoe and Waya arrived at the barn, Tom, Eli, Dustu, and Adahy were already loading hay. "You must have gotten an answer from Sergeant Anders."

Tom explained. "Tim told the private on duty that the authorization was for him to transfer five hundred bales of hay, not to get five hundred bales of hay, and that he needed one hundred thirty-two more bales and two hundred and fifty more pounds of grain to transfer the whole requisitioned amount. The private didn't even argue. It was a logical request.

"We decided to get six hundred bales of hay. Tim got us five empty grain sacks. We're going to divide the grain into ten bags and put one on each wagon. Each wagon will start with almost five thousand pounds. That's a lot, but every day we'll take ninety-two pounds off each wagon as we feed the animals.

"We bought packs to carry all the people food and our supplies on our own backs, and we'll walk.

When we get to Fort Gibson, we'll divide our six hundred bales of hay between five wagons and sell one wagon and one harness.

"We won't feed our mules grain the last morning before we get to Fort Gibson, we'll buy hay and grain at the stable that evening and the morning before we leave. We won't have to give the mules grain again until the next morning, and we don't need to feed them grain the day we get home.

"Tim said we could keep any grain left from what he gets here. We should have thirty-four pounds, so we'll only have to buy one fifty-pound sack of grain at Fort Gibson to get home.

"We'll be twelve pounds short of grain, but we can give them just a little less than a pound a day, and they'll be fine. We will have used up only sixty-six bales of our six hundred by the time we get home."

Roscoe accepted the plan. "All right. I see we've got somebody verifying how much hay we're putting on each wagon. Any of us also counting?"

Eli explained how they were keeping track. "Yes. In this wagon, we can only get eleven bales in each layer. After we've made eleven layers, we'll add two more bales, then cover it with the tarp. We'll have one hundred and twenty-three bales per wagon."

Dustu and Adahy placed the last two on the first wagon. Eli tossed them a tarp. They unfolded it, dropped the sides down, then climbed off while Tom,

Goodbye Hideout

Eli, Roscoe, and Waya tied the ropes in the tarp grommets to the wagon.

Eli placed a half-filled sack of grain onto the floorboard of the seat.

At noon, when they went to the infirmary to eat dinner, Sergeant Anders and his men had all four military wagons loaded. Roscoe, Tom, Waya, Eli, Dustu, and Adahy had also filled four wagons.

FIFTY THREE

In the forest, Ke put on his gloves and picked up a walnut. His fingers punctured the husk's thin skin and penetrated the squishy black below. "Yuck." He threw the thing against the tree. The black goo splattered in every direction. Specks of blackness covered his face. He pulled off his glove and wiped his face but only succeeded in smearing the dots into streaks.

The squirrels peacefully hibernating inside their cozy nest in the assaulted tree awakened. Small, furry faces looked out to see what horrible fate had befallen them. They loudly chattered and scolded the being below who must have been the one who had disturbed them.

Ke, Gad, and the women looked up. Four squirrel faces voiced their unhappiness that those below were stealing the nuts on the forest floor. Their small brains only thought to attack. The animals threw nuts that they had in their nest at the people stealing their winter food. A nut bounced off Gad's shoulder. "Stop that, you little pest," he ordered them. He picked up a few more of the squishy nuts and tossed them in the tub.

The squirrels came out of the hole and descended partway to warn the people from a closer and more threatening location. "Chip! Chip! Chip!" they hollered at the thieves below to no avail. They ran back into their nest and threw more nuts, one of which hit Hanataywee in the back of the head.

"Stop that." She threw one back at them. It impacted beside the squirrel nest and exploded into droplets of black goop that splattered the squirrels' faces. They scolded more vigorously, ran down to the ground, and then darted at the horrible beings stealing their nuts. Quickly, they veered away before the people were close enough for a successful counterattack.

Ke chased them back to the tree. They tried to descend again, but Ke tossed a nut at them and ducked before the goo landed in his face. The squirrels raced to the back of the tree. "I chased them away," Ke announced triumphantly. They continued collecting the walnuts.

Helen informed Ke of his misconception. "You didn't win. They may hide for a short time, but they'll be back and attempt to run us off."

No sooner had Helen spoken the words than Sally felt a bite on the back of her ankle. Happily, the thick mukluks protect her flesh. Attempting to dislodge the vermin, she shook her leg. Its tiny claws and teeth held on as it fearlessly attempted to sink its teeth into her. Ehawee and Ke tried to swat it off, but couldn't do so with Sally flailing her leg.

While everybody focused on Sally, the other three squirrels scurried to the tub and filled their mouths with nuts before they dashed back to the tree.

Ke saw them scamper up the tree with swollen faces. "They're taking our nuts!"

Sally finally shook the creature off. Gad declared war. "This is going to have to be a military operation. Ke, you and I will keep guard. If you see any of them coming, throw nuts at them, chase them, or do whatever you need to do. Just keep them away. Hanataywee, Ehawee, Sally, and Helen, you scoop up the nuts as fast as you can and get them in the tubs." They took up their assigned duties. Ke and Gad hurled nuts at any squirrel that dared to approach.

The squirrels dashed here and there, trying to breach their defenses. Sally informed them, "They attack like tiny coyotes."

"There comes one. Get him!" Gad commanded as he skirmished with another of the rodents.

For three hours, they fought the forest dwellers. They loaded four ten-gallon washtubs of gushy black slime, and most of the walnuts the squirrels had left on or thrown to the ground.

Ke threw one last nut at the locals before he

retreated. The squirrels had finally chased away the intruders and chattered their victory. Ke watched them gather the remaining nuts as they drove away. "I think they believe they won."

Gad informed Ke of a military secret. "It's best to leave your opponent thinking he won even if you have accomplished your objective. You don't want them to feel the need to get even."

Hanataywee agreed, "We surely don't want a forest full of retaliating squirrels. I'm sure there are too many for us to make a successful defense."

Helen passed out the ham, cheese, and bread slices. "We don't know how Luyu's hand is doing, if we can stay in the infirmary tonight, or if we'll have to leave. I think we should start working on the nuts."

Ehawee took her share of food. "The nuts look nasty. Let's do it after we eat."

Once they got started, they found the old rotting husks easily scraped off the shell. Helen took off her gloves to take a turn reading <u>Paul Clifford</u>. She discovered the walnut juices had soaked through the leather. "Look." She held up her stained hands.

Sally looked at hers and discovered they were as dark brown as Helen's were. "Let your hands dry before you touch the book. Doctor Seibel hasn't told us we can have it."

Ke started opening the inner shells with one of the large pliers Gad had brought. He removed the nuts inside, then ate them, or dropped them into a smaller goo-free bucket they had brought until he had eaten all the nuts he wanted. At that point, he decided he made a better driver and Gad a better nut opener.

FIFTY FOUR

When the walnut gatherers arrived at the fort, they removed the tubs of husks and the pails of nuts, swept the shells out, and then loaded the last of their hay into the final wagon. Helen, Hanataywee, Ehawee, Sally, Gad, and Ke carried in a ten-gallon tub of mushy walnut husks and four pails of nuts, which they set down in the hall that ran from the infirmary door to the hospital ward at the back.

Sally walked into the room and found the doctor dissecting a book. "What are you doing to that book?"

With a scalpel and the skill of a surgeon, he carefully cut the strings holding together the sections of the book. "I'm giving sections to people who can copy them."

Sally looked at the pages already completed. "Very nice."

Helen looked at the drawing of a flayed arm displaying the inner workings. "I can't draw this well. Give me a section of words to copy."

Tahatankohana explained what they were doing. "Luyu has been reading each section aloud, and I have been telling her what to copy. Then we switched to Doctor Seibel copying the instructional material because he knows what is important to copy and what can be left out. Luyu has been copying the explanations of the illustrations. I think she has them all done."

Roscoe was already helping in the way he enjoyed. "I told Tahatankohana I could copy a picture or two, but I'll stop and make the medicine with the mugwort, cloves, and walnuts."

Sally immediately piped up, "I can copy pictures. Give me the next one." She took a sheet of paper from the pile. The doctor removed the middle page from the section he had just cut loose and handed the folded page to Sally. She noticed they were short on supplies. "We need more pencils and erasers. I think I have time to hurry to the store and buy some." She put the page aside until she got back.

Gad offered his services. "It's better if you don't go alone. I'll go with you."

"Thank you." Sally hadn't taken off her coat.

Neither had her escort. "Let's go."

"Just a minute." She went to her bed, unstrapped the loaded revolver, and packed it into her bag.

Knowing they would never again see each other after Sally left and that their time together was short, the two went together. Sally chatted about nothing in particular. The young soldier walked silently beside her and tried not to move his jaw, which was feeling sore after the day's battle. Sally asked, "What's the town like? Do you ever have problems in town? Do you have fair justice?"

"Sure, we have problems but nothing major. Especially if it's civilian problems, everybody knows Judge Atwood won't take any excuses."

Sally dropped the subject. Gad had confirmed that the judge was there. They enjoyed the trip to the store and returned with a dozen pencils, an equal number of erasers, and another four quire of paper. A guard stood at the locked infirmary door. Sally sweetly requested entrance. "Please open the door. We need to go in."

"Sorry, ma'am. Once the gates have closed, this door is not to be opened until the gates open in the morning."

Sally stated the flaw in his argument. "We just walked past them, and they were open."

"If you look in that direction, you will see the gate is closed." They turned and looked. Between the time they walked past and had arrived at the infirmary, the gate had been closed.

Gad entered the debate. "For pity's sake, Henry. You know me. Just let us go in and then lock the door behind us."

"No. I'm following the colonel's orders."

Sally changed tactics. "You are absolutely right." She turned and walked away.

Gad followed her. "We can't stay out here."

"I know. Come on." When they were out of view, Sally circled to the back of the building. When the guard was not looking, they ran across the road to the space behind the infirmary. They knocked on one of the hospital ward windows.

Doctor Seibel spoke with them from the other side of the open but barred window. "What are you doing out there? They already locked the door."

The people in the room heard Doctor Seibel and went to the window. Sally explained. "We didn't get back from the store fast enough. The guard says his orders are that the doors stay locked from the time the gate closes until the gate opens. Is there any window we can come through?"

The doctor contemplated for a moment. "There is a small window without bars in the storage area above my office. I think you can fit through, but it's high."

Gad wanted Sally to be safely inside with her family. "I can get her higher if somebody can pull her the rest of the way up. I'll go to the barracks."

Tahatankohana said, "Show us the window."

In his office, Doctor Seibel pointed at the scuttle hole to the small storage space above. He got a stepladder from the closet. Tahatankohana climbed through the small hole into the space above. He crawled to the window that took up most of the three feet of space between the floor and the roof. He opened it and stuck his head out. Sally and Gad stood below. "Two more of you come up here." Adahy, Dustu, and Eli climbed into the room. Tahatankohana told them, "I'm going to lay here with my arms out the window. When I have Sally, you pull me backward."

Gad leaned against the infirmary wall and formed his hands into a cup. Sally put her foot into his hands. He raised her. "Step on my shoulder." Sally did so and reached up as she leaned against the wall.

Tahatankohana grabbed her wrists. "Hold on to my wrists too."

Sally wrapped her fingers as far around his wrists as they would go. "Ready."

Tahatankohana repeated, "Ready." The other three men pulled Tahatankohana's feet. Gad felt Sally leave his shoulders. They had her up to the window. "Her arms can't flex around the window."

"Hold on." Eli crawled to the window, put his knees on either side and knelt above Tahatankohana. He reached down to Sally's elbows. "Gad, push her up as far as you can." Gad turned and pushed up on the bottom of her feet.

Eli pulled up and held her with her arms above the bottom of the window.

Tahatankohana reached out and got her under her armpits. "I have her. Pull her in."

Eli let go. She put her arms inside the window and leaned in over Tahatankohana. Eli pulled her through the window.

Sally turned around to talk with Gad. "I'm sorry you won't get to hear more of the story. Thank you so much for getting me in here. You're my hero."

Gad told her what was in his heart. "It's my pleasure to help such a fine person."

Henry came around the side of the building to investigate the knocking sounds. "You want to go in too?"

Gad spun around. "Are you going to report me?"

"There's nothing to report. My orders didn't say anything about people going in through a window."

"It would be a lot easier if you opened the door and let me go in. It's stupid to make me climb in through the window."

"I will not go against orders. Go get a ladder."

"Land sakes alive, Henry!" Gad hurried away.

FIFTY FIVE

Tahatankohana and Eli returned to copying John and Charles Bell's anatomy books. Sally, Dustu, and Adahy remained in the storage room. Henry kept watch at the open window. Nobody was getting out of the building from anywhere on his watch.

Gad returned, set up the ladder, and then climbed up with the supplies they had bought. He passed Sally the box holding the paper, pencils, and erasers then went in through the window. Gad apologized to Sally. "Sorry you had to get in the hard way."

"It's not your fault. You're still my hero."

As soon as Gad was inside, Henry, being the soldier he was, told them what he felt compelled to do. "Close and lock the window. I'm going to report that this window needs an additional guard."

"Of course, thank you, Henry." Gad locked the window closed. They lowered themselves down through the shuttle hole onto the ladder. Sally went out last, so Gad could help her. The soldier closed up the opening before they joined the others in the hospital ward. He carried in a chair and sat it beside one of the adjustable food tables.

Sally sat in the chair and adjusted the table's height. "Where are Luyu, Hanataywee, and Ehawee?"

Helen told her, "There weren't enough pencils, so they went to prepare supper and the medicine. We showed Luyu our hands. She said she was going to use the medicine anyway."

Gad picked up the folded page with the illustration for Sally to copy while she got a blank paper from the box. She placed the sheet in the proper position on the table with the eraser beside it and held the pencil in her hand.

Gad opened the page to look at what she was about to draw. "Sally will not be copying this page!" He stalked across the room. "Give her another!" He handed the opened page to Tahatankohana. Tahatankohana looked at the picture of an undressed male with his abdomen pulled open, displaying the veins inside. The image showed other external parts as well.

"All right. Get another."

Gad took the next picture out of the book. Arteries and muscles of the thigh. Charles Bell once again made the drawing of the lower extremities complete. "What is the purpose of this?" Gad handed it to Tahatankohana then looked at the next illustration of the back of the leg and hip. It passed inspection. He took it to Sally. "This one is more appropriate."

Sally looked at it. She didn't know what was wrong with the other illustrations, but this one looked fine. She lay the picture in front of her. "Much obliged." She put her pencil to the paper and started on the intricate drawing.

Later, when Doctor Seibel walked out of the room alone, Sally put down the pencil, stretched, and then left the room. She caught up with the doctor on his way to the water closet. "Do you live in town?"

"Yes, I could stay here, but I like getting away from military life."

"Do you have nice neighbors?"

"Very nice. There's the store owner, the judge, and me."

"What part of town is that? I bet you picked a good view."

"It's down at the far end of town. I can watch the river from my porch. It's beautiful. The problem is that nothing stops the wind coming down the river. It blows right through the walls. I've seen it blow out a candle inside my house."

"It's a wonder it hasn't blown off your roof. You can go first." Sally allowed the doctor to precede her since she didn't actually have to go anyway. When the doctor came out, she said, "It was nice talking with you. See you back in the hospital room." She went into the small room with a new contraption to handle the business hygienically. Mounted high on the wall was a tank with a chain you pull to let the water drop and flush out the bowl. The first day she had flushed it twice just to watch it work.

When supper was ready, Sally still had a long way to go to finish the leg drawing. The pictures of the heart, hand, and arm with their arteries, as well as the corresponding chapters of John Bell's companion book, had been completed.

All copying ceased while they ate. After eating, they resumed the work. Roscoe copied one of the drawings rejected for Sally's viewing, and Tahatankohana started the other. As they worked, Luyu read Paul Clifford with her maggot-free, blackened hand inside the no longer white glove.

Eli, Tom, Helen, Doctor Seibel, Hanataywee, and Ehawee went to the other end of the room because it was hard to copy the words from the medical book while hearing Paul Clifford.

Gad and Ke listened to the story with the people who were drawing. Dustu, Waya, and Adahy decided to try copying pictures of the head.

From time to time, Tahatankohana compared the progressing drawings with the originals. He was pleased with all their work. Not very far into the night, Ke fell asleep, listening. Gad picked Ke up.

Goodbye Hideout

"Will you read more? I will never hear any more after you leave."

Luyu consented, "I will read to the end. You know, if you learn to read and write, there are so many other wonderful stories you could read."

Gad carried Ke to his bed. He lay the boy in the bed and pulled the cover over him. He looked at Ke for a moment. *It would be nice to have a son of my own.* "Who could teach me?" Gad asked loudly enough for Doctor Seibel to hear.

"If you want to learn, I will teach you."

"Thank you, Doc. I do want to learn, but for now, Miss Luyu, please continue."

Luyu read through the night while the others copied. At two in the morning, Luyu read the last word of <u>Paul Clifford,</u> then went to bed. One by one, the others finished their work then also went to sleep.

At four in the morning, minus only the unnecessary commentary, the books had been copied. Tahatankohana closed the curtains over the many windows in the room and crawled into his bed.

FIFTY SIX

Four hours after sun up, they woke. Gad spooned the thinned porridge through the narrow space between his teeth. Roscoe ate a much thicker portion laden with raisins. "I'm sure the horses have had their morning feed. After we eat, I'll go buy the horses."

Tahatankohana felt tired. "Just be sure you get young, healthy, strong horses already conditioned to pulling heavy loads."

Gad said, "I didn't tell you what happened to my jaw. A horse kicked it. I help care for them. This time she broke me, but I'll break her when I'm healed. I know our horses well. I can tell you which you should buy."

Roscoe put on his pack and walked with Gad to the infirmary door, which had been unlocked for hours. No guard stood at the door or by the small window of the storage area. As they walked to the barn, Gad asked, "What are your plans for your animals? Do you have any horses already? What do you have now?"

Goodbye Hideout

"We want to breed the horses and our donkeys, goats, and sheep as well. The horses, mules, and donkeys have to be able to pull heavy wagons. We have a miniature male and female donkey, one standard size jack, three donkey geldings, four female donkeys, twelve male mules, eight female mules, one male and three female goats and the same of sheep, three male horses, one gelding, twelve mares, and one dog." When they arrived at the barn, Roscoe asked the attendant about his animals. "Did you give them heavy grain, hay, and unlimited water this morning?"

"Yes, sir. You paid me for it. I brought them in, fed, and watered them. I've kept them in and didn't turn them out into the field just as you asked."

"Thank you. I appreciate that." Roscoe was glad he didn't have to round up twenty-two mules.

Through his wired mouth, Gad asked his fellow equestrian handler the location of the horses. "Are all the horses in the field on the lower end?"

"Yes, they're down there." Gad was great with horses, but he couldn't read the authorization papers, and the soldier on duty knew it. "These people are authorized to buy no more than two horses from the sellable stock for fifteen dollars each. I wonder which the sellable ones are."

"We shouldn't sell the horses the officers prefer to ride or the big draft horses. What do you think?" Gad wanted to know if the horses he was considering would be considered sellable or not in someone else's thinking.

"I'd say that's right."

"Good. We're going to look at them." He took two harnesses with lead ropes attached off the pegs on the wall. They walked across the field in the cold air. Gad told Roscoe, "One is a three-year-old female. She's a Morgan accustomed to working. I know you said they have to be already able to pull a heavy wagon. The other is only eighteen months and hasn't ever been in a harness, but she's a fantastic quarter horse that hasn't come to anybody's attention but mine. Nobody will care if I sell her. She's the best horse you can get for breeding."

"Let me see her. I'd like to take her if I can get her into a harness. We need all of them ready to go, so let's try."

In the infirmary, Sally prepared to leave while Tahatankohana, Waya, and the doctor looked over Luyu's hand and arm. She took the loaded revolver out of her bag, strapped it on, and then put on her coat and pack. Sally walked out of the infirmary alone.

Gad caught the Morgan first. He slipped the halter over her head. "This is Biscuit." He handed the lead rope to Roscoe. She compliantly followed.

Gad was glad he had started working with the quarter horse. He knew she would take a bridle and saddle with no problem. He hoped she would go into a harness too. "I call this one Promise. To me, she is a promise of a fantastic horse. If I could have any horse here as my own, it would be Promise."

Tim and his men had spent their last night in town. They got up with the sun, assuming they would move out early. They had been ready for hours. He saw Roscoe coming across the field. As soon as he was in range, he called out. "Why in all tarnation are you just now getting ready?!"

"We were up and busy until very late."

"Get everybody out here. Let's go."

"They'll be here any minute. I'll harness one team. If they aren't here by then, I'll get them."

"I'll go now." Tim walked out of the barn and started toward the fort. He thought he saw Sally, rapidly walking down the road toward the far end of town. *Couldn't be.* He opened the door of the infirmary.

Tim heard Ke by the water closet. "Sally?"

In the hospital ward, ten full packs lay on the beds. Tahatankohana stood beside Doctor Seibel, looking at a bed top full of papers. Tim spoke up. "Are you ready? We've wasted half the morning."

Tahatankohana looked up. "As soon as Sally is ready. We're looking for her."

"I saw her walking across town."

Eli asked, "Where?" as he came back into the room to get his pack.

"Toward Doctor Seibel's home."

The doctor thought that explained it. "I told her I had a beautiful view of the river from my porch. She must have gone to look."

Hanataywee defended her. "Sally wouldn't have done that. She knows we're leaving this morning. What else did you tell her?"

"She asked me who lived around me. I told her the store owner and the judge."

Luyu quickly realized the significance of what she had seen earlier. "She strapped on a revolver!"

Eli dropped his pack. "Oh, no! God, please stop her! Doctor, show me your house! Now!" Eli ran for the door. Doctor Seibel grabbed his coat.

Ke picked up the book Paul Clifford. "Doctor, are you giving us the books?"

"Take them." The doctor answered as he and Tahatankohana dashed out the door behind Eli.

Tahatankohana needed information. "What would be the best way to shoot Judge Atwood?"

"What?!"

Eli forcefully instructed the doctor, "Just answer the question!"

"If she wants to get away, she would have to shoot him through the window, but he would see her standing in the field between the river and the house."

Tahatankohana knew better than that. He had taught Sally himself. "He won't see her, but she's there."

Goodbye Hideout

The doctor asked, "Why?"

Tahatankohana and Eli explained as they hurried to stop Sally from administering retribution.

Back in the infirmary, Tim looked at Sally's family. "What's going on?"

Ke started to tell what he knew. "She must blame–"

Tom picked up his son's pack and stopped Ke midsentence. "It's a family matter. We're leaving now. Bring that pack." He pointed to Tahatankohana's.

"I'll carry it." Tim put it on.

Luyu scooped up the drawings on the bed and put them in the binder.

Ke hurried to Doctor Seibel's office. Through the barred window, he saw several soldiers and the blacksmith leaning a ladder against the building under the unbarred window above. He got the other four books Sally wanted and the three books Tahatankohana wanted from the desk. He carried the stack of books out the door. Outside he heard Tim say, "Surely Sally couldn't actually hit anything."

Ke corrected him. "Sergeant, I've seen Sally shoot flying geese from the sky with a gun and an arrow. If she shoots at something, she'll hit it."

Tim was surprised such a dainty, lovely woman he thought he knew could be so deadly. "But, she wouldn't shoot anybody, would she?"

Tom just said, "I hope not, but she has good

reasons to want to. Tahatankohana and Eli might even be tempted to help her."

As he walked with Luyu and his grandsons, Waya asked in Cherokee, "What is this about?"

Tom explained, "Judge Atwood is the one who, knowing they were guilty, let some criminals go free after they shot up the Williams home. Later, those men burned their entire farm to the ground. They caught the men and tried to take them to Little Rock because they knew they couldn't go to Judge Atwood.

"The judge in Little Rock realized Ann and Tahatankohana were married. In white man's law, an Indian can't marry a white. To his face, Ann told the judge she was right before God, that he was not, that he was a horrible person, and that she was going to fill the world with Tahatankohana's babies.

"Judge Hall wanted to whip her on the spot, but the sheriff of Harmony, who is their friend and was with them, got the judge to sentence them to hard labor. The two of them had to rebuild the Cadron Ferry landings and the ferry by themselves.

"It took months, but they did it. Because the man who runs the ferry is their friend, they made it even better than it had been beforehand. Tahatankohana tried to do what the judge said. He ran away from Ann, so she wouldn't have to go through that again, or be whipped.

"Ann, Sally, Stephanie, and Eli tracked him down

and reunited. They've been running ever since. Judge Hall has been trying to find Tahatankohana and Ann. Because of this, Sally lost the man she loved."

Dustu remarked, "That's senseless and unfair. I'll help her shoot him."

"The whites will execute her or anybody else who kills a white judge even if he's as guilty as sin itself," answered Luyu.

On the other side of Fort Smith, Roscoe and Gad were both happy. Gad had thirty dollars to turn in to the quartermaster from the sale of two horses. Biscuit and Promise stood passively in the harness behind Beauty and Dollie. Gad's favorite horses belonged to people he liked, who knew their value and would take good care of them.

Mules 7 and 8, and Brandy and Starlight were ready to go in the harnesses of the next wagons. Gumdrop and Glory, and Honor and Justice were harnessed to fourth and fifth wagons when Tim returned. The four military wagons, Ezra, Ham, and Morgan, had been ready to go for hours.

Roscoe thought it was best to be prepared. "Sell me a bucket of liniment."

Gad walked to the tack room. "Help me mix up a batch."

FIFTY SEVEN

Sally lay behind a tall, frost-covered stand of grass in the field behind Judge Atwood's house. She watched the man in a rocking chair, reading a book. *A man who doesn't administer justice fairly should not be allowed to continue to ruin lives.* It would be an easy shot. She looked for witnesses. *People are dead because he let his brother-in-law go free.* Her finger tensed. She stopped. *He must have known Roy would kill somebody one day. If he would shoot up a home like mine, he was more than comfortable with killing people. It was only because we saved ourselves that the man didn't kill us. He wanted to murder us when Gus threw that flaming oilcan into my house.* A word caught her attention. *Gus threw that can. Ben, Charlie, Pete, Al, and Gus shot up my house.*

Judge Atwood left the room. While Sally waited for him to return, his wife came into the room and sat in the rocker. Judge Attwood returned with two cups of tea, handed one to his wife, put the other on the small table beside the chair, and then kissed her cheek.

Goodbye Hideout

He pulled a chair over and sat close beside her. He reached his hand over and took the hand of his wife. They sat together, looking out at the river, drinking their tea.

Sally asked herself, *do I want to be the one to ruin a life?* She looked at the woman whose life she would destroy when the blood of the man beside her suddenly covered her.

Tahatankohana and Eli searched the field with their spyglasses. They both looked at the spot they would have picked to shoot a person through the window facing the river. It was hard to spot her, but they did. They signaled for her to desist and leave.

Sally had decided she would let Judge Atwood live before she saw her brothers. She slid an inch then stopped, and looked at the couple behind the window.

Eli said, "She's coming. It's going to take a long time."

Sally didn't move until the focus of those in the house was not toward her position. She pushed a few inches forward, looked toward the window, and then waited again.

Judge Atwood stood up and left the room. He returned with Doctor Seibel. Mrs. Atwood walked toward the doctor, who purposefully directed their attention away from the window. The doctor, however, could see outside. Sally stood and saluted, then walked across the field, out of view.

Both her brothers put their arms around her. Eli ordered, "Don't ever think about such a thing again."

Tahatankohana added, "You are worth much more than everything any of us has lost or suffered."

"It's been eating me up for the last two years thinking about him getting away with what he did and all the horrible things that happened because he let them go.

"I could have doled out the consequences he deserves, but his wife doesn't deserve that. I chose to give them Grace and decided to let him live. I'm at peace now." With her walnut-blackened hands, Sally took the hands of Tahatankohana and Eli. "Let's leave this place." They left Judge Atwood, the past, and all the pain behind.

They walked into the barn. Eli said, "Everything is well. We're ready to go."

The person walking beside the lead animal of each team urged them forward. "Forward, ho."

Gad knelt beside Ke. "You are a skilled fighter. I am glad to have fought a battle with you."

Ke replied, "I enjoyed it too. I wish all men were like you." He hugged the soldier who had proved to him that every man was an individual to be judged by his own merit.

Gad said, "Goodbye," to Ke, then all the others. He walked beside Sally. "I'm glad I got to know you. I hope whatever was bothering you this morning is all right now."

Goodbye Hideout

"It is. Much obliged for the trip to get the walnuts. I enjoyed the squirrel battle."

"Me too. Ke is so much fun. I've known your family for only two days, but I'm going to miss you terribly. Ke brought your books. Doctor Seibel said you could have them. Please send him the replacements. He is going to teach me to read. He said he would let me read your books."

"We will do everything we can to get them here. Thank you for getting me into the infirmary last night. I will miss you, and I won't forget you either." She kissed his cheek.

"May I kiss you better than that?" Gad asked.

Sally stopped walking and turned toward him. Gad kissed her very well, even with his jaws wired shut. "Goodbye, Sally. I hope you have a glorious life."

"You too." Sally left behind another man who could not go with her as she walked away with her family.

FIFTY EIGHT

Promise walked beside her lifelong companion. Biscuit wasn't complaining, so Promise didn't either. Roscoe walked beside them with Tahatankohana. "What do you think? Gad said these are the best they had. He was especially glad we took Promise. He said she is the best for breeding we could find anywhere, and he wanted us to have her. He said Biscuit is a great all-around horse and able to work hard continuously."

"We'll see. They're doing well right now, and they are nice-looking horses."

Tim dropped back to walk beside Sally. He wondered if she was as good of a shooter as Ke has said. "Would you like to hunt together?"

"If either of us sees something we can cook for supper, we can see who gets it." When the sun was in the noon position, they had only been traveling for a few hours, so they didn't stop. They arrived at the regular campsite the military used when traveling

Goodbye Hideout

between the two forts and then set up camp for the night. They were thirteen miles from Fort Smith, but neither Sally nor Tim had seen any game. As they doled out hay and grain to the mules and horses, Sally told Tim, "Guess you still don't know if I'm any good or not."

"I'm not trying to find out."

"Yes, you are. Tahatankohana, what do you think of Promise and Biscuit?" Sally walked away.

Tahatankohana ran his hands down Promise's legs. "She doesn't seem to have any swelling. I'm still going to rub her legs with liniment. Please give her extra hay and grain."

Sally pulled another flake of hay from the open bale and put another half scoop of grain in front of Promise. Suddenly, she drew the Lefaucheux revolver and fired. She walked fifty yards out, then held up a hare by the ears. "Do I win?"

"Only if I can help you eat it."

"We'll divide it sixteen ways. Everybody can have a few bites. I'll skin it." Sally flipped over a Dutch oven, flopped the rabbit across it, and made short work of gutting and skinning the creature. When the fire burned just right, she roasted it on a spit.

Ezra had seen Sally cook and hunt. What he had never seen was the Sally she had been at Fort Smith.

Tim, Ham, and Morgan had met Sally at Fort Smith. They didn't know the Sally that Ezra knew. Tim thought, "This is going to be an enjoyable trip."

Tahatankohana looked at Luyu's hand. "Maybe this wasn't a good idea. I can't see if it's red. How does it feel?"

"Still hurts, but it does feel much better. I've been thinking about Chetan being injured, you and Sally getting thrown into the river, and the wolves attacking me. Maybe we shouldn't try to cross the country. Joe Smith is dead, but Judge Hall still believes he's hunting for you, so he won't send anybody else. Maybe we should live in Fort Arbuckle or one of the Cherokee villages. Being outside all the time leaves us wide open to everything. I don't know if we'll be safe tonight. Maybe we should sleep on top of the wagons."

"Grandmother, it was terrifying to be attacked by wolves, especially alone. I was terrified when the coyotes attacked, and there were six of us. I was terrified for myself but more so for the people I love. I understand, but I don't think anything will attack us here. Still, we always post guards anyway."

"Think about what I said."

"I will."

The next five days went the same. They watered the animals and gave them hay and grain to eat while the people made and ate breakfast. They traveled five hours before they stopped and allowed the animals to rest and graze on any dry prairie grass they could find for a few hours. The people ate cold food and tried to stay warm. After dinner, they traveled four more hours and then stopped where they knew there was plenty of water.

Even though there was also prairie grass they could eat, they gave the mules and horses hay, rubbed liniment on Promise, and soaked Luyu's hand in the anti-parasite medicine. Except for the two pregnant women, including Tim, Ezra, Ham, and Morgan, they all swallowed a morning and evening dose of the medication they had made at Fort Smith.

They ate a hot meal every evening consisting of food they brought, combined with whatever any of them killed or gathered along the way.

Luyu remained fearful. She insisted on sleeping on top of a wagon every night. Right on schedule, they arrived at Fort Gibson in the afternoon of the sixth day. Sally didn't know how Luyu was still walking. She knew Luyu wasn't sleeping, that she desperately needed to, and that she had to be inside to accomplish that. Sally remembered how Waya and James had stayed in the stockade during a storm. "Tim, how can we get Luyu into the jail for the night?" Sally asked.

Tim also remembered James and Waya spending the night in the stockade. They weren't going to be able to go about it the same way. They could try her needing to be in the infirmary, but her hand was much better. He couldn't think of a reason.

The sun was still up when they arrived. All ten

wagons entered the fort with all forty animals and sixteen people. Tim went directly to Colonel Howland.

The private on duty outside the colonel's office knocked on the door. "Sergeant Anders has returned with his report."

"Send him in."

Sergeant Anders stepped into the room and closed the door behind him. He handed Colonel Howland a sealed envelope from Colonel Habersham and several unsealed sheets of paper. "I have a message to deliver from Colonel Habersham and a written report from myself on the status of the Creek and Choctaw relations. Five hundred bales of hay have been delivered to the barn. I will also debrief you on the events that occurred. My scouts will give you an oral report if you desire to speak with them personally."

"Get them." He unsealed the letter.

Sergeant Anders left the building. "Luyu, the colonel wants to talk with you and Waya."

"All right." She told Waya in Cherokee that the colonel wanted to talk with them.

When the three of them reported to Colonel Howland, his door was open. He saw them. "Come in here." He remained behind his desk.

"Scout Luyu, report what you saw on your mission." As Luyu spoke, she moved her hands about to emphasize one thing or another.

Goodbye Hideout

The colonel noticed one hand wore a black glove and one a dingy white glove. When her report was complete, he knew why her hand was black and that all was well between the Creek and Choctaw Indians. The colonel stood up and walked across the room. "May I look at your hand?" Luyu took off the glove and held out her hand. "So this color is from cloves, mugwort, and black walnut husks and you also drink it to get rid of intestinal parasites. Do you mind if I pour water on your hand?"

"Go right ahead."

"Come." He picked up a pitcher of water on their way outside. He poured water over her hand and rubbed her fingers. They did not get one bit lighter. "How long does this color stay?"

"A few weeks."

"Let's go back inside. Do either of you want to add anything to Luyu's report?"

Tim thought she had been very thorough. "No, sir."

Luyu asked Waya if he wanted to give his report. He did. Luyu translated everything. His information was very specific about what he saw and why he made the conclusion that there were no problems brewing. Other things he had observed he did not report because they were not relevant to the mission. She repeated the last thing he said, "Waya says he knows other things, and so do I, but he will not tell you, and I will not either. You will have to put us in jail, then we will tell you in the morning."

"So only after a night in a nice safe cell where no wolves can get to you, and you have slept well for at least one night, you will tell me the other information."

Luyu said, "Yes, please." She held her husband's hand to her cheek. Moisture filled her eyes. He had slept on top of the wagon with her for five nights, and now he was trying to help her feel safe, so she could sleep. She loved him even more.

The colonel ordered their imprisonment. "Don't stand there, Sergeant Anders. Incarcerate them."

"Yes, sir. Right away." He took Luyu and Waya to the stockade. "These scouts refused to give a full report. Colonel Howland wants them jailed."

The guard took the keys out of the desk drawer and walked to the back. He opened the first cell door. "Get in there, lady."

Luyu stepped into the cell. Tim stepped in behind her. "I don't want you to contaminate these. You'll have to use your own. I'll bring them." He took the sheets, blankets, and pillows. He knew her own would be more comfortable and warm. He stepped out of the cell and closed the door. Luyu liked the sound of the door locking the wolves out.

The guard opened the second cell. "You next."

Waya walked into the other cell. Tim took his

bedding too. Luyu told Waya in Cherokee why Tim was taking the blanket, sheet, and pillow.

Tim handed the guard the bedding and gave him further instructions. "I'll bring their bedding. You fold these up and put them where they will remain clean and non-infested. I'll have their supper sent over." Sergeant Anders left Luyu and Waya right where they wanted to be.

He went back to the barn where Tahatankohana, Ke, Hanataywee, Ehawee, and Sally were putting the sixty-eight bales of hay that belonged to their family onto their other five wagons. Ezra, Ham, and Morgan unloaded the forty-four extra bales that belonged to the army. Tim told them, "Waya and Luyu are in jail for the night because they would not give a full report. I will take them their bedrolls, so they'll be more comfortable."

Tahatankohana handed him Waya's bedroll. "Thank you."

Sally got Luyu's. "I appreciate that."

"You'll have to thank Waya. He's the one who made it happen. They're not in any real trouble. Colonel Howland understands, and I'm having supper sent to them." He walked away with the two bedrolls.

Tom went to the store to complete the sale of the one wagon and harness. Eli, Helen, Roscoe, Dustu, and Adahy paid the private at the stable to keep their animals in the stable during the night, to rub down all their legs with Fort Gibson's liniment, and to feed and water the animals that night and in the morning. They also bought one sack of grain. They used bags emptied during the trip from Fort Smith to split the grain they had left from the trip and what they had just bought into five equal portions. Sally loaded them on the wagons. "I hope Luyu has a peaceful night's sleep."

Tom joined them with the money from the sale. "Ma, do you want to come with me to the bakery?"

Ke said, "I sure don't, but I'd love to try a danish this time."

Helen replied, "Thirteen danishes coming right up."

Eli told his father, "We're done here. We're going to go set up."

Tom replied, "Go to the store and see if there is anything you want to buy."

"I'm sure you bought anything we need."

"Son, I'm telling you to go to the store and look."

Eli realized his father thought there was something there that he should be the one to buy. "All right, Pop. I will."

Ezra said, "We'll see you tomorrow before you leave."

Tom and Helen left the barn for the bakery. Eli went to the store. The rest of them walked to the forest to gather wood to make a fire. Eli stood in the store and looked around. *Pop didn't say buy eggs or something particular. What does Pop want me to notice?* He walked past sacks of grain, flour, salt, sugar, peas, and other dry goods. Eli looked at the knives, cooking kits, hatchets, and other tools. He looked over the section with raisins, dried apricots, and canned vegetables.

He saw canned peaches and stopped in his tracks. He thought about the first time Stephanie had truly grabbed his attention. Back when she and her sisters lived in the farmhouse James had built. Stephanie had come into Yates Mercantile, and he had helped her get a jar of canned peaches from the top shelf.

He remembered how her long, blond hair had gleamed. Her very shapely well-toned body was only inches from him as he had stretched to reach the treat she wanted. He had looked into her beautiful blue eyes when he had handed her the jar. She had said, "I love peaches. Ann said I may have one jar."

Eli wanted his wife to know he remembered that day. He wanted her to remember it too. He bought four jars of canned peaches and then left the store.

Outside, Eli saw his father and grandmother headed toward the river. He held up a jar of peaches as he joined them. "Is this what you thought I should buy for my beautiful wife?"

Tom smiled. "You're a good husband."

Those gathering wood joined them, they built a fire, and fixed supper where they were allowed to be after dark. Sally thought *Colonel Howland is a good man to make that accommodation for Luyu. Too bad everybody doesn't think like him.*

In the morning, they ate breakfast, then broke camp. They went to get their animals, which they hoped had already been fed and watered. Roscoe smelled fresh liniment on all their legs. He hoped Promise would not balk when he tried to get her into the harness. As he led her to the harness, the four men who had accompanied them from Fort Smith arrived to say goodbye.

Morgan said a quick, "Goodbye. Have a safe trip. God's speed," then left.

Ham joked with his friends, "If there's ever anybody else you want me to detain with a good rumble, I'll be glad to do it," but he meant what he said.

Tahatankohana shook Ham's hand. "Hopefully, it won't be necessary, but I'm much obliged for you holding up Joe Smith."

Tim shook each of their hands. "It's been a life-changing summer, fall, and winter since you and the others in your village came into my life. Goodbye and good luck to all of you."

Each of them offered their best wishes to the men. Tim and Ham left to perform their morning duties.

Ezra lingered. "Goodbye, my friends. This time I guess we really won't meet again. I will miss you. I wish people had not mistreated you. I pray for the very best for all of you."

Tahatankohana shook Ezra's hand. "You have shown us what a good man looks like. I count you as my friend. Thank you for not telling anybody my other name, and thank Ham for me. You know I couldn't tell him while Tim was here."

Sergeant Anders took Luyu and Waya from the stockade to Colonel Howland. "I trust you had a peaceful, restful night?"

"Yes, thank you," Luyu answered gratefully.

The three of them stood before Colonel Howland. Luyu told the colonel what her family had asked her to say if she got a chance. "You're a good man, and so are the four men we have gotten to know this year. You, Sergeant Tim Anders, Privates Ezra Knuckles, Morgan Finch, and Ham Blanders are fine examples of how soldiers, and people in general, should behave. I don't know if our opinions matter, but my family and I think very highly of them and you, and we appreciate all of you very much. We hope life brings God's blessings to all of you."

"Your opinion matters. Colonel Habersham wrote me a letter commending my men. Especially Sergeant Anders and Ezra Knuckles. He said, 'They are true leaders.' He recommends that I promote them. He also said you three wrote him an excellent report of your mission and thanked me for sending people who did such thorough recognizance. He said you have the duplicate copies of the report."

Luyu motioned to Waya to give the colonel the papers as the two of them stepped forward. Each of them passed the colonel a copy of their report. Waya spoke what Luyu had taught him to say. "Night in jail convince me. Give all knowledge."

The colonel thought Waya's report would have the best intelligence, coming from a seasoned Indian warrior. He read it over. "This is very helpful. I did not know three of the Creek Micos are dying. I agree it might take some fights to the death between people in those villages to determine who will be the next Mico. We might have gone charging in, thinking there was a problem, and then created an actual problem. I believe you have prevented much trouble."

Luyu translated the colonel's words.

Waya was glad he had done something good for all the people. "You are welcome."

Next, the colonel read Luyu's report. She had written that the Creek and the Choctaw harvest had been good and hunting as well because the buffalo had returned. There was plenty of food and wood in the lodges, and the people had plenty of furs to keep warm. The men had plenty of women. Women had enough men. There was no reason for anybody to want to make a problem.

The colonel believed this was useful information. "Domestic life is directly related to tranquility. This is good to know. I'm glad you decided to cooperate. I want you and your whole family to know this has been an excellent year. We have established good trade relations with the Quapaw and the Cherokee. I've learned quite a few things of value.

"I don't know if these will be useful to you, but I wrote letters of recommendation vouching for your qualities of good character, knowledge, and helpfulness to all people and especially to the United States Government. This assessment is based on what I know of you and what my men have told me. I made individual letters for every one of you written with my own hand. I signed them and stamped them with my official government seal."

The colonel handed Waya a stack of envelopes. He shook Waya's hand and then the hand of Luyu. "May God protect and bless all of you. You are dismissed."

Luyu remembered what had happened with the baker. "Colonel, would you request that the baker sell Ke thirteen éclairs, thirteen danishes, and four loaves of bread?"

"Why? I'm sure he can buy them."

"In front of Ke, he refused to sell that much to Eli. He had much more than that amount in the case. He said he didn't have that much to sell to Eli because Eli is an Indian lover."

The colonel wrote the request. "Sergeant, observe without being seen. If they want to do so, send Ke and

Eli to buy these items without showing this paper. If he doesn't sell respectfully, they are to show the paper. Let me know what happens."

"Thank you, Colonel Howland." Luyu saluted. Waya did the same before they turned and walked out of the room. Luyu explained everything to Waya as they walked to the stable with Tim.

Tim handed Ke the paper and explained that Colonel Howland had one last mission he would like Ke and Eli to undertake. He explained the mission. "Will you accept?"

Eli looked at Ke. "You don't have to do this. If you want to, I'll accept the mission with you."

"All right, but will you let me talk to him?"

Eli agreed. "Of course."

They moved the wagons out of the fort while Eli, Ke, and Tim went to the bakery. Tim got into position outside the bakery where he could hear. Ke stepped into the bakery in front of Eli. He looked directly at the man. "Mr. Baker, sir. You are a very good baker. I have never tasted anything as delicious as the éclairs you sold us. I very respectfully ask that you give me the privilege of buying thirteen éclairs, thirteen danishes, and four loaves of bread."

The baker thought *this Indian has learned respect and understands I'm not some servant to bake him treats.*

"I'll sell them to you."

Ke gave the baker the money. As the baker put

the pastries in a box, Ke told him something else he had thought about while he had been gone. "Mr. Baker, sir. We did not treat you like a person when we were here before. You make life so much better with your talents. I bet people don't tell you how much they appreciate what you do. I want to tell you that I do."

Since he had been at Fort Gibson, the boy was the first person who had ever told the baker that he appreciated him. It occurred to him that an Indian boy was more thoughtful than the whole lot of the rest of them. "Have you ever eaten a trifle?"

"No, never. I didn't know there was such a thing."

"Try one." The baker passed Ke a trifle with the tongs.

Ke took a bite. "You are an excellent baker, and you came all the way out here to share something wonderful like this. We are truly blessed. How much do I owe you for the trifle?"

"Nothing. It nice to serve it to somebody who appreciates what I've made."

"Thank you, sir. You are generous too. May I also buy thirteen of these?" Ke took two bags, handed them to Eli, then took the last one and passed it to Eli as well.

"Sixty-five cents."

Ke counted out the money as the baker opened

another bag and deposited thirteen small trifles. Ke exchanged coins for the trifles. "I misjudged you. I'm glad I got to know the real you, sir."

The baker looked at the boy. "Me too."

As Eli followed Ke out the door, he told the baker, "I am too."

Tim joined Eli and Ke as they walked to the gate. "Ke, you are a wise person. I know I have enjoyed the bread and pastries when I can get some. I've never thanked him, but I will now. Also, I'm happy I can report to the colonel that the baker sold you the items with no problems."

Ke had the note from Colonel Howland. "My family would like to thank you, Ezra, Ham, and Morgan. It's not much, but this says to sell to the holder thirteen danishes, thirteen éclairs, and four loaves of bread." He handed Tim the note, then opened his moneybag.

"You don't have to do that," Tim replied.

"We want to." Ke gave Tim two dollars and sixty cents.

"Thank you, Ke. You are very generous and thoughtful." Tim put the note and money in his pocket. "God bless you all and keep you safe." *There's no sense in taking a chance that I'll have to give Colonel Howland this unneeded note and miss out on the treats. Plus, I should tell the baker how glad I am to have the privilege of eating his tasty pastries.* Tim started toward the bakery.

Goodbye Hideout

When Eli and Ke joined their family, everybody was reading letters. "What have you got?" Eli asked.

"There's one for each of you." Luyu handed them envelopes.

"The colonel said this about me?" Ke asked after Luyu had read him the letter.

His grandmother put her arm around him. "Why would you think he would not notice your wonderful qualities?"

Ke put the letter back into the envelope and tucked it into this pack. "This is very nice. I'm going to keep it forever."

Lisa Gay

FIFTY NINE

Tahatankohana went back to being Noah as they drove the wagon train across the field to the ferry. Orville was already there since he knew they were heading out that morning. "Your wagons are heavy this time. One per crossing, but I'll take you for two dollars each trip if your animals run the treadmills going over. Mine will bring the ferry back."

The family immediately accepted. The first trip, Promise and Biscuit walked forward, Beauty and Dollie wore the blinders, and Sally walked in place in front of them as they trod toward the shore they were leaving.

Halfway across, Ke decided to take a turn walking in place. Thirty minutes later, Sally, Ke, Beauty, Dollie, Promise, and Biscuit exited the ferry on the west side of the Verdigris and Neosho Rivers and north of the Arkansas.

Noah helped Orville get his horses into the harnesses before he stepped off the ferry to wait with Sally and Ke.

Goodbye Hideout

Four and a half hours later, the last wagon came across. All the mules and horses had spent the morning eating prairie grass. While they waited, Luyu had soaked her hand, which was as black as pitch after seven days of the treatment. Afterward, she put on her silk gloves.

Sally, Helen, and Roscoe had dinner prepared. They ate as soon as everybody was across. Ke gave a trifle to each of them while Eli told them how nicely Ke had spoken with and complimented the baker.

Luyu took her treat. "This is what Colonel Howland, Sergeant Anders, Ezra, Ham, and Morgan saw in you. You did very well."

"Thank you, Grandmother. I meant what I said."

"I know you did." Luyu hugged him.

It wasn't far from noon. The wagons were heavily loaded, and they knew they would not get to the same stopping place they had found on their trip the week before. For six hours, they traveled slowly, stopped every two hours, and took the animals to the river for water. As darkness fell, they set up camp, posted a sentry, and unloaded the evening hay to feed the mules and two horses.

While the men rubbed liniment on all the animal's legs, Luyu climbed to the top of the fullest wagon. With fewer people around, she spent the night peering into the darkness with two fully loaded Lefaucheux twenty-round revolvers.

After they fed the animals their morning ration, each wagon was two hundred and thirty-five pounds lighter than the day before, and the packs the people carried were lighter by the amount of the food they had eaten.

At the end of the second day, they had made up the distance they hadn't traveled the first day. Roscoe and Noah examined Promise. She still looked fine. The people rubbed liniment not only on the legs of the animals but also themselves.

On the third day, they arrived at the river bend, where it moved closer to the road. Waya thought this was the place where they had left the hemp line tied to the tree. "I'm going to try to find our rope."

"You cannot go out there alone!" Luyu exclaimed.

Waya assured her, "I will be fine. I will take the revolver."

"No. Even with the revolver, you cannot fight a pack of wolves alone."

Sally spoke up. "Why don't a couple more of you go with Waya?"

Dustu answered for himself and his brother. "We will go."

Luyu issued orders. "All of you have to carry a revolver, and you have to ride over. If you see any wolves, gallop away immediately."

"We will. We promise."

Luyu still worried. When the sun set, she cried, "The wolves ate them!"

Goodbye Hideout

Just after dark, Waya, Dustu, and Adahy rode into camp. Luyu ran to them. Once off their mules, she squeezed them tight. "I was afraid you were in a wolf belly."

"We are safe, my wild dove. It was just hard to untie the knot."

Noah walked over. "I am glad you found it."

Waya knew Luyu would not be able to walk the next day if she didn't sleep for the third night. He made a suggestion. "I will stay awake beside you on top of the wagon and keep watch with this revolver. Others will keep watch too."

Sally told Luyu, "I will also take a turn. We all need to sleep some every night."

Luyu was exhausted, and she felt safer. She slept through the night, but everybody heard her cry out in her sleep.

Not long into the fourth day, Ke called out a warning. "Somebody is coming fast!"

They drew their weapons and circled the wagons. Eli climbed to the top of a wagon and looked through his spyglass. "It's Ezra."

Helen spoke the question they were all thinking. "Why would he be coming this way?"

When he was close, Ezra called out. "Ezra wants to join you!"

"Come!" Noah hollered back. When Ezra joined them, Noah asked, "Why are you here?"

"Colonel Habersham wrote Colonel Howland a letter saying Sergeant Anders and I are natural leaders. He suggested that Colonel Howland promote us. Sergeant Anders was promoted to Master Sergeant. Morgan, Ham, and I were promoted to private first class. Master Sergeant Anders said the colonel wants to make me a corporal, but he has to have a reason to promote me again, so the Colonel wanted me to go on another mission."

That didn't answer their question. Tom said, "Congratulations, but why are you here?"

"Colonel Howland told Master Sergeant Anders to find me a mission that will benefit the army. Master Sergeant suggested that I immediately acquire another wagon coated in pitch that would be able to navigate the river like a boat and then roll out onto land and travel as a wagon. And also that I could assure that an obligation made to the military doctor at Fort Smith would be fulfilled.

"It's too easy to be a mission, but they're trusting me to complete it successfully. I'll have the pleasure of spending more time with this family, and I won't have to spend boring winter days sitting in the barracks. Also, I will never ever tell anybody that you are hiding at Fort Arbuckle."

Sally looked at Noah, "It's better for us if we don't have to go to Fort Gibson again, and one more person to help guard us will be useful. You know why."

Goodbye Hideout

"I brought supplies." Ezra's second mule carried a packsaddle loaded with four bales of hay and a partial sack of grain. Ezra had his bedroll and a pack behind him on his mule.

Noah looked at each of the others, then agreed, "Join us."

SIXTY

They traveled together two days and arrived at Fort Arbuckle a day later than those inside had expected them to return. Chetan stood in the guard tower. When he saw them on the horizon, he climbed down the ladder. "They're coming!" He opened the gate. Beside him, Ann held Christopher, Bethany held Chumani, and Stephanie had Joy.

Ezra looked at Stephanie. He looked at the two babies. "She is still pregnant. Who is the other baby?"

Chetan was surprised that his family had revealed their location. "Why are you here?"

Noah went directly to Ann and put his arms around her and their son. "I'll explain, Father. Close the gate quickly."

"I'm so glad you didn't have the baby. I've missed you." Eli hugged Stephanie.

Chetan didn't see any reason to close the gate immediately. "We can leave it open for now."

Luyu spoke up. "I'm the reason he wants to close it. Please do it while I can see that nothing came in."

Goodbye Hideout

"All right." Not yet knowing why, Chetan locked the wolves outside for Luyu.

Luyu felt so much relief. "I'm going to sleep."

"Mother, are you all right?"

"I'm fine, but I'm exhausted. They'll tell you everything."

While everybody had been gone, the places where people slept had been rearranged. "I'll show you where you can sleep." Ann led Luyu to the place where they had moved her bed.

While Luyu slept, Waya told about the wolf attack, and then Ann told Ezra how she had become the mother of Joy.

Dustu told Ezra how Rose had stomped and injured Chetan. All Chetan could say was that he didn't remember any of it, but that he knew it had happened by the condition of his body.

Ke told about the squirrel war and the baker at Fort Gibson.

When Ke told about the trip down the river, Ezra thought about riding the river home. "Maybe I could sedate my mules and float the wagon home."

Eli had been on both trips down the river. "Every time we've traveled the river, we've had a problem that would have been disastrous if there had not been other people to help. You shouldn't do it alone. We'll give you the extra three bales of hay, so you can ride back."

"All right. I'll have more time doing something interesting if I take the road back to Fort Gibson, and I can read one of those books on the way."

The next day, the hay move began. Since Noah agreed he would unload the wagons alone when he had wanted to copy the books of John and Charles Bell, he started the work by himself. Ezra joined him in the stable and started unloading the hay from the wagon the army was buying.

Shortly after they started, Chetan and Bethany went to help regardless of what the others wanted. Ezra gave Chetan the silver coins he had brought to purchase the wagon and harness, then he and Noah put the bales on the conveyer belt that must have been brought to the stable with Mac and Amanda's hay.

Bethany cranked the handle that rolled the wide belt and moved the hay to the loft where Chetan stacked it. When they started on the third wagon, Noah asked his mother. "How is Father? I don't want him to help any more if he still needs to heal."

"It's been twenty-nine days. He can do it for a while, but not all five wagons."

"I should have thought about him not letting me do this alone when I agreed to do it."

No sooner were the words out of Noah's mouth than the rest of the family walked into the barn. Dustu spoke for the group. "Some of us wanted to help you right away, but I told them not to because I wanted to see if you were willing to do what you said you would do. You've already unloaded two and haven't asked for help. I see that you are a man of your word. We are not going to make you unload all of this alone."

Ann and Stephanie sat in the stable with Joy and Christopher while Ezra and the rest of the family, except Sally, unloaded hay. When most of the feed was in the loft, it was time for dinner.

Sally joined the others. "I can't find the books."

Ann asked, "Did you look in the building where we put everything we wouldn't need this winter?"

"That was the first place I looked."

Bethany said, "What about the trade items room?"

"I looked there too."

Noah said, "I guess we need to search everywhere. Let's wait until after we eat."

Each of them named a room they would search. After dinner, a great search began. After hours of looking, every nook and cranny had been examined without finding the books. The sun sat just above the horizon.

Dejectedly, Sally closed the last crate. "I guess we have to return the books we got from Doctor Seibel."

Luyu woke. She rose from the pallet on the floor and walked into the outer room. "Anybody here?" She heard no answer.

Defeated, Sally walked across the courtyard.

Luyu opened the door and looked outside. "Sally, where is everybody?"

"Everybody is searching. We can't find the books we're supposed to send to Doctor Seibel."

"That's probably my fault."

Sally's spirits rose. "You know where they are?"

Luyu stepped out the door. "I think so."

Sally followed Luyu back to the room where they had put the trading items.

Sally sighed. "I already looked in there."

"I doubt you would have seen them. I laid them on a bolt of cloth then put the other bolts on top of them." Hanataywee joined them, as Luyu explained. "We carried them into the room. Everybody had already read them, so I left them there." Luyu walked straight to the bolts of cloth. "They should be between the bottom two bolts." She picked up one end, and Hanataywee got the other.

"There they are!" Sally joyfully retrieved the books. The three women carried them to the room where they ate. As they entered the room, Sally informed the others, "Luyu knew where they were!"

"Wonderful!" Ezra took the books. "It's late. I'd like to stay until the morning."

"Of course," Noah answered.

Ezra hated that he had to leave at all. He fell asleep thinking about how much he liked these people, especially Sally.

In the morning, they ate breakfast before they

Goodbye Hideout

loaded the books with the bales of hay Ezra needed to get home. They gave him bear sausages, salted goose legs, half a smoked salmon, smoked antelope, walnuts, dried corn, beans, apples, apricots, cranberries, limes, okra, dried tomatoes, sweet and white potatoes, and two butternut squash to eat on the way home. He hitched his mules into the leading slots of the four animal harness that he had also bought from the family.

Knowing they could go nowhere, Ezra kept his feelings to himself. He hugged them all, started toward Fort Gibson, and then turned to look at his friends one last time. He waved goodbye to the people on the ramparts of their hideout.

SIXTY ONE

Four weeks later, Luyu's hand was almost completely healed. Even so, she became agitated when anybody left the fort. She could barely breathe until they returned. Therefore, they rarely left the safe space inside the high stockade walls of Fort Arbuckle.

Ann made the dress she had wanted to make with Canada goose wings she had gathered back in Noah's village. Others tanned the wolf hides. They made mukluk inserts out of blanket remains to replace those Noah and Sally had lost in the river.

February 21st, on a peaceful but cold and snowy day, Stephanie felt a pain. *Is it time?* After several contractions, she was sure. She put down the book she was reading. "The baby is coming today."

Sally also put down her book. "I'll get Eli." She hurried to the barn where the men chopped wood.

"How far apart are the pains?" Luyu asked.

"Pretty far."

Bethany said, "Let's start timing them."

Goodbye Hideout

Eli returned with Sally. "Should you start boiling water? Do you have everything you need? How much longer? Is everything all right?"

"Yes, Eli, everything is ready. It will be a long time."

After the other men finished chopping the tree, they carried the wood to the buildings they were using, then went to the communal building to find out how Stephanie was doing.

Eli was calmer than when he had first joined Stephanie. "It will probably be a few more hours."

Everybody sat down to eat. Stephanie thought it would be better not to eat anything. After the meal, the other women cleaned up, then got Stephanie and Eli's room ready.

Mid-afternoon, Eli and all the women went to Stephanie's room. The walk across the courtyard helped to move things along. Only an hour later, Stephanie cried to push her first child into the world.

Eli was amazed at how much pain accompanied the process. *Why do women want to have children?*

At 3:29 pm, a baby girl entered the world.

Eli watched his child leave the body of his wife. Even covered in blood, his child looked beautiful.

Luyu took the new arrival into her hands, pushed the blood in the umbilical cord toward the baby, tied then cut it off, and handed the child to Sally. The baby cried as Sally wiped her niece clean with warm, salty water, wrapped the baby, then gave her to Eli. "Your daughter, my brother."

As Eli took his child, Helen said, "You should name her Hattie after your mother."

"Thank you, Grams. I would like that if Stephanie does." He handed the baby to his wife.

Stephanie took her child. "Hello, Hattie." She remembered how Christopher had cried when he was born. "Go on and cry, my daughter. Your arrival was harder on you than me."

Eli said, "Poor child. I saw how hard that was on you. I'm sorry I made you go through that."

"My darling, I want to have another as soon as we can." She brought the baby over to nurse.

Ann told them, "Congratulations on a beautiful daughter. I'll go tell the others." She left because she also wanted to see how her babies were after an hour away. She walked into the room where everybody waited for the news. "Stephanie and Eli have a beautiful, healthy daughter. They have named her Hattie. You can see her tomorrow."

An hour later, guarded by Luyu, Sally, and Helen, Stephanie and Hattie slept.

Eli went to tell the others about his daughter. "She's here, and she's beautiful." They all congratulated him. Before long, Eli went back to his wife and child.

It was a very happy day for the family.

SIXTY TWO

Luyu decided she needed to talk with Waya. "I don't want to go across the country. Look at what has happened outside our village. Rose almost killed my son. Noah and Sally almost froze in the river. Dustu and Hanataywee were almost swept away. Noah was almost hung by white people, almost frozen in a river, almost put in prison, and almost killed by coyotes. Wolves almost ate me. We will never get to the far sea. I want to go home."

Waya had thought about what would happen when it was time for them to leave. He knew Luyu was too afraid to travel outside day after day for months. "Our family will break up."

Luyu had convinced herself. "We can make them stay."

"Some may decide not to go. We all know that Noah, Ann, Sally, Stephanie, Eli, Helen, Tom, and Roscoe will surely leave."

"I do not want to lose anybody, but I cannot travel all the way to the western sea."

"Let me talk with Dustu and Adahy."

Adahy said, "We promised Chetan we would go to the western sea."

Dustu said, "I won't leave Hanataywee, but I would be happier staying here where I know how to live."

Waya went back to Luyu. "They say they promised to go to the western sea to marry their wives."

"I will talk to my son." Luyu found Chetan alone and explained why she wanted to go home.

"Let me talk with Bethany. She will not want to lose our oldest son. I don't want to lose him either, or Christopher."

Bethany decided to ask her daughters what they would prefer. "Luyu is too afraid to travel across the country. Would you want to go home to our village or go across the country?"

"Father will take away our husbands." Ehawee started hyperventilating.

Hanataywee said, "We need to all talk together."

They met secretly and decided to pray about it individually, then talk about it again the next day. Bethany cried all night. One way or the other, her family was about to be ripped apart. She prayed that somehow they would stay together.

The next day, they sneaked away and talked again. Adahy and Dustu disagreed for the first time in

Goodbye Hideout

their lives. Adahy wanted to see the western sea. Dustu wanted to stay where they were. In the end, they all knew that Luyu could not travel across the country. They decided to go back to their Quapaw village but not tell anybody else until it was time to leave in the spring.

Lisa Gay

SIXTY THREE

The beginning of March, before the melting snow prevented them from crossing the Arkansas, Noah brought up leaving. "We should start packing the wagons, so we can leave in the next few days."

Luyu looked at the others. They all slightly nodded their heads. Ann noticed, but Noah was looking at his plate.

"Tahatankohana," Luyu asked for her grandson's attention.

He looked at her. Luyu stated, "We are not going with you. I am very sorry."

Noah looked at his mother. "Mother?" Tears streamed down Bethany's face. He looked at Chetan. "Father?"

Chetan looked directly into his son's eyes. "Luyu can't travel across the country. She is too afraid. She was almost killed, and so was I. What if Ke or Chumani had fallen in the river?"

"But I saved you. What if I hadn't been there? You need me."

Goodbye Hideout

Luyu replied, "These things would not have happened."

Noah reminded them, "Mina's parents drowned in the river right beside the village." His family remained silent. "Who isn't going to go?" Noah asked.

Luyu said, "None of us are going."

Noah was shocked. "You already talked about this and decided together? How long have you known you weren't going?"

Chetan replied, "Since Hattie was born."

Noah stood up, left his breakfast on the table, and strode to the door.

Bethany cried, "Noah, please stay!"

Her son slammed the door and then stalked across the courtyard and left the fort. Night fell, but Noah hadn't returned. Everybody was concerned. Luyu was frantic. Ann told herself *Noah can take care of himself.* At the end of the second day, Ann was just about as distraught as Luyu. Just before dark, Noah returned. He hugged Ann, Chris, and Joy. "I'm sorry. I'm sure I scared you being gone so long."

Ann knew how horrible he must feel that his whole family was deserting him. "I was very concerned, but I'm not mad."

Noah did not talk to any other person. He locked himself in his room. Bethany went to his door and knocked. Noah did not answer. She pleaded with her son through the door. He didn't answer. She asked for help. "Ann, talk to him for us."

"What will I say? Don't be hurt that your family doesn't care about you. What did you expect?"

Everybody spoke to Noah through the door. Chetan tried to explain that Luyu couldn't keep herself from being afraid and that it was his obligation to take care of his mother. Luyu tried to explain how terrified she felt. Bethany said she had to be with her husband. His sisters said they shouldn't take their husbands away from the only parent they had ever known.

The next day, Ann read them a letter from Noah. "I understand. Take the wagon I bought from the village, your horses, one of the horses I bought from Petang, and enough provisions to get to Fort Gibson. Buy whatever else you want. Have a wonderful life full of children, joy, and peace. Goodbye."

Ann handed Bethany the letter and Chetan the three hundred and thirty-three dollars that were Noah and Ann's share of the thousand dollars they had gotten from the sale of dynamite when they had fled their village. "I told him he would regret it if he didn't hug and kiss you. He said he couldn't do it."

Everybody in Noah's birth family left for Fort Gibson the following morning. Noah stood on the rampart and watched them go. He couldn't believe they were actually leaving him.

Two hours later, he jumped on his horse and charged down the road. When he caught up with them, he hugged his mother. "I'm going to miss you so much. Thank you for being a wonderful mother. I love you."

Bethany held him tight, "Thank you for coming. I want us to be together. I tried to get them to change their minds. I'm going to miss you more than you'll ever know, but my place is with your father. Please understand that I love you."

"I know you love me, and that you're afraid somebody may be hurt even worse than grandmother and father."

"I love you, Father. Thank you for all you have taught me about being a man. I will miss you terribly." Noah hugged his father.

Chetan kept his arms around his son, "I wish it didn't have to be this way. I love you, and I could not be prouder."

Noah picked up Chumani, who didn't understand what was happening, and told her he loved her. He hugged each of his older sisters, his brothers-in-law, and Waya, and assured them all that he loved them. He got down on his knee to speak with his brother, whose heart was broken.

Ke hugged Noah's neck. "I thought you didn't love me anymore."

Noah wrapped his arms around Ke. "I love you very much, and I know you are going to be a good man. I'm glad you're my brother. I need you to help Father and the rest of the family for me. Will you?"

"I love you too, and I'm glad you're my brother. I promise to take care of our family."

When Noah got to his grandmother, he held her the longest because he knew she felt responsible for his pain, and they both knew she was. "I love you. I forgive you. I couldn't have a better grandmother. I understand because of Sally. She is slowly overcoming. I hope you find a way as well. Thank you for not telling me until the end. It was merciful."

"I'm sorry, Noah. I wish I was able to not be afraid, but I can't. It's not that I don't love you."

"I know, and I love you." He turned again to his mother and hugged her one more time. "Goodbye, Mother. I love you so very much."

He knelt beside the dog. Gihli licked Noah's face and happily wagged his tail. "I see you decided to go with Dustu." Noah didn't want to draw out his sorrow. He patted Gihli on the head before he got back on Eyanosa. "I love you all. I will miss you. Goodbye."

Noah went back to the place where he had been forced to say goodbye to his birth family. The Goodbye Hideout. He returned to the family he had found in Harmony. "I guess this confirms what I said on the mountain at Fletcher Creek. This is the family I belong to. Thank you for staying with me. I need you to know I love all of you very much, but I will only completely trust God not to let me down for the rest of my life."

Goodbye Hideout

They wrapped their arms around Noah.

After a few minutes, Noah asked, "May I take the babies and be alone?" Ann walked toward a cradleboard, but Noah stopped her. "I want to carry them in my arms."

They put warm clothes on the babies. Noah held his children to his chest. Ann opened the door.

As Noah walked away, Ann heard him say, "I won't leave you no matter how scary or dangerous things get."

Ann knew Noah's heart was broken, and no matter how hard she tried, it was something she could never mend.

Acknowledgments

I acknowledge God the Father, Jesus the only begotten Son, and the Holy Spirit as my savior and inspiration.

Chapter Heading

Brady, Cyrus Townsend, Plan and Perspective View of Boonesborough, Border Fights & Fighters; stories of the pioneers between the Alleghenies and the Mississippi and in the Texan Republic, New York, McClure, Phillips & Co., 1902, page 126, modified.

Follow Me Online

https://www.ChanceandChoicesAdventures.com

Did you like this story?
Please write a review!

https://www.amazon.com/Goodbye-Hideout-Lisa-Gay/dp/1945858176

Chance and Choices Adventures
by Lisa Gay

Pray for Justice
Choose Your Consequences
No Remorse
Means of Escape

Torn Hearts
Xida People
Stone Cold
Goodbye Hideout
Along the Way
The Western Sea
Sally's Sketchbook

Books by The Traveler

Provence: a land of lavender and olives